Svetlana the Last Princess

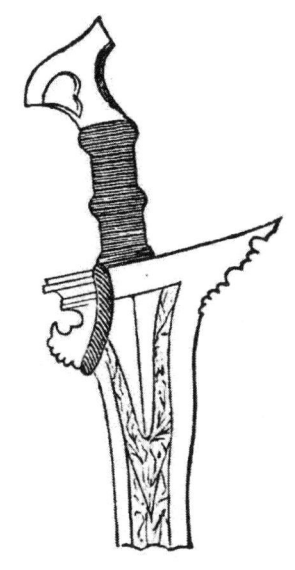

Morena Stamm

This is a work of fiction. Names, characters, places and incidents are products of the author's imagination or are used factiously and are not to be construed as real. Any resemblance to actual events, locales, organizations, or persons, living or dead, is entirely coincidental.

No part of this book may be used or reproduced in any manner whatsoever without written permission except in the case of brief quotations embodied in critical articles and reviews.

FIRST EDITION.

Copyright © 2020 Morena Stamm

All rights reserved.

ISBN: 978-1-9990345-8-0

Imprint: Independently published

To my mother who may not always understand where my ideas come from but accepts and loves me completely for it. Not only do you accept me, but you helped me grow into the confident, strong, independent young woman I am today.

PROLOGUE

⌘

Ten Years Earlier

SVETLANA BRACED herself against the wall hoping none of the servants would see her. Father wouldn't like hearing that she had spied on him and mother.

But she *had* to know.

Mother had promised her that this summer she would get to learn to ride a horse. How to *really* ride. Not the side saddle that the old stinky man kept trying to get her to do on her pony.

She inched closer to the door, waiting.

"You are not leaving this city because I said so. It is final."

He sounded so angry. Svetlana chewed at her lip, worried. What if father wouldn't let them go? She hoped not. Mother had promised!

"Alerik, you may be king, but he is my father. And he is dying. You will not deny me his last days. Or Svetlana from meeting her grandfather."

"That is precisely why you are not going. I don't want that old crow giving *my* daughter any ideas."

"Ideas! She deserves to know her history. My history! Or are you ashamed of me, your wife?"

Silence.

Svetlana's nose began to tickle. Oh no! She couldn't sneeze now, or they would hear her.

She held her small hand over her nose, squeezing her eyes shut. Please don't sneeze, please don't sneeze.

"Svetlana is already eight years old," her mother's voice was low. Svetlana had only heard it like that once when her mother was angry with her father. Normally she was always happy and smiling, airy as the short summer nights. "You promised me when I was pregnant with our daughter that I would be allowed to bring her to my father's estate."

"I thought you would have another child!"

The tickling in her nose disappeared and Svetlana sighed. Thank the gods. But then she heard something strange. Sniffing. Was…was mother crying? Svetlana worried her lip again.

Her mother had only cried one other time, but the young girl couldn't remember why. It had been something important. It must have been.

"Anichka," her father mumbled quietly. Svetlana strained her ears trying to pick up what they were saying. But only quiet whispers filled the air. Then heavy footsteps came towards the door.

Oh no! Svetlana picked up her skirts and ran down the hall back to her own room. She bounced on her toes, silent as a cat, just as mother had taught her to do.

She bounced onto her bed and crawled under her sheets. A lead weight sat in her stomach. She knew that they weren't going to her grandfather's.

Big fat tears rolled down her cheeks as she cried for a man she didn't know. Why wouldn't father let them go? Her young mind still couldn't understand her father's reasoning.

Hours later, deep into the evening, Svetlana was woken by someone shaking her shoulder. She came to groggily, not understanding why her day dress was still on her.

"Mina?"

Svetlana turned and looked into her mother's black eyes, a mirror of her own dark eyes. She smiled at the pet name. Only her mother used it. Svetlana had never heard any of the other servants and courtiers in the castle use it.

"I wasn't listening, mother, I promise," She said looking down at the ice blue sheets on her bed.

Anichka reached her hand out and with a single finger pulled her daughters' chin up until she looked back into Anichka's eyes.

"You should never lie, my daughter. It is better to say nothing."

Svetlana nodded seriously, tears pricking in the corners of her eyes.

"Now, mina, I need you to pack quietly, just your play clothes, into a dresser. Lem will come take it down to the carriage. Do you understand?"

Svetlana scrunched up her eyebrows, confused as to why she needed to pack. Father had said they were not going. Mother never went against father. Ever.

"But-But I thought father said we couldn't go."

A shadow crossed her mother's eyes before she turned back to Svetlana. "Your father had a change of heart."

Anichka pulled her young daughter into her lap, basking in her warmth. She sniffed Svetlana's hair, remembering when Svetlana had been younger how her hair smelled of fresh child. It was unlike anything Anichka had ever smelled before. She craved it. Yet, the gods had not seen it fit to gift her with another child.

With her jaw set, she tightened her hold on the little girl before speaking, "I love your father very much, mina, but he is not the only love in my heart. My own father holds a special place in my heart. The king understands and has given us leave of the castle for one month."

Svetlana bounced off the mattress and hurried to follow her mother's orders.

To soon, she sat beside her mother in the cramped carriage as they both watched the moon glitter from the sky. To excited at the thought of meeting her grandfather, Svetlana bounced on the cushion.

"Mama," she finally squeaked out, only calling her that because they were alone. Father didn't like it when Svetlana used their names. He liked it best for her to call them 'your majesties' but that didn't sit right in her young mind. Instead, she thought of them as mother and father.

"Yes, mina." Anichka stroked her daughter's dark hair lovingly. It was too bad that her father would meet his only granddaughter under these circumstances. But one could not always choose better circumstances. She had learnt that difficult lesson early on as Alerik's wife and queen.

"What does grandfather look like?"

Anichka leaned back and let her mind wander to pleasant memories of the scent of hay, the soft kiss of a horse's lip on her hands, and of her father's dark eyes as he watched from the stable.

"It's been many years since I have seen your grandfather. But I remember his eyes being black as night."

"Like mine!"

"Yes mina, like yours and mine. And like those before us."

Fiddling with the edge of her cloak, she asked in the loud voice of a child, "Why doesn't father like grandfather."

Anichka sighed. She had worried her young daughter might have heard the hurtful words Alerik threw at her. She rubbed Svetlana's back as she replied gently, "It isn't that your father doesn't like your grandfather. Your father doesn't like who my father is and what he can do."

Dropping her cloak, Svetlana sat up and pulled at the curtain of the carriage, pulling it wider. Moonlight spilled into the carriage and bathed the pair in pale light.

"Isn't that the same thing, Mama?" she asked, staring up at the sky full of stars. They had already cleared the city, which sat atop the only hill for miles around. The moonlight glittered off the short shrubs and shorter grass of the land. Soon the winter winds would howl through the flats and bring with the snow and ice, making it impossible to travel between the great city of Issha and the outer lands held by the seven lords of the old families.

"Oh Svetlana," her mother's smile wavered as she watched the land with unseeing eyes, "No, it isn't the same thing."

Svetlana chewed on her lips as she looked up at her mother. She didn't understand at all, but she didn't like seeing her mother sad. No, she wouldn't ask her about it again.

As she curled up against her mother's side, she was slowly rocked to the edge of sleep. She dreamt of riding a great black stallion, her hands free in the sky and her mother and a dark eyed man watching from afar.

CHAPTER ONE

⌘

Sneak Attack

"DARKLING! WAKE UP!"

Carien shook Darkling's shoulders, desperate for a response. Bodies poured in from the forest wearing thick furs and axes at the ready.

"Please!" She begged, tears dripping down her face and onto Darkling's. She watched the arrow lodged in Darkling's chest, hoping that her hunch was right. That the arrow had missed her heart.

"Ugh."

Ashta shook her head; spots clearing from her vision as blinding pain pulsed in her chest.

"Don't move."

Blinking, Ashta looked up into Princess Carien's ashen face, her caramel eyes filled with fear.

"Wha…"

"Look out!"

Carien ducked, an arrow just missing her head. Ashta tried to sit up but stopped when she noticed the quill end sticking out from her chest. She turned her head and watched in horror as one of the Tripsian soldiers was cut down by a Bbrskian berserker.

Her father had found them.

She had been so sure that he would be distracted by his siege on Naankdoen that he would forget about his other daughter.

The last living one.

"Carien, help me up."

"I can't," her voice shook as she backed up, fear widening her eyes.

"Look at me," Ashta hissed. Once the princess's eyes were on her, she leaned forward, gritting her teeth against the pain. "I need you to be strong for the both of us. We are not safe here."

"But what can I do?"

"Get me up."

With shaking hands, Carien gently settled her shoulder under Ashta's armpit and her left arm anchored on her waist. It took two tries before she finally had enough momentum to get both of the girls onto their feet.

"Now what?"

Ashta forced her breath through her nose, trying to work past the pain. She needed to be aware if she was to protect the princess.

"Carien I need you to reach down the back of my skirt, you will feel the handle of my half sword."

She reached down and carefully pulled the sword out from Ashta's clothes. Ashta reached for the sword with her free hand just as a berserker came running towards the pair with his axe swung back.

Ashta lunged forward burying the sword deep in his chest before jerking back.

Carien steadied her even as her stomach turned at the blood dripping from Darkling's sword.

"There's nowhere to go! We're surrounded!"

Ashta ignored the panic in Carien's voice and took in the small clearing. Four of their own soldiers were already dead on the ground. The other lionesses fared better, but Mintia's arm hung uselessly as she parried against two enemy soldiers. Trice was nowhere to be seen.

"Darkling! This way!" Kkaar shouted as she came barreling towards the pair with her own horse. Kkaar leapt off the horse, cutting down to berserkers before running towards the pair.

"We're surrounded, there's no way we will all make it out alive," Kkaar shouted, continuing to hold off the berserkers. Ashta watched in despair as the soldiers and lionesses were slowly being overwhelmed. The noon air was filled with screams of death and despair.

There was only one way.

Ashta turned to Kkaar, "Get the princess on your horse and get out of here."

Kkaar stared back at her, slowly shaking her head. "I won't leave you behind Darkling."

"You have to. It's the only way."

Carien watched, tears spilling down her cheeks. This couldn't be how it ended. They had escaped Naankdoen; they should have been able to make it back to Tripsia.

A berserker ran at the trio, axe swung high. Before Ashta could shout out a warning a spear sliced through his back and pointed out his chest, lodging him to the ground.

Behind the man was Luci with her own horse and Starson. She jumped off quickly and kneeled down beside Ashta.

"Help me get her on," Luci cried, reaching under Darkling.

"We can't," Carien cried out, shaking from shock.

Luci swiveled her head between Carien and Kkaar before taking in the arrow lodged deep into Darkling's chest. She grimaced. There was no time to cut it out. They needed to act fast or risk dying.

"Cover us Kkaar!" she yelled, pulling out a short blade. She sawed off the end of the arrow, leaving the point lodged in.

Carien pulled off her headscarf and handed it to Luci without a word.

Luci looked up at the princess gratefully before wrapping the scarf around Darkling's chest. With the point secured, there was no worry of the other woman bleeding out.

"Can you ride?" she asked Darkling tersely, trying to ignore the clamber of steel scraping and clanging against chainmail.

Ashta gritted her teeth before pulling herself up. For a moment she swayed, the world darkening before coming back into focus. She would not leave the princess. It was her duty to protect her. "Yes."

Luci gave her a short nod before helping her over to Starson.

"Hurry! Their soldiers are overwhelming us!" Kkaar shouted, sweat dripping down her arms. She prayed to every god she knew hoping they might get out alive.

Before Luci could boost Ashta onto the horse, Ashta pushed away from the girl. She gently touched Starson's forehead.

His wide eyes calmed as he watched her.

I need you to kneel.

Carien and Luci watched in awe as the horse knelt down, allowing Darkling to climb on before she slumped over his neck. The pain was manageable. Barely.

"Let's go!" Kkaar shouted, grabbing Carien around the waist and jumping onto her own horse. Luci mounted quickly and without a backward glance they rode out from the camp and straight into the heart of the desert.

The shouts of death and pain followed them as the hot sun beat down on their bare shoulders. The horses panted as sweat dripped down their sides, never slowing from their quick gallop.

Ashta gripped Starson's mane with all her strength. If she fell off, she knew that she would not be able to get back on. And she could not die.

Not now.

Not like this.

For long hours, the only sound that could be heard was the pounding of hooves as the four traveled further into the desert bordering Tripsia.

As the sun slowly set in the west, leading them hopefully to the palace, Kkaar pulled back on her reins allowing the horses a rest as they gently trotted. Luci pulled up beside her while Starson stayed behind, careful to keep his master on his back.

Luci looked back worriedly before turning to Kkaar. "How long until we are at the palace?"

Kkaar watched as the last rays disappeared behind the great sand dunes. "A couple weeks. A week if we make good time and find food."

Carien shuddered, leaning forward against her guard's strong back. She didn't dare mention that she was thirsty. They were all thirsty, even the horses. But it was either run into the desert or risk being run down on the long winding road meant for the wagons and trade.

The horses gentled to a slow walk, their heartbeats slowing. Carien was the first to break the silence. "Do you think anyone survived?"

Luci turned in her seat, squinting behind Darkling but she could not see anything except more sand dunes.

"No, my princess," Kkaar finally answered. She had been so focused to get to Darkling in the fight that she hadn't called out to Trice. One moment the northerner had stood at Kkaar's shoulder pointing towards Darkling, the next she had disappeared into the melee. It was better for Trice and the other men and women to die than to be captured. That much Kkaar knew, her own capture still fresh in her mind despite the many years that had passed.

"We should let the horses rest," Luci said, her voice carrying across the silent desert.

Kkaar rubbed her hand, the scar from the lion's teeth still tight. She worried that if their party stopped, they wouldn't be able to continue.

"How much water do you have on your saddle?" Kkaar asked, knowing her own canteen was full from the stop they had made earlier.

"A half a canteen, maybe?" Luci called, checking her bags then glancing at Darkling's slumped form. She could barely make out her chest moving. At least the other woman was breathing Luci thought grimly. "With Darkling's we have two and half canteen's."

"And food?"

Chewing at her lip, Luci shook her head.

That was what Kkaar had been worried about. She had nothing on her own horse either. They could survive for two days; three if they stretched the water out. But eventually they would have to get Darkling help, or the woman would die.

"I have some dried meat and berries," came a rough voice.

Both Luci and Kkaar jumped as Carien squeezed Kkaar around the middle.

"Darkling!" Carien called.

Kkaar slowed her own mount down until they walked in step with Starson and Darkling.

"How are you doing?" Kkaar asked, taking in the glistening sweat on the dark-haired woman's forehead. She looked feverish. This wasn't good.

"I've been better," she mumbled giving Carien a weak smile. She grimaced as Starson jostled her as he slipped across a flat rock. He twitched his ears, continuing to pick his steps across the sinking sand, careful of his master.

"What are your thoughts. Should we stop?" Kkaar asked.

The stars glittered above, lighting up the barren wasteland.

"No…" her voice was hoarse. She tried to speak again but couldn't find her voice.

"Go in closer Kkaar," Carien demanded pulling out the water canteen. Her legs brushed against Starson as she leaned over and held the canteen to Darkling's mouth. The other woman took several sips before turning her head.

"Just walk…" Ashta finally managed, before her vision blacked out and she floated in a sea of darkness.

"I don't know how long she will make it," Carien worried aloud.

Kkaar pulled her horse ahead and came up beside Luci. "Darkling is made from tough leather. It takes more than an arrow to kill a Bbrskian." At least she hoped so. She turned to Luci. "We will keep walking."

"But what about the horses?"

Kkaar didn't want to worry about that yet. But it was a problem. She shrugged in answer. "I'll stay awake for the first part. Be sure to tie yourself in."

Luci nodded. It would be a long night and her hips already ached. Carien nodded off first to the gentle sway of the horses' step.

The next day passed in utter silence, not even an eagle's cry could be heard across the barren land. Heat sat on top of them as an oppressive weight, trying to drown them in exhaustion. Kkaar was careful to only take a few sips of water, leaving most for the princess.

By the second day, she began to see shadows playing in the corners of her eyes. Hazy visions of dragons and wolves nipping at the horse's feet.

Carien sat silent, dreaming of water and the sweet cooling mists in the mountain air.

Starson walked carefully, the only one aware of the hell that Ashta's mind was caught in. Every so often, she would jerk in her fitful sleep, her mind almost coming to consciousness before she was sucked back into her nightmares of past memories.

On the third morning, Luci's mount stumbled before falling to its knees. Kkaar jerked her own mount to a stop. She watched dispassionately as Luci slit the horse's throat, catching the blood into her canteen.

They passed around the warmed blood, drinking it without thought. Carien's cracked lips barely opened as she poured back the blood. Don't think of it, she kept telling herself, you need to stay alive.

Kkaar pointed to Starson before kicking her own horse back into a walk. They wouldn't make it far, her hazed mind thought. It was only a matter of time before their horse fell to.

Luci held the canteen to Darkling's dried lips. Blood dribbled down her cheek and stained the horse's black coat. Only after Darkling had taken several swallows did Luci pull the canteen away and drain it herself. She kept pace beside the tall warhorse, thankful for his shadow.

Before the sun had fallen in the west, Kkaar's mount's leg buckled. Her quick reflexes pulled her off in time before the horse fellow over, its heart burst.

She lay there, panting, the princess in her arms. Please. *Please.* "P...please."

Luci jogged over; her own legs wobbly. Carefully she helped the princess up, shouldering her from one side. Kkaar stood slowly, taking up the other side.

Slowly, painfully, the three limped behind Starson as the sun kept beating down on them mercilessly.

Kkaar watched blindly as Starson's mighty bulk stumbled before falling to his knees.

Ashta's limp body slipped off his great back, not even a groan slipping from her parched lips.

Kkaar stumbled towards her. She fell to her knees and stared down into the sunburnt face, almost unrecognizable. She watched, panting, for any sign of life.

Please, she thought, please not her. We need this one.

Luci stopped behind her, swaying with exhaustion. Had it been all for naught, she wondered. Was there anything different they could have done?

A shudder racked through Ashta's burnt body. Everything hurt and all she wanted was for it to end.

No.

But it hurt, she thought. Wouldn't death be easier?

No. You are not done yet. You are still needed little one.

Who are you? She asked. Was she going crazy?

You already know who I am. Have always known. Now open your eyes, little one, and find me.

But she didn't want to open her eyes.

Now!

A pulse of energy shot across the land and Ashta's chest raised off the heated sand. She gasped in a deep breath as her black eyes shuddered open for the first time in days.

"Darkling?" Kkaar asked, worried about the other woman. But Darkling looked past her to something over her shoulder. Following her gaze, Kkaar gasped.

A child.

Not ten paces away stood a young boy. His skin dark from the sun, he stared back at the small group in silence. With a nod, he turned and began walking north, away from the setting sun.

"Luci," the other girl jerked herself straight, "Follow the boy." She followed Kkaar's pointed finger and took in the slowly disappearing figure. Luci pulled the princess closer before jerkily following the boy.

Kkaar turned back to the prone body before her. "Can you stand?" She asked.

But Ashta was too far-gone.

Darkling had made it this far, Kkaar thought; she would make it a little further than. With the last of her strength, Kkaar lifted Darkling up before settling her arm around the thin woman's waist.

"Come on Darkling, just a little further."

Ashta's eyes fluttered closed.

Listen to your friend.

Scrunching her eyebrows, she peeled open her eyes. Happy? Ashta demanded of the voice. This time it was quiet in her head. She stayed awake as Kkaar half dragged her limp body across the sand.

Before them, from the hazy sand, emerged a small grouping of dark huts. As they came closer, Kkaar could make out the animal hides lashed around the round tents. The four women stumbled into the middle of the grouping of tents where the lone boy stood watching them.

Finally, only steps away from the boy, Kkaar collapsed onto the ground. She watched as people emerged from the tents.

CHAPTER TWO

⌘

Desert People

Silence reigned in the center of the ghostly tent village. Slowly, people emerged from their tents until a circle of men, women and children surrounded the four women.

Carien likened the people's dress to memories of her own village she had grown up in the alps. The rough white cloth that twisted and hung off their bodies, kept them cool while protecting them from the sun. Well at least the women, Carien thought, her lip twisting up at the corner. The men wore loose fitted pants. That's it. Their bare chests were dark from the unrelenting sun.

The boy that had led them to the village disappeared into the crowd. Uneasy, Carien shifted from foot to foot as the silence reigned. The people just stood there and watched, not saying a word.

"Do you think they can even speak?" Luci whispered, barely moving her cracked lips.

Too afraid to move, Carien barely moved her head in a nod.

A loud groan wracked out of Darkling's chest, shaking her body. Kkaar, crawled over to the other girl's prone body. Her hands shook as she tried to adjust Darkling's body.

"Don't."

All three girls turned to the smooth voice that was at odds with its owner. A grizzled man, his skin sagging, and blue lines faded all across his chest, pushed through the crowd. The boy was not far behind the older man.

The old man gently pulled Kkaar's shoulder back before kneeling down beside her.

He placed an ear over Darkling's mouth and watched her chest.

The women watched, waiting.

He then placed a hand on Darkling's forehead.

With a sigh, he turned to Kkaar.

Four men from the crowd came forward and began lifting Darkling away.

Kkaar tried to stand, not wanting to leave her friend alone.

A soft hand stopped her.

"The arrowhead must be removed. She will not make the night otherwise." His smooth as honey voice soothed her. Her shoulders relaxed as she kept watching the old man. He flicked a glance at Luci and Carien, who still held onto each other's shoulders. "Amkan will bring you to your sleeping quarters and give you water. You must be tired from your journey."

Helplessly, Kkaar nodded in agreement following the man's orders with dazed confusion.

It was Carien that shook her head and turned to the man again, her eyes narrowed. "We are not leaving her."

He nodded, gently herding them towards the boy, "Of course, she be brought to your Yer after the arrowhead has been removed."

Satisfied, Carien nodded before turning back to Amkan. The boy led them to the outside of the little village where a small tent, a Yer, stood proud against the rising night winds.

Amkan held the flap open for the women. Kkaar, with Luci's help, stumbled past the boy into the darkness. Before Carien stepped through, she turned to the boy and asked, "Whose tent is this?"

He just looked up at her, his face clear as a cloudless sky.

Giving up Carien followed her guards and was pleasantly surprised by the coolness inside. It took a few moments for her eyes to adjust. She made out furs and what she assumed pillows littered along the outside walls. In the center stood a pot over a small fire. A ladle handle hung off the end of the spit.

Carien stumbled in her eagerness for liquid. She grabbed the ladle and dipped it into the pot, greedily gulping the spiced soup down her throat. After another ladle full, she walked over to where Luci huddled over Kkaar's stretched out body.

"Here, give her this before she falls asleep."

Luci took the ladle from Carien's hands. She carefully held Kkaar's head before ladling a sip full of liquid into the other woman's mouth. A bit of water dribbled down Kkaar's chin. The other woman's mouth cracked open giving Luci the opportunity to pour more lukewarm soup in her.

Once all three women were full, they lay down together, seeking warmth and comfort from the terror of the past few days.

In another Yer, close to the middle of the village, Ashta lay prone on some furs. Her dark hair was knotted and splayed across the white hides of Elkm rA. An eerie grey green color shone through her sunburnt skin.

Four men, all young and of the same stature, stood near the entrance of the Yer, waiting. The healer, jHora, would call upon them when he needed them. But for now, he heated the water, allowing the clay vessel to bob around.

As he cut away the bloodied and dirtied bands around Ashta's chest, jHora marveled at the young woman's muscles. Her limbs were strong, molded by years of hard training and battle.

He grabbed a rag and washed away the blood and dirt around the small nub where the arrow had entered. A small gasp from the direction of the four men had his hand pausing over his work.

Not now, he chastised, continuing to clean around the wound.

jHora frowned as he got a closer look at the arrow shaft. Black liquid seeped from the wood. It wasn't blood. This was not good.

Amkan, go get the Ruutka. There wasn't much left, jHora grimly thought, but it would have to do. The village would come to some more soon enough. The Alpen people sometimes traded their Ruutka for the zMun people's obsidian and other treasure's his people found in their travels through the desert.

He searched in his bag for the necessary tools for the upcoming procedure. He pulled out two large wooden spoons.

Carefully, he dipped each spoon into the now boiling water. Then he fished out the clay vessel, gently cracking the top all the way around. He pried off the top, clay crumbling and falling into his lap.

Amkan ran into the Yer, bowing down to jHora as he dropped the dried bag of Ruutka at the healer's feet. Quietly, the boy disappeared back into the evening light.

jHora poured the dry Ruutka into the open clay vessel filled with liquid hot honey. He stirred the honey with the Ruutka carefully with first one spoon, then the other.

It is time.

All four men stepped away from the wall and came to kneel down beside the slight woman. One man watched her with interest. Her hair was blacker than he had expected. Her skin golden.

A sharp word from jHora had the man shaking his head as he took up his position by her head. He carefully pulled her hair to one side then placed his hands down onto her shoulders.

The second man straddled her hips, his hands locking her legs into place. The last two men kneeled beside each other.

jHora gave each of the last two men a sticky spoon.

The men carefully worked their spoons into the wound, widening the wound as they worked it in and over the arrowhead.

Once both had their spoons in place, the men waited. jHora chanted quietly, sending a prayer out to the god above and the god below. Let this one live, he thought, glancing quickly at the young man at her head.

With a sharp nod to the men, jHora reached down to the arrow shaft and held. The two men at her head and feet tensed. The last two pulled their spoons apart, widening the wound to a gaping hole.

Ashta gasped, pulled from her unconscious state. Heat poured out of her chest as her whole body tingled. With a scream stuck in her throat, she jerked and pulled at the arms restraining her.

jHora pulled the shaft hard, ripping through the last bit of tissue. He threw the bloodied arrowhead to the side of the Yer, quickly grabbing the still hot clay vessel. He poured its contents into the wound as the two men slid out their spoons.

This time Ashta did scream, the sound wrenched from deep within her soul. For a brief moment, her eyes shuttered open. Firelight flickered across the stretched animal hides above her. Then she glanced back and was caught by twin orbs of purple.

Her brow crinkled in confusion. *What the…?*

But before she could finish her thought, she was pulled back under into dark oblivion. jHora grimaced as her tense body slackened immediately.

He bandaged the wound before pouring some heated water down her throat. Lastly, he swiped some sweetened honey across her lips and inside her cheeks. With a nod to the men, he turned back to the fire, dropping the hot spoons into the pot.

The three men carefully lifted her while the purple-eyed man held open the flap to the Yer.

Moonlight bathed Ashta's body in the now late night, her body swinging slightly. The man grimaced as his hand gently swept a tear from her temple.

Please, he prayed, begged.
Please.

Her nose itched. Ashta tried to move her arm but nothing happened. *What the…?* Forcing open her eyes, she blinked several times to rid herself of the gritty dry feeling in her eyes. When she could focus them, she found herself staring up at a cloudless blue sky.

"You are awake!"

Barely turning her head to the right, Ashta's muscles screamed in protest. Carien looked down at her with watery eyes.

Ashta tried to talk but all that came out was a croak.

"Don't try to talk yet," Carien warned as she screwed open her water pouch and carefully poured it's contents into Ashta's mouth.

Her heart burst with happiness to see the dark-haired woman awake, her eyes clear. They had all been worried that Darkling wouldn't make it.

The cart that they were seated in jerked, causing Carien to fall back hard, water spilling down the wooden slats. She scrambled to close up the canteen and sit back up.

Meanwhile, Ashta brought her head forward so she could see straight ahead. Or straight behind, she amended, taking in the various people walking towards her with packs on their backs. But she was moving to. She turned to Carien, arching a brow.

"Do you remember arriving at the village?"

Ashta shook her head.

Carien pursed her lip, trying to find an easy way to explain a not so simple people. Or, at least not as simple as she, Luci, and Kkaar had originally thought these people were.

"We had been riding through the desert for days and had used up the last of the water. Starson had died from exhaustion," Ashta felt a twinge of guilt at the ugly death of her trusted companion. "We thought for sure we would die when Amkan, a boy from the village, found us on his search for cacti. He brought us back to his people, the zMun people. Their wise man was then able to remove the arrowhead from your chest." Carien hesitated, not sure whether she should continue.

Ashta's stare had her continuing, except in a rush. "The next morning, they had the village packed up and moving. Except you had come down with a bad infection and have been in and out for a week. Yesterday your fever finally broke. And now here we are," she finished with a flourish of her hands.

Ashta blinked, still stuck on one fact. A week. Seven days. Not including the first few days when they had wandered through the desert. It was enough time for the news of what happened in Tripsia, and of the attack, to have reached the king.

Grimacing, she tried to shift her weight but was blinded by pain throughout her chest. Taking in small rapid breaths, she blinked up at the continuous blue sky above her.

The color haunted her, the exact shade as a certain prince's gaze. The same warmth.

Did I make the right choice? She wondered, knowing that the prince would be stuck in Naankdoen for the remainder of the foreseeable future; Either the city would have to fall or the Bbrskian army be decimated. Neither had ever happened in the history of the known world and the Midloean kingdoms before.

Ashta worried that in her lifetime one of those facts would be proven wrong and that no matter which side won, her soul would pay the price for it.

CHAPTER THREE

⌘

Traveling With Company

ASHTA WATCHED THE sun slowly rise into her view as their company followed the sun's trail across the sky slightly to where it slept each night.

She passed the time by carefully stretching and relaxing each of her limbs, first with her fingers until she finally got down to her legs. Her muscles cried out in pain from disuse, but she gritted her teeth and pushed through it.

Carien sat beside her, dozing in the sun. Ashta worried about the sun and its damages to the princess's face but knew there wasn't much choice they had right now. They were at the mercy of the zMun people.

Even as Ashta chewed at her lips, she kept her mind busy, cataloguing how many villagers she could differentiate, and how many of those were able bodied. Surprisingly, even the old in the group had hardened muscles from years of strenuous use. They were a people that could hold their own in a fight. Yet, Ashta saw no knives, swords, or bows. The occasional spear was slung across someone's back with heavy packed hides hanging from each side.

It made sense, she mused, there wasn't much wood available in the desert. A bow and arrows required lots of wood. Also, the desert people didn't have enough wood to make a forge and bend metal into knives and swords. Most of their weapons would have been something they traded for.

jHora glanced over at the young woman who now lay awake in the back of the cart. Her mind was a bright spot amongst his people. Yet he could feel a darkness edged around her essence. As if there was something horrible, she refused to think about. In time, jHora hoped, the girl would learn to clear her mind of such memories. For a darkness such as that could poison the mind if left untouched and unhealed.

With a nod to zHeezek, the man that had held the girls legs down, jHora stopped and began unloading his great pack. Men and women around them also stopped, dropping their packs as the children ran to the yack cart to gather what water the peoples still had.

Flung to a stop, Ashta carefully reached up with her arm and rubbed at the back of her head.

"What's..." Carien began, startled from her nap. Her cheeks and ears were pink from the sun.

"Midday meal, methinks," Kkaar replied, dropping her load of furs beside the wooden spoke. She leaned on the cart and glanced down at the dark-haired woman. "You are awake."

With a nod, Ashta slowly pulled herself upright before dropping her back against the wall of the cart. She looked straight across at Kkaar, whose skin was already darkened from the beating sun. Before Ashta could open her mouth to speak, a young girl jumped onto the cart and grabbed onto a large barrel at the end. Two more kids jumped up to help the girl pull the barrel to the edge. Carien shuffled to the edge of the cart and jumped off stretching her legs before leaning against the cart with Kkaar.

She looks comfortable, Ashta realized. A tension she had never noticed the princess held in her usual gowns was gone. Her Tripsian day dress had been traded in for a tunic like the other women.

Ashta and the three women stayed quiet as they watched the people busy themselves with making up a fire from some desert brush and boiling up water with herbs and dried meat. Ashta's mouth watered. Despite the burning heat from the sun, she shivered in anticipation for some food. Even some papna would be delicious right now.

A man separated from the grouping of villagers and wound his way towards the women. He balanced two bowls in one hand and a clay vessel in the other.

Something about the shape of the vessel pulled at a memory, but Ashta couldn't quite piece it together.

He nodded to the lionesses and the princess. "There is broth for you," he said to Carien, Luci and Kkaar, glancing back at the fire before turning towards Ashta.

His voice was smooth and soft like honeyed rose tea. Yet, even his voice tickled something in her mind. It was familiar. His whole body was familiar, like she had seen this man before. But that's impossible, right? She worried quietly to herself.

zHar smirked, placing the bowls onto the cart. He carefully hopped up without jiggling the rickety wooden floor. Once he was seated beside the dark-haired woman, their faces towards each other, he pulled the bowl of broth onto his lap.

He lifted a spoonful to her mouth and waited for her. But Ashta just stared at the man. His eyes were bright purple. They glittered like strange gemstones.

"You need to eat," he encouraged, touching the warm metal to her lips. They opened automatically, even as she kept staring at him, questions swimming in her eyes.

They sat in silence until she had finished her bowl. Then he dipped the spoon into the clay vessel and lifted it to her mouth. She sniffed it and could smell hints of honey and something else.

Her nose wrinkled.

Ruutka.

"It helps. The infection is not gone yet."

Reluctantly, she accepted the spoonful, swallowing convulsively as the spiced sugar slid down her throat. She leaned back and watched as the man took the same spoon and started to eat from his own bowl.

The wooden slats of the cart jiggled and Ashta glanced up into Kkaar's eyes. This time Luci stood beside her. Reflexively, Ashta searched behind them for Carien. When she saw the princess seated with some women, chatting and eating, she let go of her breath. Good.

Turning back to Kkaar, she nodded for the other guard to begin.

"We need to go over what happened. And I'm not talking about just the desert, but Naankdoen."

Ashta shifted a glance at the strange man, who still ate his broth silently watching the women. An errant black lock of hair curled on his forehead, making him look almost boyish. *He's cute.*

She shifted her focus back to Kkaar, missing the smile that played across his mouth.

Kkaar waved her hand, dismissing the danger of speaking in front of the stranger. "The zMun are safe," she leaned forward her arms crossed over the cart edge. "What happened in Naankdoen, Darkling?"

Ashta noticed his quirked brow, but ignored it, answering her fellow lioness. "As you remember, the king had demanded our presence in the castle. He-" she hesitated, glancing over at Carien. The princess's caramel hair glowed in the sun, her whole presence happy and joy filled. The important part was she was out of earshot. "He sentenced Princess Lillian to death." She recalled flashes of white fur splattered blood red. Blood dripping down the cobblestone path. Sobs cut off followed by awful silence. The grim faces of Bbrskian berserkers lit up in the night by fire.

Shaking her head, she forced herself to continue. zHar frowned, rubbing at his chest, his broth forgotten.

"After her body had been disposed, an emissary from Bbrski landed on the dock. He laid down terms, the live princess for the safety of the city."

Luci gasped. Kkaar laid a gentle hand on the smaller woman's shoulder, still watching Darkling's pale face. "And so, they attacked."

"Yes."

"How did you escape with the princess?"

Ashta shrugged, "All that matters is that the princess is safe and alive. We need to get her back to the safety of her father and the rest of the white lionesses."

Kkaar nodded in agreement, not asking about what Darkling wasn't saying. If it were important, the other woman would have said it aloud. "We could be months out from the ruined city, plus we have no food or water supplies."

"Our people can take you part of the way."

All three guards turned sharply to the new voice that joined them. jHora stood to the side of their party, aloof.

With their attention, he continued, "We are on our normal migration to our winter site. We will be crossing into Tripsian desert in a week. From there you can separate from us. It should be no more than two days travel to the ruined city from there."

Traveling with the zMun would ensure their safety for the next week, as well as food and water. Plus, the people knew their way through the desert. It would be safest option and the fastest. They couldn't afford to be lost in the desert again.

"Then we shall travel with the zMun until we reach Tripsia." Luci and Kkaar nodded in agreement with Ashta's statement.

Pushing back the blankets that covered her legs, Ashta stood up, using the cart edge for support. The purple-eyed man's eyes widened before he grabbed the bowls and hopped off the back of the cart. He hurried away, lost amid his people.

Kkaar and Luci lunged forward as if to help, but Ashta dismissed them with a wave. She toed her way to the edge of the cart before hopping down onto the sand. Her landing jarred her wound. She rubbed at the bandage as she gritted her teeth. Across from the trio, Carien stood, pale and gaping.

Ashta forced her shoulders to relax and a smile onto her lips, then she turned to Kkaar. "Spar with me."

The other woman shook her head, her hands up. "I-I can't. You are still healing."

Steadying her breathing, Ashta walked with slow measured steps until she stood right before Kkaar. "You know as well as I, that lionesses can't afford to take time to heal," she hissed into her ear.

Kkaar shivered, before finally nodding in agreement. "You should stretch first, if we are going to do this."

Ashta didn't bother replying, taking a few steps away from the cart before folding herself over her legs, her hands flat on the sandy ground. With focused breaths, she stretched each tight muscle until she felt fully in control of the pain. Her chest would hurt. But that was something she would just have to work through.

"Ready."

She stood on the balls of her feet, bouncing slightly in the loose ground. It was unlike anything they had trained in. But it brought memories of the pit and the trial. Her lips tugged up at the corners as she waited for Kkaar's move.

Luci sat to the side, in the shade of the cart, and watched the two women as they sparred. For once, the fight was even, Darkling having to compensate for injuries. But even then, it was just barely even. The dark-haired woman was born with a talent unlike anything Luci had ever seen. Her movements weren't as graceful as their friend and fellow lioness Ceerie. No one could be as graceful as a woman with the touch of elf blood running through her veins. And yet Darkling had sharpness, and a raw strength that made it impossible to look away.

Luci noted that many of the zMun people watched the sparring match.

"She is good."

Jumping slightly, Luci was shocked to find the purple-eyed man beside her. She shivered. A guard should never allow someone to sneak up on them. It spelled death. But the shifty eyed man had snuck up on her many times the past few days.

"She is," Luci agreed, watching her lover. Kkaar wasn't as strong, or as quick as Darkling, but she was consistent. She didn't tire. She didn't anger. She just fought.

Luci frowned, knowing their few stolen moments would disappear once they arrived at the ruined city. Their love was forbidden but ignored for the most part by the lionesses. But there were others who watched in the sprawling underground compound. And Kkaar had said she did not want to risk Luci.

Kkaar dropped to the ground before coming up with a roundhouse kick. Darkling just ducked out of the way, but her face tightened with pain. Luci watched the other woman's tense jaw as Darkling got up to deliver right after left fist, barely deflected by Kkaar.

She was something else.

Rustling canvas had Luci turning back to the seated people. Except for the purple-eyed man, the other people were now standing and helping each other put their packs on.

Luci signaled to Kkaar. The other woman nodded before taking a step back.

"Draw."

Ashta's nose wrinkled as she gasped for big lungsful of air. She was out of shape, and only after a few days. The idea disturbed her. If she wanted to remain alive as a guard, she could not afford even a day without training.

She nodded to Kkaar, before walking over to the cart. The purple-eyed man stood beside Luci, a bowl of broth waiting in his outstretched hands.

She lifted a hand to stop him. Gingerly, she hopped up onto the back of the cart and sat on the edge, her feet dangling, as she tried to slow her heart.

The man came over and stood between her legs. Ashta stiffened but didn't pull away. She told herself it was because of the spoonful of broth he already had halfway to her mouth. But her body shivered with another reason.

She ate in silence, watching the other man. His arms were toned from hard use and dark from the sun. A slight blue smudge flashed at her each time his hand came up to her mouth. The sun glanced off his hair, bringing out streaks of bright red in his otherwise black hair.

When the bowl was finished, Ashta opened her mouth to thank him but he had already turned away and disappeared.

Strange, she thought, rubbing her aching chest. Her eyes caught on the princess, who was walking towards the cart.

Ashta pulled herself all the way up the cart before settling back into her spot in the back, this time without a blanket. She would have walked with the others, but she knew she couldn't push herself that fast. In another day, maybe.

And so, as the party moved further Southwest following the setting sun, Ashta dozed off into a deep dream filled sleep.

CHAPTER FOUR

⌘

The Lioness

"HIGHER LENTIA!" Remina yelled at her sparring partner.

The other woman wasn't focusing, her eyes clouded as she tried to kick her leg high enough to reach Remina's leg.

And failed.

It had been over an hour of training and the other woman had still not worked through her problem. She wouldn't get anywhere today.

Holding up a hand, Remina ended the fruitless sparring session. She took her time with her stretches before walking out of the training room and walking back to the lioness's barracks.

Lentia was still sitting on the ground when Remina had left. If she kept it up, Remina worried the other woman would find herself on the wrong side of the executioner's axe.

"Remina the Lion!"

Remina stopped, standing at attention to the messenger boy. When he didn't continue, blushing bright red, she quirked a brow.

Finally, he choked out his words. "T-the Baron Attel has arrived at the castle and requests your services for the duration of his stay."

Remina refused to show any emotion even as her chest warmed. Justus was back. With a sharp nod she dismissed the boy and walked right back out of the barracks. If Justus was here, he would be at his summer residence.

She wound her way through the stone alleys of the palace before slipping out of the walls and into the surrounding city Trian. The great city of Tripsia that stood above like a shining gem over its vast emerald green rainforests. The cliff face brought with it the salty smell of the sea and its temperate winds, making Trian the perfect place to grow fruits and flowers of every kind.

Smiling, Remina passed the market filled with its food and wares for the morning. She grabbed an orange from Arita, an older woman whose son she had saved from the King's wrath. Arita smiled, waving at her.

Oh, life was good. Remina had gained the king's favor and could walk through the city as she pleased. The itch at her neck reminded her she was never truly free to leave. The king had ensured that, tattooing a collar around her neck for all to see. But it didn't matter. No slave had ever been released from Tripsia's hold. The most Remina could hope for was a quiet life protecting the nobles of Tripsia and then become a teacher for the next generation of cubs.

She ducked through the back entrance of the sprawling complex owned by the baron Attel. The cooks and servants didn't even look up from their stations, use to the Lionesses that walked among them. Remina kept walking through the servant halls until she came to the bedroom. She hesitated at the secret door for a moment.

She knew she shouldn't do this. Nothing good would come of it. Yet her heart ached.

Straightening her shoulders, she pushed through the door and came to a stop in front of the Barons bed. Too soon, Justus walked out of his dressing room. He didn't pause at her appearance, walking straight to her and pulling her in for a long-drawn-out embrace.

"I have missed you, my Mina," he whispered into her ear. She shivered at his hot breath, before coolly stepping back.

"The great city of Trian welcomes you, Baron Attel."

He frowned at her severe expression and took a step back as well. Had he been gone to long, had she forgotten him? Them?

"Mina?"

There, a small spark in her eyes, almost unnoticeable if one was not sure where to look. But he knew. She was his Mina, his love.

Remina turned away, trying, and failing miserably, to keep her rigid stance. "Oh Justus," she let out on a breath, unwillingly. "We can't do this anymore."

"Why? Have you fallen out of love for me?"

She shook her head. What she felt was not the point. There union was forbidden. The King's wrath was the only thing holding her back from what she wanted to do with Justus. But she knew the King's feelings for her were more, even if she felt nothing for him. He would not stop at just punishing her. He would punish Justus and his family. And that was something she could not risk.

"Please," She begged, "Please try to leave us behind. We can never be."

Justus knew that he could not change her mind. At least not right now. Give her some time with him and she would see it his way. That he couldn't live without her. He had tried to live without her all winter, for her sake and for his aging parents. But he could not forget the girl with haunted blue eyes.

So, he stepped back from her, nodded his assent, and left the room. He knew she would follow, as she had followed him the last five years.

He made his way downstairs, where his finances man was waiting. They had a meeting with the King this afternoon, and Justus had already wasted too much time. The King had a short temper.

As their small party made its way back up to the great palace, he could not help but wonder. There must be some way where they could find happiness. Somehow.

Remina grimaced at the edge to Justus's thoughts. She knew he wouldn't give up on them. It was one of the things she loved about him. He never gave up on those he believed in.

But she was too far out of reach for even him to help.

As the great palace doors swung open to greet them, she began to feel a prickle of unease at the back of her neck. The columns stood tall, following them down the hall, reminding them that they were mere mortals to the immortality of the kings. But Remina knew the truth of royals. They were not above mortals and could feel pain and die just like a common soldier.

Soon they stood before the great throne, sitting high above them. The small, rounded body of the king squirmed in the large seat. He had come to his kingship young, King Atticus. He was barely thirty summers old, a mere three summers older than Justus. Yet Remina knew the two were infinitely different. Where Justus was wise, kind and caring; Atticus was not.

"Remina the Lion," His voice squeaked, betraying his surprise.

She stepped forward, giving him a slight nod before stepping to the side. Remina grimaced as she listened to the change in the King's thoughts. He was suspicious of her presence with Justus. She didn't know what had occurred over the winter, but the king had become more and more possessive of her.

Thankfully, he ignored her for the majority of the meeting, instead paying attention to Justus and his man. Remina tried to ignore what she heard, but it was hard to ignore the state of Justus's land. They were losing money. Badly.

Finally, the king dismissed Justus. Remina turned to follow him.

"Not you, Remina the Lion."

She stopped before turning slowly towards the King. She saw Justus hesitate before continuing. Even he had heard tales of how volatile the young king was to those that did not do what he wanted.

Atticus walked down the long staircase before stopping in front of Remina. With him so close, she noted the difference between him and Justus. The King stood the same height as her, with the help of heightened shoes. His skin was pale from lack of sun. Even the short walk down from the raised thrown had sweat beading on his temple.

Justus, she easily recalled, had skin as golden as the desert of her home. His hair was black as night setting off his black eyes. He was tall, a full head larger than her. She dreamed of running her fingers through his hair, before running her hand down his wide chest.

"I had a gift made for you," Atticus said, his voice to loud.

Remina nodded, still lost in her daydream.

Oh Justus. If only.

With a nod, a servant came out from behind a column and held out a sword that lay across his hands. Surprised at the quality, Remina reached out without thinking. At the last moment, she glanced over at the King.

"Please. It's for you."

Remina still hesitated. She shouldn't further his affections. Yet, even the King could not hope to do anything with a white lioness.

Forbidden to marry.

Forbidden to have relations.

The laws had been set long before King Atticus and his people would not let him forget.

With that comfort, she pulled the heavy great sword into her hands. It was tall, its sharp edge gleaming. Even as she swung it, she could feel its balance. Not too bulky, but heavy enough to do damage.

As she looked over it, her eyes caught on the pommel. Opal. Remina rubbed the stone feeling her power strengthen, as she heard not only the King and his servants, but also commoners in the streets below. And Justus on his way back to his summer compound. Her heart pounded. So much power.

She jerked her hand away from the stone, pushing it back into the servant's hands.

"You don't like it?"

Remina had enough wits about her to understand the danger of the situation as she took in the king's reddened cheeks.

She bowed low before answering carefully. "The great sword is beautifully crafted and masterfully balanced. A lowly slave is not worthy of such a high prize."

Blustering, the King waved his hands, "I want you to have it. I don't care about your status. You are one of the best guards, and the best swordswoman Tripsia has ever seen. It seems only fitting that you have a worthy sword for your skill."

Remina nodded, knowing herself beat. She accepted the sword and belt. She carefully belted it to her back, the tip coming down past her hip.

"I accept your praise, your majesty. With this sword I will continue to serve you and your house faithfully," With another bow she took a step back, "Now I must return to my station."

With that, she turned and left the columned palace and its pale prince behind. She couldn't risk his recklessness. It was only a matter of time before something had to give.

Rubbing her wrist with its familiar blue mark, Remina wished for simpler times. When she had been a little girl, free to run through the streets naked without a worry for herself. But that time had passed.

As she snuck back into Justus's residence and stationed herself in his office, Remina was filled with unease. Something had to give.

Justus's black eyes looked up at her before catching on the opal pommel. "Nice sword," he commented.

Remina shrugged then focused her eyes on a spot on the wall, tuning out Justus and his men. Something had to give, and she feared this summer would be the last calm summer.

CHAPTER FIVE

⌘

A Familiar Feeling

ASHTA RUBBED HER arms, the hairs standing on end. Since the dream, her body had become hypersensitive to charges in the air. And for some reason the desert was full of them.

Nice sword.

Shivering again, she quickened her step, passing the yak cart. Carien only gave her glance before settling back in the cart. It would have been easy to stay on the cart with the princess, but Ashta knew the best way to get her body back into shape was to push it.

Every day when the party broke at midday, when the sun was its highest and strongest, the village would stop for their meal. Ashta would seek out either Luci or Kkaar and spend most of it training.

A familiar silhouette appeared beside her, keeping pace. She slanted a glance over at purple-eyes – as she called him now to herself. His body was covered in a fine sheen of sweat. Ashta knew it wasn't from the walk, as the exertion was minimal. He must have been doing something else. Scouting ahead?

They walked in silence together, the morning sun slowly rising behind them. Ashta didn't mind the heat on her back. What did bother her was she couldn't make out purple-eyes face. As if hearing her, he angled himself to her, allowing her to make out half his face. His mouth was pulled up at the corner in a familiar smirk.

A prickle at the back of her neck had her suspicions up. Maybe there was something familiar about him, about the zMun people.

Her curiosity won out and she broke her own rule of silence. But only because she couldn't properly assess the threat without speaking to the people. At least that's what she told herself.

"What are you called?"

He was silent for a few steps, not turning away but neither turning towards her. Her ears almost rang with his voice because she listened so intently for his words.

"My name is zHar."

Ashta quirked a brow. Even his name was familiar, tickling at the back of her mind. She had heard it before, she was sure.

Pushing the thought away, she asked another question that had been plaguing her since they galloped straight into the heart of the Naankdoena desert. "How can you be sure that we are not being followed?"

"We are not being followed," he replied firmly. His voice was filled with confidence that Ashta almost believed. Almost.

"But how can you be so sure?"

He pushed a hand through his locks, setting his hair up at haphazard angles. Ashta's fingers tingled to smooth them back down. She clenched her hand instead to stop the urge.

"I…I just know."

She turned to look up at him and was caught in his gaze. Not only were his eyes an unfamiliar shade, but they were also filled with a warmth that Ashta had never felt before. Well not never, she amended, it reminded her of her mother's gaze. Or her grandfather's. Filled with understanding, admiration, and love.

That last one made her shiver. There was no way zHar could feel that for her. They had only just met.

She broke off their gaze and continued walking, comforted by his closeness.

That was one thing she didn't understand about the man. Since the first moment, she felt safe with him. Her whole body loosened and her mind relaxed as if he was a familiar friend. But he wasn't, she tried to remind herself sternly.

There was another thought that had been nagging at her mind. A story she had heard in the Naankdoen palace.

"I-" she hesitated not sure how to continue. But his silence encouraged her to speak, especially with the noise of all the people around her. "I had heard that the desert people of Naankdoen had moved to the city Kiang Don. I didn't realize that there were some still in the desert to this day."

"There isn't." His answer was so quiet that at first, she didn't hear the words.

"But the zMun are a desert people? And we did find you within the Naankdoen kingdom."

He nodded.

She waited for him to continue.

Instead, the silence grew.

He took a step closer, then began telling a story that was all too familiar.

"Our tribe's leader zHella, lead the people to the old city where the young princess waited. With her father's blessing the two married, and with their union zHella was able to protect our people. For a time.

We had enough food and water to fill our bellies and soften out skin. But too soon the people became antsy. The walls became too crowded, the people in the city too many. And then the city's people began stealing the food the King had ordered for us. They threw dung at our heads. The final straw was the night the city people tried to burn our Yer, killing some of our children. zMun went crazy, and attacked the city people, not caring who they killed.

Only our tribe leader, zHella, could quiet the pain in our hearts. He came out to the city edge, to the wall we had set our Yer against. With a quiet finality, he banished our people back to the desert, warning us to never return.

The tribe was broken.

From that day on we never flourished, barely surviving each year. Just as we survive now.

In answer to your question, we are not the same tribe as the one that entered the city that fateful year. We…" And for a moment, Ashta believed he would continue his story. But instead, he shook his head, his fingers grazing down her arm and lighting a fire in her belly.

Shivering she pulled away and returned to walking beside the yak cart. Carien laid back, the sun baking her royal skin to a golden brown.

The story of the zMun was a sad one. She remembered the first part, when she had stood in the hall staring up at the creation banner on the Naankdoen castle walls. Before everything in her life had gone upside down.

The zMun had suffered the worst drought in their history and were dying, with no water and no food to hunt.

Meanwhile, the first princess in the history of Naankdoen to be born used her powers to come into contact with the tribe leader. They fell in love and when they met in person, the king, ready with his army realized there was nothing he could do. And so, the people were saved.

For a little while it seemed.

Ashta's mouth pulled down into a grimace as she thought about her own story. For a time, being sold to the Tripsian kingdom as a slave had saved her. She had been free from the shackles of her past, from being princess Svetlana.

But that notion had been shattered in Naankdoen. Ashta would never be free of her past. And when they did return to court, she knew that her history would come into play. Especially if her fears about her father's true reasoning for sending his other daughter, Princess Lillian, to Naankdoen were true.

Her father was not a benevolent leader. He ruled with total power and fear. But making his own people fearful of him only worked for so long before the grumblings of revolution would begin to murmur through the ice Kingdom.

Ashta stretched her arms back, comforted by the cold steel on her body. Whatever her father had planned, Ashta was ready. This time she would be able to fight him, with her mind and with her body.

The Yak cart came to a sudden stop, throwing Carien into the back by the water barrels. Ashta jumped up quickly and offered to help the princess, but Carien just waved her off.

"It's my own fault," she said through a smile, rubbing her head where it had hit the barrel.

She scrambled off the cart and quickly joined the women making the midday broth.

With a sigh, Ashta jumped off as well, not surprised when Kkaar appeared beside her.

"How's the chest?"

"Healed," Ashta said truthfully. The stitches tugged but she could feel the skin knitted together, a few more days and she would take them out. A little training wouldn't rip them open.

The two women quickly fell into their fighting stances.

Their sparring had gained quite an audience, the young boys and girls sat watching while the men and women stood back, watching with half an eye.

Ashta didn't mind. She made sure to slow her moves and practice technique, giving the young ones time to see what she was doing. Kkaar understood what she was doing.

They cycled through punches, kicks, until finally doing throws. Ashta didn't mind the throws but she felt the tug of her stitches reminding her to take it easier. Ripping through stitches never helped the healing process.

As they separated to begin their cool down stretches, a little girl jumped up and asked, "Why don't you ever fight?"

Ashta straightened up and gave her whole attention to the child, dirt streaked down her chest, her hair light from the sun. "A fight does not serve well to practice and hone in on skills."

The little girl wrinkled her brow, not satisfied. "But when you fight someone, they don't give you time to practice."

Ashta walked over to the girl and crouched down until they were eye level. The girl's dark brown eyes were filled with questions, but at the back Ashta could feel a small thread of fear.

Fear she understood. Fear was what had her jumping in the water despite her half-sister's attempt at drowning her. Fear was what had her jumping onto a torash without thought to chase down the princess before she died.

But this little girl didn't need fear.

"No. In a fight, the other person doesn't give you time to practice. But by then, your body will be used to fighting that when your brain is scared your body still knows how to fight. Would you like to see?" She asked gently. When the child nodded slowly, Ashta got up and turned to Kkaar.

"What do you say?"

"I wouldn't mind a fight. With your wound I might still win," Kkaar grinned.

Ashta smirked at her cockiness, "In your dreams."

And with that, she ran at the other woman, not holding back.

This time there were no pulled punches, there was no softness in either woman.

zHar watched in silent awe as the dark-haired woman parried and kicked, her fists so fast they were a blur. But the other woman kept up.

Without thought, Kkaar grabbed Ashta's leg from a kick and threw her down, grappling with her in the sand. But Ashta didn't let the move stop her.

Winded, she pushed through the pain radiating through her chest and flipped over until she was the one on top.

When the dust settled, Ashta lay atop Kkaar, the other woman's arm pulled back to the point of dislocation, her body held in a vise by Ashta's leg.

Finally, after a few seconds of struggle, and Ashta pulling back just slightly on Kkaar's arm, Kkaar tapped her free hand.

"Yield," she choked out.

Ashta loosened her hold and quickly jumped up. She reached down and helped Kkaar up.

"I almost had you," she grumbled, massaging her stretched shoulder.

"Not a chance," Ashta replied with a smile before walking over to the young child. She crouched down again and this time there was no sign of fear.

"The body has memories separate of your mind. If you practice both you will always be ready."

The girl nodded gravely, then reached her hand out touching Ashta's chest. Ashta looked down to see the bloodstain seeping through her bands. Shit. She ripped her stitches.

With a sigh, she rose up and walked over to Kkaar and Luci. zHar stood close by, two bowls in his hand.

Without thought, Ashta unrolled the blood soaked bandage.

Luci hissed as the mess of skin and stitches came to light.

A clink of clay had Ashta turning to zHar. He quickly disappeared into the crowd. Ashta puzzled over his disappearance before focusing back on the wound. She picked out the stitches she could find. Two stitches at the top of the wound still held, but the other eight bellow were gone. Plus the wound had split further down.

"Here," a honeyed voice comforted.

Ashta stared into his violet eyes, shining with something. She took the cloth, the familiar scent of Ruutka in the air. She cleaned up the blood and held the cloth with pressure on the wound.

zHar held a needle, as he carefully threaded it.

When he glanced down into her black eyes, he almost forgot what he was doing. With a shake, he gestured her towards the back of the yak cart. She hopped on to the edge, sitting, her feet kicking out as she balanced.

"May I?" he asked, standing between her legs again. He felt the same blast of heat as last time, but he held it close. She wasn't ready. The challenge in her eyes said as much.

Slowly, she lifted the cloth aside and waited.

He leaned forward, ignoring her soft skin, as he began the first stitch. She was strong, not even a gasp of pain as he tugged the stitch tight. As he went to cut it, he realized he had forgotten a knife. *Amkan.*

Before he could continue the thought, Ashta reached up into her hair and pulled out a small thin knife.

At first, he didn't grab it, to shocked at the appearance of the knife. He had known about the other blades on her chest and legs. But her hair. He shivered at her lethality. Then took the knife, cut the thread, and continued onto the next stitch.

Ashta forced herself to breathe through her nose. The pain was manageable.

But the heat that flushed through her body from his nearness. That was something else. If she hadn't been desensitized from nudity from the Nursery, she might have blushed at his nearness to her breasts. But it didn't matter. His face was contorted in concentration as he carefully made each stitch over her heart.

Once the stitches were done, he carefully dabbed the Ruutka infused cloth over the closed wound.

"There." He said quietly, and for a moment they stood like that, forgotten by time.

A gentle shake through the cart reminded Ashta that there was an audience, a very large audience. She reached up her hands and pushed his bare shoulders until he stepped back.

The moment her hands had touched his skin, she gasped. A familiar shock of fire and energy raced through her hand and to her center.

And then she realized why zHar was so familiar. Except for his bright twin violet eyes, he looked exactly like prince zHavier.

Same hair, same strong jaw, same electricity.

She jumped down and walked over to Kkaar who held out an extra chest band.

Not the same electricity, she amended. The reaction zHar had brought out in her body was ten times as strong as zHavier's.

She shivered at the thought.

She didn't want anyone to have that kind of power over her body, over her.

CHAPTER SIX

⌘

Old Majik

CRACK.

It was just the slightest noise, yet every one of Ashta's senses came on in high alert. She kept her breathing the same, not moving from her spot beside Carien's body. They must have been asleep for a few hours. Ashta's internal clock told her it was just past midnight.

Not hearing anything, she decided to get up and investigate. Her senses screamed at her. Her gut clenched hard with unease. Something was not quite right.

She carefully pulled back the fur she slept under, making sure not to jar Carien. The other two guards slept peacefully, their limbs entangled. For a moment Ashta watched their still bodies, her heart aching knowing that their love could never be.

She slipped her leather skirt on, not bothering with the boots or her bandages. She took out the short half-handed sword before approaching the entrance.

Ashta waited, holding her breath, but she could hear no movement outside. Not even a lone bird cry. All was silent in the night.

Taking a small breath, she pushed the flap aside and stepped out.

Before she could gasp, zHar grabbed her sword, and covered her mouth.

Only when her heartbeat slowed down did he release her. With a nod, he turned around.

Ashta hesitated, not wanting to leave Carien unprotected. Yet, there were two guards sleeping in her tent. And the zMun had shown no aggression to their small party. They should be safe, she comforted herself with.

Nodding, she followed him on light steps. The moon stood high in the night, lighting up the Yer as a million stars lit up the sky.

Her hips swayed with each step, forcing her long-unbound hair to brush against her back. The tickle unnerved Ashta, no longer used to her hair being free. Not since she had lived in the Nursery.

Ahead, past zHar's shoulder, she could make out people standing. A large group.

As they got closer, the hair on her arms and the back of her neck stood on end. All of the tribes people, from young children to the old, stood silently, watching her and zHar walk closer.

Only a step away, the people parted, allowing zHar and Ashta to walk by until they stood in the center of the group.

Unnerved, Ashta stepped close to zHar, her arm brushing lightly against his.

She turned to ask him what was going on but was stopped by his shaking head.

Frowning, she instead turned and stared at the only other person standing in the center. The woman who stood before Ashta looked no bigger than Trice, her arms and torso thin from not enough food. Her hair hung down past her knees but in one sleek wave. Its dark colour absorbed what little light the moon gave off.

But that's not what had Ashta's hair standing on end.

Blue sparks flashed and fizzled around the woman's hands.

And then she began a slow dance. Her body twisted and twirled, slow as a leaf in the wind. She went around the circle once, twice, three times. Each time a step closer to the very center.

Ashta was mesmerized by the other woman's hands. It was only when she stopped, that Ashta realized what the woman had done. In the sand lay a perfect circle of runic symbols and letters, twisted within each other as if lovers.

The woman crouched down, whispering words that Ashta had never heard before. The woman's hands flared before lighting up the indents in the sand. Scared, Ashta stepped back.

Straight into zHar's chest.

Before Ashta could wonder about his sudden movement, he pushed her forward until she stumbled into the circle. The flames sparked higher at her intrusion as if fueled by her.

With her focus on the other woman, Ashta stepped through the circle, the flames licking at her skin. Their heat blew Ashta's hair around, and yet she did not feel the sting of burning flesh.

She walked forward until she stood directly across from the woman. The healer, Ashta knew now instinctively, pulled her into the center, and then began dancing around her, faster this time. The flames jumped and flared to the unknown beat, blinding Ashta to anything but their flickering blue light.

And just as suddenly, as they had flared to life, the flames disappeared. Ashta gasped, stumbling back as the healer suddenly stood before her. Before she could fall, the woman grabbed her wrist. The blue sparks and flames flared, and this time Ashta did cry out as the unmistakable sting burned its way down her arm.

The last thing she saw was purple eyes, flecked with silver and blue.

Then everything went black.

Rumbling of wooden spokes. The chuff of the yak as he strained against the yoke. The creak of water barrels.

Ashta blinked open her eyes, shocked to see it was almost midday. How had she overslept? She rubbed her eyes, her fingers getting caught in her hair.

Why is my hair braided?

She remembered pulling it out of its braid last night, as was her ritual each night. And yet, it now was held back in its snail shell shaped braid. As she sifted her fingers deeper, she felt the ends of her throwing knives.

With a start, she pushed back the blanket and looked down at herself. Her legs were encased in their leather leggings and skirt. Her breasts were bound back. As she patted her hands down and around her body she felt all her knives and swords were in place.

Shaking her head, she couldn't seem to shake the buzz from her sleep. Or had it been a nap and she had forgotten where she was and the time, she wondered.

"You're awake!"

Ashta jumped at Carien's voice, realizing that the woman sat on the edge of the cart, her legs dangling over the moving ground.

The other woman's smile diminished as she took in her guard's confused state.

"Darkling?" she asked quietly, shimmying back to take a better look at the dark-haired beauty.

"How… what…where?" her voice was higher pitched than normal, panic seeping through. Then she stood up, her legs shaking from the cart's movement. She quickly spotted Luci and Kkaar walking slightly behind the cart. With wordless understanding, Kkaar nodded, jogging to catch up with the back of the yak cart.

Before she could jump up, Carien yanked on Ashta's wrist. "Has this always been here?" She asked, more curious than disturbed. Ashta looked down at her wrist and noticed the strange runic markings circling her wrist. Only one hand width, the blue marks stood in stark contrast to her sun darkened skin.

Ashta shook off Carien's hand and ran her own fingers over the marks. They stood slightly raised, no different than the tattoo on her ribs.

Freaked out, Ashta shook her hand and jumped off the cart. Kkaar followed, wisely staying quiet. Even she could feel the strange energy coming off the woman in waves. The tribes people were unusually quiet this morning.

"How did I get dressed?" Ashta asked first, in a terse whisper.

"We found you like that," Kkaar answered honestly. The fear from the morning still tangible. She had turned over that morning and noticed Ashta's body gone. After a quick search of the tents, she had finally stumbled upon Ashta's prone body.

"What do you mean?" Ashta asked even more disturbed. She had a faint recollection of blue flames. But nothing concrete. She glanced around at the other tribes people, noting the strange mark on her wrist was on every other person around her. Everyone except Kkaar, Luci, and Carien.

But the strangest part for her wasn't the mark itself. She had seen it before, that strange blue marking. It tickled her brain from a place deep inside of her. She had seen it.

Ashta finally shook herself, realizing that Kkaar had been speaking.

"…and there you were, dead asleep. I didn't want to wake you because I figured something must have been up for you to dress and patrol. Should we take up a watch tonight? Do you think the Bbrskian threat is still imminent?"

"No."

Her voice was certain. Her father was still a danger, but she didn't think he would send berserkers into the boiling desert. They weren't built for the heat.

"No," she said again shaking her head. "I thought I had heard something, but it wasn't anything. Just a loose flap."

Kkaar quirked her head but didn't question their leader. The woman wouldn't lie. With a nod, she slowed down again and walked beside Luci once more.

Ashta pushed the fear and the faint memories deep inside her, locking it away. There was no time to think about these things, she needed to be ready for Carien's sake.

With a sigh, she followed behind the yak cart. Carien had returned to her seat on the edge, smiling wide, up at the sun. Ashta couldn't remember seeing the princess this happy before. Not in Tripsia, and definitely not in Naankdoen.

This time she felt his presence before zHar walked up beside her. She nodded in acknowledgment of him. He didn't say anything and so neither did she. It was a comfortable silence, despite the simmering fear below her surface. His presence had that effect on her.

Ashta turned to take him in, his strong profile. She could make out faint lines around his mouth, like he smiled often.

A twinkle of blue had her eyes refocusing, past his profile. For a moment, she stared into the pale eyes of the short woman. Ashta's mind froze then filled up with memories of the night before, the circle, her dancing, and the fire that didn't burn – until it did. Ashta rubbed her wrist, staring back.

Then the next blink of her eyes the healer was gone, lost amongst the people.

And yet, Ashta was sure she had never seen the woman before amongst the people.

Suddenly, she stumbled over her feet before coming to a halt. The midday meal had been called. But this time zHar did not disappear.

They stared at each other, neither moving.

"Hey!"

Ashta broke the stare first, looking to Kkaar.

"You ready to spar?"

Ashta's reply was to fall into her ready stance. zHar backed up against the yak cart, taking in the smooth movements of both women. It was an elegant yet deadly dance. One wrong move and either could kill the other, especially since they did not hold their punches today.

He watched Darkling with pride, her grace, and strength evident from years of training. His heart ached for the time she had lost, but it was necessary. The future depended on the past, but more than that, it depended on her. On this woman's decisions. He could only hope she chose wisely.

The two women broke apart, taking a quick moment to breathe and shake out their limbs, now limber, and ready for the hard training.

zHar took his queue and stepped forward. Ashta turned to him, her mouth already pulled down. Her black eyes challenged him. He didn't back down, taking another step forward. "I want to learn."

Kkaar's eyes widened as she took in his tense form. She glanced between the two rigid bodies before shrugging. With a nod to Luci, she picked up the sparring match from where Darkling had left off.

Ashta forced her stance to relax, taking zHar's question seriously. "Why?" His answer would determine more than just their training.

He watched his feet, legs spread shoulder width part, feet planted. Like a man, not a soldier. Definitely not an assassin.

Yet, as Ashta took in his body, she could see the opportunity for a warrior. She knew nothing on whether the zMun fought and trained. The legends of the desert people even more unknown than the Naankdoen people.

"When the time comes, I need to be ready."

Ashta nodded to the cryptic words. Her mind had already moved forward, imagining throwing the tall tribesman over her shoulder and onto his ass.

"First get into the ready." She adjusted his stance before standing across from him.

Then she spent the rest of the midday meal going through simple moves that with time would make him deadly. Not as an assassin but as a warrior.

Carien came over with two bowls of broth for the both of them. Ashta smiled at the princess, murmuring her thanks. She didn't try to reprimand the other woman for doing something beneath her. Soon enough the princess would be forced back into her glass gilded cage.

CHAPTER SEVEN

⌘

Fever

THE SUN ROSE and set and the days blurred together into one long hot haze. Ashta knew that soon enough they would be separating from the people, their migration taking them farther east than the ruined city of Tripsia.

Each day, zHar's reactions were faster, his body memorizing the motions easily. Ashta couldn't help but admire his physicality. The man's body had been built for fighting. And his presence was calm, a necessity for war.

Yet, with each passing of the sun, Ashta watched the other two guards more carefully. At first, she thought it was Luci and Kkaar's relationship bringing them closer under the hot sun. But then little nervous ticks began. Luci bounced on the balls of her feet, never stopping her constant movements.

Kkaar's eyes widened until the whites all around the iris could be soon.

Ashta chewed on her lip, worried about the women. It was now coming up to five days. The midday meal had just ended, and they had begun their long trek once more. But Kkaar kept looking over her shoulders, then turning to Luci, whispering furtively.

Looking behind her and zHar, she saw nothing out of the ordinary. The children walked close behind having watched todays training session.

Then Kkaar stumbled and began screaming. Luci stood to the side, her arms whaling around, fighting an invisible opponent.

The yak driver stopped, halting at the same time as the rest of the villagers.

Ashta reacted.

Something was wrong.

She ran to the yak cart and pulled out spare rope for the Yer. She quickly ran at Luci, tackling her to the ground. She trussed up the small woman before turning to her close friend, her only true friend left from their days as cubs.

Kkaar's eyes were rolled back as a high keening noise continued to drive out of her throat and fill the desert air. Carefully, Ashta pushed Kkaar over before tying her arms behind her neck and her legs together. Normally the other woman would easily be able to slip out of the bonds, but Ashta didn't think she would be capable right now.

"zHar!"

She didn't have to look to feel his presence at her elbow.

Without another word, he took Kkaar's legs and Ashta her torso. They carried the body before throwing the deranged woman onto the back of the yak cart. After Luci's body was also thrown onto the cart, the column of villagers renewed their pace.

Ashta tried to carefully lay her friends back, making sure they were both comfortable. With one last glance, she pulled the light cloth over their faces to protect them from the sun.

Ashta sat on the edge of the cart, comforted by the now familiar rough wood under hands and the gritty crunch of the sand beneath the spokes. She made out Carien's head in the back of the column with two other women. The princess was fine. Her guards were guards were anything but.

Rubbing her aching chest, the wound pulsing for the first time in days, Ashta stared out sightlessly over the unending sand horizon.

A dip in the cart warned her of company.

After a long while of silence, she felt his warm arm reach around her shoulder and pull her into a half hug. Her body stiffened at first before relaxing into his arms.

After a while, Ashta pulls out of the comfort offered in his arms. His arm dropped and he said nothing, both staring behind them at the many people. The sun slowly blazed down over the west to sleep for the night.

"Kkaar, Luci, what happened to them, do you know what it is?" Ashta asked, unsure of the right words.

"Yes."

He didn't continue right away so Ashta turned to stare up at him. He quirked his brow looking down at her, his violet eyes twinkling with mirth.

Ashta frowned. What affected Kkaar and Luci was no laughing matter.

Her mouth opened to say as much but zHar spoke first.

"They call it desert fever."

Ashta waited for him to continue. But instead, he reached down and grabbed her right hand, playing with her fingers in his lap. She shivered at the sparks of heat that shot down her arm. But she didn't dare pull away, wanting to hear the rest of his answer.

"It keeps everyone but the true wanderers away from the land of sand."

With his answer, she pulled her hand back to herself. Ashta rubbed her fingers, mulling over his words. "So…It's called a fever because those affected get hallucinations and visions-" She looked to zHar, who nodded in assent, "Which is why none of you are affected and the p-Carien…Why is Carien not affected?"

She thought about it, understanding that Carien's upbringing was not in a desert. Neither was her own childhood. Yet, Ashta knew that the frozen tundra of her homeland was not far off from the sandy wasteland she traversed through now.

But her upbringing had been in a castle.

If anything, it was Carien that had grown up as a nomad. And Ashta could see the other woman loved it, had watched the proof of it these past few days.

zHar leaned down, tempted to kiss that impossibly soft skin. To soon. Instead, he brushed his lips by her temple before whispering in her ear. "You know why she isn't affected. Why *you* aren't affected."

Ashta tried to shake it away. She didn't know!

"Look inside yourself, all the answers are already within."

He brushed his lips once more across her ear, reveling in her shivers and her sun scented hair. Not now.

zHar backed away before jumping off the cart. He needed to speak with jHora. He would know what to do.

Ashta stared after him, suddenly cold without his heat beside her. It was too easy. She could see herself falling.

But she knew she never fell in love with another person. Like zHavier and Ceerie, Ashta only fell in love with being loved. It was intoxicating. It was something only her mother had given her, and those were meager bits in comparison to what her mother gave her father.

Rubbing her chest again, this time she tried to soothe a deeper ache. One that had existed long before she had been sold to Ennris and the Tripsian slavers.

A muffled cry from behind her had Ashta sliding back, further into the yak cart. Kkaar's body thrashed, only the whites of her eyes visible. She would hurt herself if she kept it up, Ashta worried. She pulled the woman's body into her arms, restraining her arms and torso.

At first Kkaar struggled more against Ashta's body.

Mind made up, Ashta sang in a low voice the lullabies her own mother had sung to her. The songs that she remembered from her one visit with her grandfather.

Kkaar's struggling lessened, her body relaxed within itself. Then she curled herself around Ashta's body. Ashta kept singing, sifting her fingers through Kkaar's hair. The woman's eyes had calmed and were now beginning to droop.

A quick glance over at Luci showed that she to was feeling the effects of the lullaby.

Ashta continued singing, knowing that rest was the only cure for the two guards' unsettled minds.

As she sang the old words, Ashta could make out a quite hum. Just barely noticeable, she cocked ear. There it was. She glanced surreptitiously over the yak cart's walls, noting that none of the villagers sang with her. And yet the quiet hum sounded like that of many people humming, all in perfect harmony.

Shaking her head, she focused back on the two women in front of her, not stopping until their breathing had evened out and their eyes no longer flickered beneath their eyelids.

Ashta carefully extracted herself from Kkaar's body, careful not to drop her head. Once free, Ashta jumped off the yak cart but didn't stray too far. The women were asleep and defenseless. It was her duty, her personal promise, to watch over them now when they could not look out for themselves.

She kept an eye out for zHar but did not catch a glimpse of him the rest of the evening. To soon the party had stopped, twilight having settled a purple glow over the land. Every hand helped pull bags apart and tighten ropes until forty or so Yer stood in the moonlight.

Carien and a few other women set up their tent.

Ashta helped at first before dragging Kkaar and Luci inside. She didn't dare to loosen their bonds, unsure if they would still be affected the next day.

Unable to sleep, Ashta paced around the inside of their tent.

"Could you just stand still," Carien sighed, falling back against the hard sand. She fidgeted and wiggled until the sand molded to her body.

Ashta tried to stop, her energy working itself into her hands, which she tapped a quick beat against her thigh.

"Stop already!" Carien cried, this time sitting up to glare at Darkling.

"I can't," Ashta growled, frustrated. Her fingers ran back into her hair, getting caught in the braid before cutting themselves on the hidden knives.

"Then go outside and do something. Don't come back until you are ready to sleep," the princess threatened, falling back into the sand. Ashta glared at her before looking over at the two other motionless figures.

She could probably leave them in the tent. Nothing had happened so far. And Carien could always call out and one of the people in their neighboring tents could run and help.

Mind made up she, turned and stalked out of the Yer.

The full moon hung high above her, its light so bright that it felt like day outside. Ashta kept walking until she was at the edge of the little tent village. As she stared out at the cold sand dunes, she couldn't help but notice how disturbingly similar they looked to the Bbrskian frozen tundra. It was unnerving. Ashta had to turn away to stop the images of berserkers pouring over the hills. As she walked through the tents, kids began to follow her.

At first, it was just a little girl. Then a young boy who could barely walk joined her. By the time she made it to the middle of the tents, more than twelve children stood around her. She stared each child in the eye, unsure of their game.

The little girl who had first approached her, stepped forward and grabbed her hand. Ashta shivered at the contact, at the heat within the small child's fingers. Surprising, considering the cold night air fogged her own breath before her.

Show us.

Ashta jerked back, realizing the words had not been spoken aloud. Yet, she had heard each word clearly. Not just that, she had seen memories – not her own – of Ashta sparring with Kkaar and then with zHar.

Squeezing her eyes shut, she tried to stop the images.

"Please," the girl whispered; her voice picked up by the slight wind tickling through the air.

Ashta opened her eyes and took in the child. Her arms thin, her eyes huge in her face from not enough food. As she circled around, looking into the face of each child, each kid looked hauntingly similar.

Her heart ached at the hardships these children had already suffered and lived through.

They reminded her of the other children in the nursery. The ones that were more afraid of the unknown test than of the known terror of sharing their bodies. Their eyes had been glazed; the souls having vacated after the first few years in the humid building.

Ok.

The kid's eyes all brightened as if having heard her thought. Ashta shivered but didn't dare ask aloud, or even think, the one question that plagued her about the tribes people. She had already had a tough time dealing with the Naankdoena people reading minds. She didn't want to know if the zMun people could as well. Ignorance was bliss in this instance.

Pulling the girl in front of her, she helped the girl place her feet and balance on her knees. The other kids tried to follow suit.

The full moon wound his way across the sky, lighting up the sparring session of children into the early morning. When dawn came and the first rays lightened the sky, Ashta dismissed the children to their tents. She walked back to her own tent, her agitation from the evening now dissipated.

As she snuck into the tent, she glanced down at Carien's still figure. Her body moved with the regular rhythms of breathing. Good. She wouldn't know something was amiss. Ashta snuck over to her own blanket, folding it up and beginning the take down of their Yer.

Soon enough Carien joined her. The princess never asked if she had come back to the tent, and Ashta never told her what she had done through the night. Silence filled the air and Ashta reveled in it. Today was their last day with the zMun. And then they would be on their own.

CHAPTER EIGHT

⌘

Separate Paths

IT WAS JUST before midday when the party stopped. Ashta was by the yak cart, Carien not to far behind. zHar came over, the first time she had seen him since yesterday. She gave him a quick smile before looking past his shoulder to the old man.

jHora.

"This is where our paths separate, dark girl."

His voice rung in the otherwise still air. He tapped the ground, Amkan jumping out from behind him. The boy jumped on the yak cart and began rolling barrels to the edge. Others helped shift the barrels on to some of the other carts. They left one half empty barrel for the four women.

"It should be enough to last you to the ruined city.

Ashta nodded. It was Carien who stepped forward and bowed low. "We thank the zMun people for their kindness. When the time comes, the crown and my family will be indebted one favor to you and all of your people, now and those to come." Bowing low again, she didn't rise until jHora put his hand on his shoulder.

"The zMun have heard your words." His voice was rough but even Ashta heard the warning within them.

In that moment, Ashta realized how naïve the princess of Tripsia still was, despite the half-year long journey. There was still much for her learn.

Ashta went to the yak and pulled his lead, having him turn off from the unknown path, pointing straight south.

"Dark girl," jHora called. Ashta turned, not surprised to find the old man right beside her. She nodded. He stretched his arm up into the sky. "There, follow that star and it will bring you straight to the ruined city." Ashta could just make out the star, low in the horizon but bright despite the daylight.

Before she could speak, he turned and pointed in the direction the people had been walking. There, a little higher hung another star. Barely discernible, Ashta noted its strange purple hue.

Satisfied, jHora turned away without another word.

The rest of his people followed his movement and began hiking again. Ashta stared after them, her eyes locked on zHar. He held his hand to his heart, then pointed to his head. Before Ashta could say anything, he disappeared into the mass.

And in a matter of minutes the zMun had disappeared into the desert the same way they had appeared in front of them just over a few weeks before.

Rubbing her wound, Ashta blinked hard after them. She felt as if she had lost something, but not sure what.

"Is your wound still bothering you?" Carien asked, appearing beside Ashta.

"No."

And it wasn't. She had checked it this morning, pulling out the last stitches. The scar would be there forever. As would the memories of Naankdoen and the desert haunt her forever.

Turning away, she took the lead rope once more and took the first step towards Tripsia. To the king, the slavers, the lion pits. Back to the lioness's, to Ceerie. To the law. Their time in the in-between had come to a distinct end and in as little as a day, her freedom from her past would be gone to.

"Come on, we need to make good time while the sky is light."

Carien nodded, following behind the cart. Neither woman said anything as the sun sank in the west. There were no worries for food. They were glad to have the water. Carien jumped up onto the back of the cart, carefully dripping the water into Kkaar and Luci's mouths.

When it was dark and Ashta could no longer feel her legs, just the pain of cold in her chest, she finally pulled the yak to a stop. She unyoked the beast, rubbing down his sides before murmuring her thanks into his ears. He chuffed before settling down beside the cart. As Ashta fed and watered the beast, Carien stretched out the furs the people had left them, carefully tucking Kkaar and Luci under one.

Ashta climbed up into the back of the cart, drinking thirstily from the barrel. She barely noticed a few stray droplets stream down her chin.

"Come under the fur," Carien called, already underneath the second fur.

Without taking off any of her knives she snuggled under the fur and pulled Carien back into her arms, as a mother does to her child.

But sleep didn't come to Ashta. Instead the great sky blinked above her calling to her with answers and questions. And many untold memories.

"Darkling?" Carien whispered, her breath coming out in clouded puffs.

"Mhmm."

"What happens now?"

Carien turned over and faced Ashta, looking up into her black eyes. For the first time she could make nothing out in their depths. They sucked her in, pulling her own soul out.

Blinking hard, Carien didn't break her stare.

Ashta's nose crinkled, before she finally answered. "Tomorrow we will be back in the ruined city. Your father will have questions, and demand answers."

"And what do we tell him?"

"The truth."

Those two words rang true in the bright night under the desert sky.

Carien worried the tip of her braided hair, brushing it against her chin. Could it be so easy, she wondered. Her father didn't take well to her being in danger. He would probably take his wrath out first on Darkling and then on the other two women. Especially because it had been Darkling who had headed the journey. Everything that befell their party would fall on her.

Carien couldn't let that happen.

Not when every glaring mistake had been her fault. The almost death on the back of the torash, the attempted murder at the prince's birthday ball, the truth about Darkling's identity. The death of Darkling's half-sister, and the siege on Naankdoen. It had all been her fault.

She glanced back up into Darkling's face, Darkling's eyes staring up at the great sky. Carien knew she would protect the other woman, just as Darkling had protected her without question.

They were sisters now. That's what blood did for another.

"When I was younger I didn't understand that I was not part of the Alpen people."

Ashta turned away from the sky and watched the princess's face, noting that the night sky stripped her bare, into the likeness that of a young child.

"I remember running and playing with the other children. No one cared if I scraped my knee, or if I was gone for a night sleeping in a meadow. It was everything and yet at the time I didn't realize how much it meant to me." She played with her fingers, the memories coming on stronger than they had ever before.

"You know Darkling, I never realized how caged it felt to be a princess. I think it hurts more because I know what it's like outside of the cage of royalty. That there is a happiness in having nothing but your wit in the cold mountain air. Even the way they make me dress is a cage, the clothes covering my hair, my face, every piece of my body. How can someone live like this and be happy?"

Her voice had become frantic. Ashta reached out and pulled the woman close into her chest, gently petting her hair.

"I don't know," Ashta answered. "I've never been free," she whispered.

Carien's body stilled, hearing the heartbreaking truth. She flushed with shame.

How could she lay here and wine about the harsh reality of royalty when the woman who held her had *grown up* in the same gilded cage. And she had been sold into another, less shiny cage. But her fate, her entire life would be fulfilled in cages.

"I'm sorry," the princess whispered to Darkling's heart, the same heart of a young princess who had never played. Never had friends.

Ashta lay still, not accepting the apology.

It wasn't the other woman's fault, the misfortune of Ashta being born Svetlana. First crown princess of Bbrski. And now the only living heir.

But thankfully that cage would never be hers. The bands of her new cage were for life. Once sold, no amount of money could buy a woman from Tripsia. Only the King's word could release her.

And that had only happened once, centuries ago.

"I...I remember Liam. We spent much of our time together, despite him being five years older. He never treated me as anything less, taking the time to teach me all the plants that grew in the alps. All the different animals. I loved him." Her voice wavered, the feelings still fresh despite it having been over half a decade since she last saw him. "I never got the chance to tell him. He had been gone on his walk for a half a year, when Ennris had come for me. And then I was thrown into learning everything at once. To became a proper lady, a good princess, and an obedient woman." That last part was spat out.

Ashta continued stroking her hair. It was better the other woman get the feelings out now when there were no other ears to listen. The slight snore from Kkaar told Ashta the other two woman were in a deep sleep.

"When I was growing up, surrounded by mother's people, I felt like she was there with me. I could feel her presence, a warm breeze cupping my cheek. When they took me, I never felt her again. I thought I had lost her, surrounded by my father and his world. But during the time with the zMun people I felt her again. That warm caress in the wind. I don't know what it means, but I know it must be important. Why else would she have left me alone all those years in that cold underground palace?"

This time Ashta stayed quiet. It wasn't her place to answer. Only Carien could find the answer to those questions.

She had questions for her own mother. She had only now begun to forgive her mother for being selfish enough to take her life and leave her daughter behind.

But those other questions.

The ones about why she picked her father, when the king had never once shown an ounce of kindness to the fragile woman. There were also the questions about her mother's home and her grandfather. She had never told Ashta stories about her childhood, just the few comments about her grandfather, describing his appearance more than anything.

And so, underneath the desert sky with the scent of sun and frost in the air, Ashta sang quietly to Carien. The words came from deep within, a song whose words she remembered despite having only heard it one time from her grandfather.

Her clear vocals rang true in the air, bringing fire and life to the words.

...so fly with me, my friend,
my winged horse born of salt and water...

In her mind she saw the young boy sit atop the winged horse, asking the horse to fly to the sun so they could bring it back as a gift for the young boy's mother. And so, rider and animal flew high above the land, higher than the mountain tops, and clouds and even higher than the stars. Just as the boy reached out to grab the sun, his mount's wings burned up in flames, jolting them back. The two plummeted back to the land, the scars of their brush with the sun seen in the blackened boy and the wingless horse. From that day on, both man and horse were banished to walk for the rest of their days.

"*...and when you see the black-haired ones,*
bow and step back from the forsaken ones,
forced to wander all their days,
still reaching for the sun."

The last words dripped off her tongue like honey, sweet and good. But the taste the song left behind was bitter. A warm breeze ruffled through Ashta's hair and tickled her nose. And for a moment she felt a presence near that she had thought left the world for good.

Hot tears dripped down her cheeks as she leaned into the warmth. Her whole life she had been wandering, she saw that now. But maybe there was hope for her yet. Not in the wandering but finding warmth. Happiness.

"I love you Mama," she whispered into the wind.

And for a moment, above the sound of Carien's even breathing, she heard the words her heart ached for.

I love you Mina.

CHAPTER NINE

⌘

City of Ruins

WITH THE SUN high above them, the small party of four arrived at the edge of the ruined city. Kkaar and Luci had calmed down enough that Ashta stopped to untie both of them. Kkaar looked up at Ashta sheepishly, rubbing her wrists. Luci walked to the other side of the cart not looking at anyone else.

They walked carefully past the rubble in the streets of collapsed columns.

"The great city of Trian, the emerald of Tripsia," Carien breathed out, her arms outstretched, as if reveling in the dust of the past.

Ashta said nothing, the yak walking beside her obediently, his lead line around his head and unattached.

"They say that Tripsia used to be one lush rainforest, all the way east to Kae ol. The border indefinable between the two kingdoms, so thick was the foliage."

"Hard to imagine that, your highness."

Carien looked back at Kkaar, a smirk playing across her lips. "Yes, that it is. But it really wasn't that long ago."

Kkaar snorted, pointedly looking over at the rubbles of the outer wall of the city, now no higher than their waists. Clearly, the city – the kingdom – had fallen to ruins more than a few years.

"No really," Carien said, her laugh tinkling through the desolate city, all but abandoned, except for the royal palace. "The legend goes that Tripsia used to be the seat of power for all the Midloean kingdoms. It was Tripsia that made the peace treaty with the northern Kingdoms, stopping their raids on all of the northern regions of Tripsia. The Kingdom prospered; the people lived in excess."

"If everything had been going so well than how do you explain there being no trees in this forsaken land. Well except for the occasional oasis."

"Didn't they teach you it when you were in training?" Carien asked, her mirth deflating as she realized the other women had no clue of what she spoke of.

"No, and nor did we learn of it from our homelands. Your kingdom's name is like a bad word, to never be spoken aloud."

For a moment they all walked in silence, mulling over Kkaar's words. Ashta couldn't disagree. Even growing up as a princess, she had learnt only the essentials of Tripsia. Their language, their customs, their slavers. More than that was never hinted at.

"Well," Carien continued, her face smoothing out as she went on to explain, "the legend is that long ago, the rains came every year. If not for the rain, the land would never have flourished being so hot as it is. On the day the king released the first slave, the drought began. Since then it has never rained for more than a day each year. Slowly the plants withered and died. Their roots disintegrated and the soil dried. The winds picked up, blowing the sands from Naankdoen through Tripsia until it all looked like one long desert. Only the alps had any greenery left, their source of water coming from the mists high above in the clouds.

Since then, no slave has been released, the belief being that to do so would bring the total destruction of Tripsia. Not just the inner land, but the coastal lands to. The coasts being the only greenery on this side of Tripsia."

Ashta couldn't believe her ears. She had known as well as any cub that only one slave had ever been released, hundreds of years ago. She had not realized that it was the same time as the desertification of Tripsia.

"What else do you know of the woman?" Ashta asked, deceptively calm.

Carien shrugged. "That's the only legend I know that even mentions a slave. And I only heard of it from my Nonna, the healer from our village."

The four women walked the rest of the way uphill in silence.

Ashta thought about the legend. A slave woman released at the same time as a drought. She wondered if this woman was the connection to the flag from her training day. The woman with the violet eyes, haunted, hunted.

Yet a tickle in her mind had another connection. What if- what if that slave that was released, the one from the flag, also was the owner of the sword that hung over the underground entrance of the lioness training quarters.

Her mind stilled, sensing a truth in the three connections.

But if it was true, then where did the slave come from – and better yet where did she go? The image on the flag was not a likeness of the slave. But it must have held some similarities.

Ashta wondered if the woman had been enslaved many years, and when she was very old she had been released. That would make sense, spending a lifetime in service to Tripsia and being rewarded with freedom.

But why would a King wait so long?

Ashta wasn't sure.

And if Carien had never heard about it before, than the answer about the woman, and who she was, didn't lie in the spoken legends.

No, if her story survived, Ashta could only hope to find it in an ancient tome. The princess was the only one with that kind of access to books in Tripsia. Ashta had not found the library room, where they kept the books locked. Carien had never been interested in it when Ashta had first come to her post.

Maybe Ashta could mention it.

Shading her eyes from the late sun, she looked up as the outer walls of the palace loomed above them. Where the city had fallen to ruins, the palace still stood the same as it had for over a millennium. Ashta doubted that would change for another millennia.

She caught site of a head above the wall.

"Stop here," Ashta called loud enough for only their party to hear. Kkaar and Luci stood still, there shoulders tense and their arms hanging at the ready. Carien had tensed as well, but Ashta doubted from fear. No, more likely she felt the constraints of her title coming down over her shoulders again as certain. Like a prisoner walking into a cell, the jailers cuff on the wall calling the prisoner's wrists.

A shout rose above the wall as the women waited. A slight commotion behind the wooden gates was the only indication that the Tripsian soldiers weren't going to kill them.

Yet.

Finally, the last gate rose to bring them in view of twenty soldiers. The leader took one look at Ashta, Kkaar, and Luci's dress and hair before signaling behind him. The other three gates opened in a strange kaleidoscope of motion until Ashta could see through and behind where the path continued in the main outer courtyard.

The soldiers split in half, bowing their heads in deference to the lionesses' status. Ashta wondered if the men knew who they were or if all Lionesses were afforded the same courtesy. She doubted the second one.

Glancing over at the princess, Ashta worried at the other woman's pallor, almost gray from fear.

She squeezed the princess's arm briefly, whispering, "Have faith, the gods will deliver us from this to."

Carien nodded dazedly before finally taking in a few fortifying breaths. Before Ashta could comment on her colour, they had arrived at the front doors, which were filled.

And the King looked furious.

All around, in entrances and behind columns, nobles and servants crowded to catch a sight of the small party.

The King stomped down the rest of the steps, not taking any heed to his own guards. The two women looked at the group before recognizing the black-eyed girl.

Ashta grimaced, sometimes it was good to be memorable. Hopefully it would work more in her favor.

"Carien!" He called, his voice scratchy with emotion. Despite the princess's strange mode of dress, her open hair, she still held the unmistakable air of royalty. Something that always floated around her even in the desert.

"Father," the girl replied more calmly, stepping forward and in front of their group. She stood rigid as the king, in a rare show of emotion, pulled her into his arms in front of all.

"My daughter," He whispered, and only Ashta and Carien could hear the tremble. His voice was ripe with loss and fear and love.

For a second Ashta understood the King's need to hover and protect Carien. His match with her mother had been a love match, and to lose that made Carien that much more precious to him. Especially since the princess took after her mother and not her father.

King Roman's gaunt face, if possible was even more hollow than a year ago when Ashta and her party had left for Naankdoen. Deep wrinkles creased his face, around his mouth, lending to his ever-cold demeanor. Ashta shivered as father and daughter embraced.

The King held onto his daughter for long moments, surrounded by silence. No one dared breath a word for fear of finding his attention on them next.

Ashta noted the streaks of white in his hair peaking out from beneath his silk turban. The fully white temples that had not been there before they left for Naankdoen. The king had aged, not gracefully, in the last half year.

Finally, he pulled back from his daughter, holding her at arm's length. The man stood the same height as Carien, short by Bbrskian standard. His body was soft from age and disuse. It was hard to imagine this man held the power of who lived and who died in their entire Kingdom. Ashta's life was dependent on his mood.

"Daughter, I had thought you lost when a lone soldier from your party had come back with news of the destruction of your party."

Carien nodded, keeping her eyes up and staring back into her father's eyes. She had gained a backbone in Naankdoen. Her gaze didn't waver, and her stance stood tall with pride. She was every bit of the princess that she had hid from only a year ago. Roman the sight of his daughter in.

"How is the soldier?" she asked, brow quirked.

The thinning of the king's mouth said everything. The soldier had done his duty and was paid by giving up his life. The news didn't bode well for the lionesses. Ashta glanced over at Kkaar and Luci. They all understood, now more than ever, their lives balanced in the king's hands.

"I see," the princess's flat mouth and flared nose gave away to her true feelings of her father's actions. Carien continued, "I was always safe under the protection of my lionesses-"

"And yet none survived."

"I beg your pardon, your majesty, but there are three lionesses standing behind me who personally delivered me from the hell of the Naankdoen siege and later the Bbrskian ambush. I fail to see how these three brave souls are no one."

The king released her shoulders and for the first time really looked at his daughter. She had always been familiar to him, like her sweet mother.

But that was not the woman standing before him now. No, *this woman* had a steeliness about her, a not so quiet strength that neither her mother or her former self had. Roman rubbed at his jaw unsure of how to deal with this.

Instead he looked past his daughter, even though he didn't want to stop drinking in her sweet image. Behind her, his eyes were caught in the dark stare of his daughters first guard.

The woman looked even more angular and sharp than she had before. For a moment the king feared he would never be able to break her, but she deferred her glance and gave a slow nod.

The two women behind her stood with just as much pride but they dipped into a bow the moment the king looked at them. They also didn't look him in the eye.

He glanced back at the first woman with irritation. He shouldn't have trusted his daughter with the young untried lioness. If it had been his choice, Ennris would still be his daughter's personal guard.

"What do you have to say for yourselves, lionesses?" He demanded, pulling Carien's body behind him.

The dark eyed woman had the gall to quirk her brow at him.

"I want a full debrief *immediately* in my personal chambers. You will leave no detail out. The princess was not only in danger but degraded to wearing the clothes of a beggar!" His face was purple with rage, spittle flying as he yelled.

Ashta stepped forward again, redirecting his anger to just her. She knew she, an she alone, was responsible for the Naankdoen trip. She would not let anyone else take the fall.

"The princess was safe at all times-"

"Safe! She was almost murdered at a ball because you weren't watching her!"

Ashta's face heated at his truth. She should have been paying closer attention to the princess. But zHavier had been determined to distract her that night.

"So help me gods, I will have your bodies split and sent to the Lio-"

"Father!"

Everyone turned to the young princess. Her face was flushed and her eyes were wild with passion.

She stood toe to toe against the King, hissing out her reply. "We have been traveling non-stop for a week with no change of clothes or opportunity to rest and clean ourselves. I speak for myself, *and my guards*, that we need time to rest this night. You will get your answers soon enough. In the morning. Nothing that occurred is that urgent."

She stared for a full minute into her father's eyes, before glaring at Darkling. Then she whipped around and stalked into the sprawling palace, never looking back.

Ashta nodded at Kkaar and Luci, who hurried behind the princess. Ashta was the last to follow, bringing up the rear of their group.

Before she could pass the king, he stopped her with a hand on the shoulder. "Meet in my personal chamber within the hour. I expect a full report."

Ashta kept her eyes focused forward, nodding her understanding, as she continued walking up the steps.

The king would get his answers. But the princess's fury had Ashta wondering at what price the answers would come.

CHAPTER TEN

⌘

Slaves and Secrets

ASHTA STOOD BEFORE the king. Kkaar and Luci on either side of her. King Roman sat at the table, his fingers tapping an angry rhythm on the chair's arm. He glared at the woman with the same amount of distrust as half a year ago. Back then Carien had been trying to charm him into allowing her to leave for Naankdoen.

Now, his eyes were laced with hate. His body vibrated with the need to break something – or kill someone.

Ashta made sure to take another step forward, keeping the attention on her. "Where would you like me to begin your majesty?" she asked confidently. She knew that she would appease the king where she could. Otherwise they would all end up dead or worse.

"At the beginning," he grunted, turning his gaze to a painting sitting across from him.

Taking a deep breath, Ashta launched into an account of the trip, how many days, how the supplies fared, how the Naankdoen gifts were received, and how many attempts were made on the princess's life.

She was in the middle of relaying the torash ride. Naankdoen's famed monster. Ashta had jumped on the nearest animal, racing after the princess and just barely saved Carien from the animal's mad leap to death.

The king interrupted her.

"And how did you manage to ride a torash? It is my understanding that even a skilled rider has difficulty riding an *untrained* and *unhandled* animal." His eyes glared up at Darkling.

Ashta hesitated, knowing that the king would not accept the truth. That she had just jumped on, reacting without thought. And that her mount had followed, as all of her mounts did.

"I-I...We are trained to deal with any all circumstances. It is a testament to cub training that I had the skills to ride the torash."

"Correct me if I'm wrong, but the cubs do not have a torash in the stables." The incessant tapping on his chair's arm paused as he watched the dark-eyed woman. Roman could already imagine her head on a spike.

Kkaar sensed Ashta's reluctance to answer and stepped forward to protect her friend. "The princess had a lead and her mount was racing to the spiked wall around the riding courtyard. Ashta had no time to think, only react." Then she lied, concentrating on keeping her face clear, "and the reports were wrong. The torash was a docile female. The animal was well handled and reacted to Ashta's urgency just as a trained war horse would."

The king glared at the two women for a long minute. Then with a slight nod, he motioned for Ashta to continue her report.

Kkaar stepped back, taking a breath. She didn't dare look at Luci, even though her heart craved the reassurance. Her heart beat frantically at the king's attention. She could live the rest of her days comfortably without ever having to see the king's face again.

Ashta continued her account of the last half year. The king interrupted her again when they came to the ball.

"Why were you in a dress?" he demanded.

"It was the only way we would have been allowed a third lioness into the palace. The Naankdoena had a strict rule of only two guards per foreign ambassador. We had to respect Naankdoen law throughout the time spent there as foreign ambassador. The ball was no different. Except we knew the princess was in danger, so we took the extra precau-"

"And yet she still managed to get kidnapped and had a knife to her heart."

Ashta growled low in her throat in irritation. Why did the king bother with their report when it sounded like he already knew everything? Trying to shove her emotions down, she continued.

"The ball was filled with people and the murderer was aware of all three of our locations. But we caught the trail of the kidnappers on time, and saved the princess with no damage to her person."

He raised his hand to stop her. "I've heard enough."

He stood, his guards stepping out from the walls. Each woman stood on either side of Ashta. Ashta's skin prickled as she stood before him her spine rigid.

"I sentence you, Ashta the Lion Tamer, to death. Your crimes are for willfully endangering the crown princess of Tripsia on multiple occasions."

He walked forward until he was only two steps before Ashta. She could easily reach up and throw a knife in his throat or reach her half sword in her back and skewer him. Her fingers itched to do it, but her mind held her back. To kill him would ensure her death, to take the punishment was death. There was no way around death for her.

"And for being a traitor to the crown by withholding valuable information, your birthright as the crown princess Svetlana of Bbrski."

She felt her birthright like a noose around her neck, tightening until she could no longer breath. For a second the world darkened but Ashta clawed her way back, forcing herself to stay present as the two women tied her arms back.

Before they dragged her away, the king looked to Kkaar.

"You, what is your name, lioness?"

"K-Kkaar the strangler, your majesty," she stuttered as she bowed deeply.

"I promote you as the personal white lioness of the crown princess Carien of our great kingdom Tripsia."

Kkaar's eyes widened in fear before nodding to the King. He dismissed Kkaar and Luci, taking great satisfaction in the pain visible in the black-haired witches eyes. He would prolong her death. His hands already shook in anticipation of the long weeks of torture.

This was what he had needed.

The soldiers prolonged death hadn't been enough to erase the emotions of losing his only daughter. It didn't matter that she hadn't died, his heart had felt a thousand deaths already. And the lioness would pay for each one of them.

Ashta didn't remember much of the walk to the jail. It had been dark for most of the journey, the women never slowing even as Ashta stumbled and tried to stay upright. Eventually, heat crept through the walls until sweat dripped down Ashta's back and collected in her band.

The women turned into a doorway and climbed up a long circular stairway. At the top were six small cells. Ashta noted only one was occupied, before she was thrown into the opposite cell. The one woman closed the iron door, the key locking with a final click.

She stayed for a moment looking back at Ashta. Her mouth was open as if she wanted to say something, but the other woman smacked her on the arm pointing to the stairway.

And with that, Ashta was alone, sun pouring through the small slits in the wall. Enough to lighten the cell but not enough to make the wall structurally unsound.

In moments she had her arms freed from the ropes. Even as she checked over the ropes, she noted they weren't long enough to make a noose and kill herself.

Still, it wouldn't hurt to save them.

She dropped them into the farthest corner. Hopefully, no one would notice them.

With nothing to do but despair over her situation, Ashta slid down the wall and let out a big sigh. How had it all gone so wrong?

It was something she had asked herself often after waking up in the care of the zMun. To be honest, it had already been going wrong in Naankdoen.

A scratching noise caught her attention.

Ashta turned and looked over into the other cell. The other person was shrouded in shadow, the morning sun already setting and no longer hitting her side.

Ashta peered a little closer noting the body was very much a woman. The distinct outline of her breasts were hard to miss. She couldn't make out much else on the body, the form stretched in strange ways.

There it was again. A sniff. Was the other woman crying?

Ashta crawled to the edge of her cell and tried to see more. She could barely make out the clothes, a strange rough material with no shape. There were no identifiers on the woman. Probably a commoner, Ashta guessed.

The woman's hand came up and rubbed at her eye.

There was something about her hand that tickled a memory in Ashta's mind.

Licking her lips, Ashta cleared her throat. The woman didn't even flinch. Trying to think of the right words, Ashta opened her mouth. "How long have you been in for?"

Her words were loud, echoing throughout the small tower.

At her voice, the woman jerked her head back. Then, oh-so slowly, she turned to face Ashta.

Ashta didn't even notice her gasp, or her hand moving to her mouth. All Ashta could see; all she could hear was her.

Ceerie.

But how? And why?

Last Ashta had heard, her former lover had gone for the winter with Baron Astor to guard him at his estate.

"Ceerie?" she whispered, her throat seizing up.

This wasn't how she had imagined seeing the other woman again. She had thought they would meet again in the winter, where Ashta could politely end whatever they had left of their relationship. Maybe even start a friendship. But this, seeing her here, changed everything.

"But… how? What happened?" her voice rose with each word

Ceerie blinked before turning away again, not uttering a single word.

Ashta waited for her to say something but Ceerie stayed silent as the sun slowly sank. The desert cooled and with it came the night winds whipping through the tower.

When the last drop of sun disappeared and they were in complete darkness, Ashta moved away from the gate and lay down on the stones. Her stomach grumbled, reminding her she had not eaten since before the midday. The king might feed her, if she was lucky. The look in King Roman's eye had her guessing that she was not. Lucky that is.

"It's been awhile, Ashta the Lion Tamer."

Ashta blinked from her spot on the ground, shivering at the unmistakable voice of Ceerie. It was low and lyrical, like the elven blood she was distantly related to.

The other woman sighed.

Ashta heard the shifting of cloth and then silence again.

"Three months," Ceerie breathed out before continuing in a stronger voice. "It's been three months up here in this wretched pot of heat."

"But why?" Ashta couldn't help but ask.

Another sigh. "It's a long story."

Ashta laughed, the sound jagged and harsh, "I have all the time to listen."

"Why are you here?"

Rubbing at her eyes, Ashta had no choice but to answer. "The king sentenced me to death. For endangering the princess." She hesitated and decided not to say the rest. Her true name had been one of the big arguments between them. It was better to not to mention it than reopen old wounds.

"At least yours will happen soon," Ceerie whispered wistfully.

Ashta didn't like that. Death was not something to wish to hurry up. She still had not forgiven her mother for taking her own life so quick and carelessly.

"I might as well start the story now, and maybe it will be done before the executioners axe falls."

She hesitated.

Ashta wished she could crawl over to her and comfort her.

After a long moment, she started again. "I had been in the reserves for several months. I had even guarded the Baron several times. It came as a surprise when he approached the king to purchase me as his personal lioness. I had felt uneasy around the man before, but I could never pinpoint what it was about him. I went with him back to his estate willingly.

I was a lioness; I thought my only worries would be protecting my charge from assassins and disgruntled tenants. I never thought…" She paused, taking several deep breaths. "I never thought that I needed to worry about *him*.

It started off small. Touches on the wrist, the shoulder, the waist. As the winter drew on, he grew bolder. He pinched my butt or grabbed my breast. I didn't know what to do. Grossi and Ennris prepared us for much, but they never said what we should do if our charge was endangering us.

So, I tried to ignore it. His wife, in the meanwhile, grew in her pregnancy. A month before she gave birth, before we came back to the castle, was the first time he-he-"

This time her voice hitched. Ashta could feel the woman's despair, but there was nothing she could do. Ashta's irritation for the baron only grew. How dare he? Their position as a lioness was sacred. They had risked everything to train their bodies as shield for *protection*. If they had wanted to give pleasure, they would have become a common whore. Like most of the other slaves.

For him to ignore that and completely disrespect Ceerie's station like that? It was inexcusable. But Ashta could also feel it wasn't the end of what she feared was a very sad tale.

"Go on," she coaxed the other woman. She hoped letting the story out might release Ceerie from its torment.

"After he was done with my body, I didn't know what to do. It hurt and I knew I could turn to no one or risk the wrath of a distant king, or the wrath of the very near wife who watched me like hawk.

It only got worse after I saw you at the fire dance. His wife took up residence in an entirely different wing of the house, leaving me to his torment. I knew it would come out eventually. Especially with the way we are required to dress. I tried to hide it for as long as I could, but then it was too late." Her voice was little more than a whisper.

Ashta crawled up to the iron gate and reached out as far as she could. She knew Ceerie couldn't feel it, but she felt restless and needed to do something. To comfort the other woman somehow.

"What was too late?" Ashta asked, almost too scared to know the truth. She had an inkling, but she hoped and prayed to all the gods it wasn't true. Because only a special kind of punishment awaited those who made that mistake. Ashta and all the lionesses she knew would pay the price with Ceerie.

Please not that.

But as she heard Ceerie take one last fortifying breath, Ashta's heart dropped.

"I'm pregnant."

CHAPTER ELEVEN

⌘

A Seed

PREGNANT.

Ashta's mind had been stuck on the word through the late night. She watched with dazed confusion as the east end of the tower slowly lit up with morning light.

The light brought truth with it.

Ashta took in Ceerie's swollen body and could not deny the truth. Yet Ceerie still refused to look at Ashta. A soldier came up early on and brought food and water for Ceerie.

As much as the king hated a lioness who got pregnant, the kingdom did not blame the unborn child for the situation.

Ashta made no comment about the food and the soldier didn't offer to bring some up for her afterwards.

Pregnant.

Her mind had stalled on that word, not able to see past it to the woman who sat across from her, in pain. In light of the situation, Ashta knew she could never bring up her own selfish reasons for wanting to see Ceerie one more time.

Ashta berated herself for having not tried harder to stay in contact with Ceerie. She had found the lone gift that Ceerie had sent to her via messenger strange at the time, but now she knew. The Baron had probably been trying to buy Ceerie's silence, and Ceerie, being the unselfish woman that she was, used it to buy an invaluable gift for Ashta. That gift was now long lost somewhere in the Tripsian desert, still wrapped in a protective cloth, waiting inside Starson's saddlebag.

And she had planned to end things, Ashta screamed at herself.

Rather than write a letter back and inquire to Ceerie's health and situation, Ashta had ignored it and waited to respond in person. In a year.

A year had been too long, the damage already irreversible. Now Ceerie had to pay the ultimate price for something that wasn't her fault.

Ashta promised herself that from this day forward she would do everything she could to somehow save her former lover. Her desires and wishes didn't matter in the face of Ceerie's pain.

The clunky steps on the stone-turret's stairs warned Ashta of the approaching soldiers. She sat still, watching as an unfamiliar soldier pulled out the key to her cell and carefully unlocked the gate.

He hesitated to pull it open.

Ashta smirked, no doubt the soldier thought she would attack and fight her way out of her prison. But Ashta didn't want to. She needed to somehow talk to one of the other lionesses or Carien before they executed Ceerie. If she could somehow get word out about Ceerie's condition, she knew one of her friends would search for a way to save Ceerie. They had two months, a lot could change in that time.

What wouldn't change was the certainty of Ashta's death. She stood up slowly, purposefully trying not to scare the soldier.

He pulled open the gate and three other soldiers poured into the small cell. Ashta willingly held her arms out together.

She gritted her teeth as they pulled the tether roughly, tightening it to the point that she couldn't feel her fingers.

To soon they pulled her out of the cell and down the steps. The last sight she had of Ceerie was the woman leaning against the wall, rubbing her swollen belly as her long silver hair glimmered around her in a veil.

Ashta didn't know what to expect from the soldiers. Her gut told her that the king would not kill her so swiftly. That is why she wasn't surprised when the soldiers pulled her into his private quarters where she had stood as a lioness just last night.

She *was* surprised to see Carien seated across from the king, her eyes burning with fury. The soldier jerked her forward as she was staring, causing her to stumble before she straightened herself.

"You may leave," Carien spoke with a wave, dismissing the soldiers. Kkaar stood two steps behind, her head down. Ashta tried to get her attention. If these were her last moments, she needed to tell Kkaar about Ceerie.

Instead, Carien started in on her father. Ashta hadn't just entered the room, but apparently stumbled upon their argument.

Carien pushed off from the table, standing rigid as her hands were braced against the table top. "I understand that you were worried about my safety these last few months, your majesty."

She banged her fist against the table, startling not only Ashta but Kkaar and even the King.

He stared back it his daughter, his gaze cold and filled with something else. Calculation.

Ashta knew that look because it was how her father always looked at her mother. At her. She fidgeted, not liking that the King now stared at his daughter in this way.

"But this is inexcusable. I am of age to be married. I am of the same age as you were to rule this kingdom." Before he could cut in, Carien pushed on, "And I am more than old enough to pick and choose my *own* personal guard. And that guard will take orders from *me*, and absolutely no one else. Least of all you."

"There are other white lionesses in the reserves-"

"I don't want any woman to guard me with her life. Ashta the Lion Tamer has more than proved herself to me that my safety comes above all else. That kind of *loyalty* and *dedication* does not just simply appear overnight."

She took a step back from the table, the anger slipping off of her like a cloak. Instead, there stood a tired but determined woman.

Carien stared her father down before finally speaking. "Ashta the Lion Tamer will be my personal white lioness from this day forward. And if you ever try to meddle in my affairs again father, you will pay the price."

The cold threat slid off her tongue with ease, catching the king's attention. Impossibly, his cold gaze grew colder. With his eyes still on her, Carien whipped around and stalked out of the room.

Kkaar glanced at Ashta before following the princess. Ashta followed behind her, her body shuddering in relief at the click of the door closing.

She would not die today.

Until that moment she had not understood how very close her death had been. She shuddered again, the movement gaining Kkaar's attention. Without a word, the other woman pulled out a knife and cut through Ashta's bonds.

Her relief flooded through her body, making her knees weak. But Ashta pushed through it and followed as steadily as she could behind the princess.

"Kkaar, you are released from your duty and may return to the barracks," Carien's voice called, not bothering to turn around to give her order.

Kkaar nodded, clasping Ashta's arm briefly before turning off from the corridor they were on.

Ashta rubbed her arms as she watched Carien's rigid body in front of her. The princess was in her traditional dress again with her hair covered in beautiful silks. She looked as a cocoon, itching to break free of her silken confines.

Not a word passed between the pair as they walked past the soldiers guarding the door to the princess's personal rooms.

Ashta felt a pang of regret, remembering the two soldiers from before had more than likely died in the raid by the berserkers. Theo and Gustaf. So much had changed since half a year ago.

Once Darkling stepped through the threshold, Carien came to her and pulled the dark-haired woman into her arms. Her body was wracked with shudders as she gasped through the tears.

Ashta awkwardly patted her friend's shoulder before returning her hug. It was strange to be this close, but they had hugged when Carien had offered her friendship and family.

She murmured gentle words in the princess's ear as she held her close. Eventually the tears dried up and Carien pushed away from Ashta. She rubbed at her eyes before taking a seat in the only settee in her sitting room.

"I thought I was too late," she whispered, staring at the burning fire. A luxury only the princess and the king could afford in the great palace.

Ah. That made more sense. The princess had also been aware of how close Ashta's death had been.

"You weren't," Ashta replied tersely. It was the truth, and she thanked all the gods – her mother's as well – for it.

"I could have been," Carien whispered, her gaze never flickering from the flame.

Ashta moved until she was kneeling in front of the princess. She took her hands into her own, forcing Carien to look into her eyes. "You weren't. And even if you had, it would not have been your fault. My life, and my death, is your father's right as king of Tripsia."

"No man should have the right to another's life," she replied with passion. It took Ashta's breath away. In that moment she knew the young princess would make a good queen one day. Ashta only hoped she would be alive to see it.

"That may be, but as of right now that is how the law is written and we must all accept it."

Carien's jaw tightened but she didn't say another word about it. Instead she stood and pulled Ashta up to her feet.

"Come, I had my maids pull a bath for you. If your half as dirty as I was after the desert, then we may need to pull a second bath," she joked with a wink.

Ashta knew that the emotions hadn't disappeared, Carien just masked them well as a princess should. Ashta followed her without comment. She knew that she should say no, but her skin itched with weeks of sweat, dirt, and blood. The blood she couldn't abide the most.

Carien came into the large dressing room with her, taking a seat that was clearly for a maid.

Ashta turned her back to the woman before stripping herself of her weapons. With each clink, she felt more vulnerable. She shouldn't take the bath; it would leave the princess unguarded. Glancing back, she noted the princess was two steps away and Ashta's weapons were in arms reach.

Then she noticed the princess's gaze on her weapons.

When Ashta pulled the half sword out from her skirt, she snorted at Carien's dubious look. Once she stood completely naked before the princess, Carien finally spoke, "If I ever had my doubts about the lionesses ability to protect, they are completely erased now. I don't even understand how you can walk without making more noise."

Ashta chuckled again before commenting, "Practice."

The she pulled out her throwing knives and small daggers in her hair. The princess's eyes widened even further.

Ashta dipped into the hot water, holding in the deep seated sigh.

Despite the almost burning temperature, the hot water felt divine on Ashta's skin. As she dipped her head under, soaking her hair, she was reminded of her last fateful bath.

The first night she met prince zHavier of Naankdoen, she had been dripping wet, her bandage hastily tied around her dress and her skirt pulled on. Even then she had felt something for the blue-eyed stranger. Yet she had never expected him to be a prince.

Maybe if she had been another person, in another life, they would have met and fallen in love. But the life of a princess was long gone for her.

She finally came up for air. The two sat in silence as Ashta cleaned her body. Carien only came over to help wash Ashta's long hair.

"How is the wound?" Carien asked, using her long fingers to dig into Ashta's scalp. She almost purred with the pleasure of it.

"All healed up. Only a slight pinch if I move to quickly but it won't rip open again."

They fell into silence again, Carien carefully working through the tangles.

"Carien," Ashta asked, the princess's given name tasted strange on her tongue. She still felt it was wrong to be using her name, but the princess had been the one to ask her to use it. Taking a deep breath, she continued, "Do you know if there is any way to save a guard who is with child?" She kept going hastily, "I know the consequence that the guard must face, but I was just asking theoretically, for a friend, if maybe there was something that wasn't taught to us."

Carien was quiet for so long that Ashta became afraid that she had angered the princess.

"For a friend?" the princess asked quietly, only a hint of suspicion lacing her words. Ashta couldn't have her charge questioning her abilities in the near future.

"Not for me. I've never lain with a man."

Another long quiet pause passed before Carien spoke. "I don't remember there being, but it was only briefly talked about. But I could look into the old tomes. I'm sure my tutors would love to see me returning from Naankdoen with a thirst for knowledge."

She snorted.

"Thank you," Ashta whispered. It had been incredibly hard to ask for something from the princess. Their relationship was not supposed to be equal, but the princess had said time again that they were. And now she proved it.

Ashta appreciated it immensely, not minding as Carien jerked through a knot, pulling a few hairs out.

"I miss babies."

Darkling jumped at Carien's voice, the water sloshing over the edge of the tub.

"Oh?" the dark-haired woman asked, leaning back again.

"In our village, my nonna had me helping with the babies. Sometimes they were sick, and I had to feed them. Sometimes it was one that was just born to cry, and I would walk with it for hours to give the mother time to sleep."

Ashta could imagine it but she had never met a baby in person. A vague memory poked at her, but she was sure that she had never held one.

"But their smell. Something so sweet and fresh, it made me yearn for my own even at the young age of nine. I didn't understand the ways of men and women at the time. But I knew that I wanted my own brood of children. At least eight or nine."

"So many?" Ashta asked in shock. She couldn't imagine being pregnant so long. And to give birth so many times.

"I always wanted brothers and sisters growing up. Father never remarried so I never had that opportunity until now, with you." Her hand gentled in Ashta's hair. "But I know with my own kids that I never want them to feel as alone as I did. I'd even be okay with two or three. But definitely not just one."

A memory still tickled at the back of her mind but this time Ashta was haunted by black eyes, a mirror to her own.

"Sometimes you don't get to choose how many live."

"Maybe, but I can still dream of having ten," she said on a laugh.

Ashta smiled as well, turning to the princess. "Promise me to never stop dreaming, princess."

Carien giggled, before they fell into talk about what Carien's future husband would need to be to deal with a woman such as the future queen of Tripsia.

And maybe the mother of ten.

CHAPTER TWELVE

⌘

Legends and Firsts

"I FORGET HOW filled my days were," Carien complained as they made their way to the court.

After several days, Carien still had not found a spare moment to go to the library. When she wasn't in lessons, she was being fitted for new gowns. She hadn't even been able to sneak away early in the mornings as her father had set out extra guards by her chambers to ensure she didn't try to work down in the nursery again.

"You are handling it just fine," Ashta commented, only one step behind as custom dictated.

She saw Carien's angry glances but knew that in this it was better to observe the law. The king was still on edge about Ashta's living presence around Carien. No need to push it.

"Ah, your highness!" said a frazzled looking chamberlain. "I have been looking for you. Your father has taken todays court period. You are free to do as you will until the supper hour."

Carien was so happy that she clapped her hand together. Ashta was surprised the other woman didn't hug the portly man.

Whipping around, she headed back down the corridor they had come down. "Never look a gift horse in the eye," she said on a giggle.

Ashta smiled as well, she had hoped they could search for the answer sooner. Ceerie may be safe for another two months. But eventually the time would be up.

Don't worry Ceerie, I'm keeping my promise to you.

They continued through a maze of corridors before stopping in front of a simple door.

There was no ornamentation around the door or in the wood itself, which Ashta thought weird. Even the cubs training entrance had a fancy entrance. She would have never guessed this quiet and unassuming door protected thousands of tomes that were not allowed for the public.

Carien pulled out a key from inside her gown, causing Ashta to quirk a brow.

With a secretive smile, Carien turned the key and pushed the old door open. Its hinges whined from disuse. Holding the door open for Ashta, Carien gestured her in.

Stepping inside Ashta gasped.

It was as if she had stepped through a portal into another world. The room, a square tower, went as high as she could see, the ceiling a pinpoint faraway. As she stepped forward she looked around at the book lined walls all around. Small walkways were set on each floor before another ladder went up to the next.

And yet the entire place was light enough to see clearly. Ashta saw no windows but a familiar glint had her realizing that it was set up with mirrors. Just like the room she had her tattoo done.

The reminder had her reaching up and rubbing at the spot.

"It's something else," Carien breathed out, also taking in the view.

Despite it being a now familiar view, she remembered the first time she had come here. It had been overwhelming. Her younger self had been terrified at the responsibility of knowing all that laid between the many pages in this room. It was only later that she realized that knowing everything wasn't what she had to do but knowing where to look.

"Come on. I doubt we will have much time to go through too many tomes today but I know where the old tomes about the white lionesses are."

Ashta nodded, still staring with wide eyes around her. She followed the princess up three floors where she pulled out two tomes and a long scroll. Ashta managed to carry it all under one arm, barely, as she climbed back down the ladder to the main floor. There in the center of the main floor was a table and chair as well as a settee across from it. Ashta placed her load onto the table before stepping back to the wall.

Carien glanced at the titles before taking the larger one for herself. It was a detailed account of all the written laws about the lionesses from there creation to now. She held the scroll behind her for Ashta.

But when the other woman didn't take it right away Carien turned around. She was shocked to find the other woman standing to the side. "I know they taught you to read as a cub. We will be faster finding your answer if you take some of the load."

Ashta hesitated before answering, "I can't. Only you and the king are allowed to read from the tomes in here."

Carien cocked her head. "Where did you hear that? Because I have seen others in here before, Ennris, the Enzol the head healer. Besides, I am commanding you to take this scroll and search for any valuable information."

Still, Ashta hesitated.

Carien glared at her.

Finally, Ashta took the scroll from her before sitting on the very edge of the settee. She carefully pulled the scroll open before setting it down to read. There was no point in holding it as her arms would tire from its weight.

The first line caught her attention.

Legends of the White Lionesses.

It probably didn't contain what she needed, but she had a feeling it held other information that she had been searching for.

Glancing up, she noted that Carien had taken the seat and already leafing through the great tome.

For a moment she was hit by a pang, remembering the gifts Ceerie had given to her. They books may not have had the answer Ashta was looking for now, but she did miss them. She missed the simple act of sitting down and reading. It had been a haven for her growing up, her only savior from being tormented by Lily or forced to perform princess duties for her father. Her tutors were kind and always gave her books that were filled with legends and stories and languages. She had soaked them in, reveling in the knowledge. Especially during the time after her mother.

As a cub she had become reacquainted with her old friends, books. And through Ceerie's gift, she had been given another opportunity. And she had lost it.

As she looked around the library, Ashta knew she could have spent weeks in here happy. But she no longer had the luxury to choose what she wanted to do with her time.

Forcing her eyes down to read the words, she tried to harden her heart. There were other opportunities, she was sure, for her to acquire books for herself. Maybe when she was old, she would be one of the cub teachers. Then she could read all she wanted for the sake of her cubs.

She worked through some of the early legends of before and during the formation of the lionesses. There wasn't much about the laws and definitely nothing useful that would help with Ceerie's situation.

There was one section that caught her eye.

Remina the Lion.

The first – and only – slave to be freed.

There was a whole section about her legends, but only the ones from after her freedom.

Ashta browsed through the one that Carien had told her already, about Tripsia's continuous drought. Just after that tale came another one, with a familiar name that caught her eye.

Remina pushed through the lush green forest. If she remembered what Justus has said correctly than his estate was a week journey from the palace. But if she cut through the forest, she hoped it would only be three days.

She regretted the decision, swatting at another insect bite. It had only been a couple of days since she had gained her freedom and she was keen to get as far away from the palace, and the king, as possible. But Justus had already gone back to his estate.

The King had to allow Justus's return as his land and main house burnt to the ground by the ravaging ships from Bbrski. He had lost not only his aging parents, but most certainly the moneys from this year's crops. If his estate wasn't already indebted to the crown it wouldn't have been a problem. But with the fire, he would be forced to give up his inheritance to the crown who would give it to the next person they showed favor to.

But she needed to get to Justus before the king sent his soldiers to deal with him. With renewed vigor, Remina cut and ran through the forest.

Finally, she cut to the edge of farmland. From her high vantage point she could see the white sandy beaches and just past the great blue ocean. It still took her breath away even after having grown up within view of its great expanse.

She ran into the land and headed as fast as she could to the charred remains of the great house. No one came out to greet her.

As she ran, she realized there was no one around, not a single person. Worried that the pirates had come again, she pushed herself even harder. Please let Justus be okay, she begged the great sun god of her father's people. *Please.*

She heard the unmistakable sound of galloping hooves. Horses. The king's men were already closing in on the estate.

A glint from the beach had Remina turning from the charred remains of the great house and down towards the white sand.

Her hands were shaking from exertion, but she knew she was close. So close. Churning in her belly warned her at how close she was.

As she neared the beach, she made out a small sailboat, its sails down and waiting. A man was loading what looked to be the last of his supplies into the boat.

But that man wasn't just any man. As he pushed the boat into the water, Remina called out. "JUSTUS!"

His body jerked up and he turned to her. His expression melted to one of love and happiness. She knew she had made the right decision coming here, even if her last words to him had been less than enthusiastic. Her heart clenched at the thought.

When she was almost within steps of him, his expression changed again, to shock and fear. Remina didn't dare look behind her, hearing the thundering hooves grow closer.

"Push it further out!" She screamed, joining him on the other side. He didn't say anything as they fought against the waves until they were waist deep. They both jumped up into the boat and slid onto the floor. Remina gasped for air, her body screaming for air and a rest.

"We need to row further out." His deep voice had her shivering in excitement and happiness. She loved how low it was. And she loved the musicality of his words.

She pushed against her aching muscles and the twinge in her back. She didn't dare think, instead forcing her hands around one of the oars.

They began rowing in earnest.

For a moment, their gazes caught and Remina could feel the sparks of their attraction.

"Mina," he murmured, leaning in to place a gentle kiss on her cheek.

But he never reached it.

His eyes widened as he gasped, the arrowhead poking out through his chest.

"Justus!" she called, fear pushing her to her knees as she caught his body, narrowly missing a second arrow.

"Get…" he gasped, "Get us out of here."

"I will," she promised. "I will."

After placing him against a side wall she took up both oars and rowed for their lives. Her muscles screamed in protest, beyond done from exertion. But her mind knew that if she slowed for even a moment, the soldiers she could make out on the beach would be after her. Even now she saw as a second party of men joined the first, pointing further down the beach. She glanced over and made out the outline of another sailboat.

Shit. She needed to move faster. She quickly stood and set up the sail. It blew open catching the first wind. As she turned to steer, she realized they were headed straight into a storm.

It could kill them.

Glancing down at Justus's pale face, she realized it didn't matter. He could already be dead. But she refused to die. And she refused to give up on them. Especially now that she was free to be who she wanted to be. To love who she wanted.

And she wanted Justus like she wanted her very next breath.

Lightening flashed and she shivered as the thunder shook through her bones. Now it was time to see if her few sailing lessons from her brother and his friends could save them. And if not, at least she died free to choose.

"Those marks," a raspy voice called out, pulling Ashta out of the legend before its end. She was surprised to be staring straight into the ancient eyes of the healer who had done her tattoo.

The ancient man moved incredibly fast despite his stooped back, capturing her wrist in his hands. He turned it over and leaned in close to study the blue marks. "Incredible," he whispered, the marks almost glowing under his attention. He ran his fingers over them before pulling back.

Ashta glanced up into Carien's shocked gaze. Neither of them had heard the screech from the door. Yet Ashta knew if she glanced behind her, she would find the door wide open.

"I've only seen these marks once before."

He glanced up into her eyes. His watery gaze cleared for a moment and Ashta wondered at the man's true age. Was he saying…? No. That wasn't possible.

She jerked her hand out of his grasp, rolling up the scroll before his wandering eyes could read what she had been reading. With a nod at Carien, Ashta stood and threw the scroll down on the table.

"It must be already supper time," Carien spoke out to no one. She stood with grace, closing her tome nonchalantly.

The Enzol stared at the two women but said nothing else.

Carien walked around the table and out the door, Ashta hurrying a step behind her. Once they had put lots of space between them and the library, Carien stopped and leaned back against the wall. She let out a breath she obviously had been holding.

"I don't know how he snuck in their without either of us noticing, especially with your cat senses."

Ashta shrugged, still at loss for words.

Carien grasped her shoulder and squeezed gently. "I didn't find anything that could be of use for your question."

Ashta let that sink in. *I should have left the scroll earlier and picked up the second tome.* She beat herself up over it, realizing that she had fallen for her selfish wants. Hadn't she promised Ceerie? And there she was wasting an afternoon reading about the freed slave Remina the Lion.

Her heart skipped a beat as she thought of the name, so similar to her own.

But then again, half the lioness's had Lion in their name. Ennris the Lion Killer. Remina the Lion. Ryce the Little Lion. It didn't make her special, she reminded herself.

"But don't worry, I will keep looking for you, Darkling."

At her quiet words, Ashta took solace in the princess's warm gaze. She knew that she had slipped up today, but Carien would not stop until they had an answer.

Or Ceerie was dead.

Ashta hoped for everyone's sake it was the former.

"Now come on, let's get supper out of the way so we can focus on the other court games my father has set up."

The princess's eyes rolled at her father's attempts to distract her. If only he knew how smart his young daughter was becoming.

CHAPTER THIRTEEN

⌘

Connected

DAYS PASSED WITH no progress. Carien managed to sneak an hour everyday into the library to no avail. With each day, her face became more grim and Ashta became more desperate. She helped read through scrolls and scrolls of history and law, from all across the Midloean kingdoms. And not a hint of an answer came up in the words.

On one of these days, Ashta ran across an interesting piece of law. She looked up from her scroll to see Carien still hunched over her own tome.

"Your highness."

No movement.

"Princess."

She still did not stir.

"Carien!" She whisper-yelled.

Finally, Carien looked up from the work blinking hard. "What?"

"Come here, I found something interesting."

"Is it about the lionesses?"

"No."

Ashta said no more, waiting for the princess to hunch over the scroll beside her. Carefully pulling the scroll close, Carien whispered aloud the piece of law.

"*If no heir is procured, then Tripsian law allows a one-year period of potentials from the great families to come forward and take a series of tests. Whomever survives to the end is crowned as the King or Queen of Tripsia and their family line becomes the new ruling family.*

But this doesn't matter. My father has an heir."

"I know. But mine does not, I wonder if Bbrski has something similar in place."

For a moment the two women stood and considered it.

For Ashta, it made sense because it allowed someone to rule without fear of the other families. But she was sure that the council of Bbrskian families appointed a ruler if there was no heir. The Tripsian law made more sense. It weeded out the weak and the greedy. The ones that had power only through their network and not on their own merit.

Carien returned to her tome as Ashta continued reading, learning that the series of tests made Ashta's test to become a white lioness look easy.

That anyone could survive was a feat alone.

But the law stated that until a person completed every last test, then the tests continued and the council ruled until a leader – a King *or* Queen – was found.

A sigh rose from Carien. "Come now, Darkling, it is dinner again. We will not find our answer today."

Ashta was grateful that Carien had taken up the cause. But their answer did not come that day or the next.

Becoming antsy, the next time the two women are cooped up in the library, Ashta got up from her place.

"I'm going for a walk. Lock up behind me."

Carien nodded, following her to the door.

Only when the click of the lock in place could be heard did Ashta release her breath. She knew the princess was safe in the library but leaving her alone went against all her training and her instincts.

But Ashta couldn't sit in the musty tower chamber a moment longer. Hope was slowly giving out and they had a little over a month before they *needed* an answer. And Ashta simply could not accept failure.

So, she roamed the halls. Every time she heard voices approaching, she would duck into a darkened doorway, waiting for them to pass.

Minutes passed by as her brain ran in circles, trying to find something they might have overlooked. But she stalled every time. The laws were clear on the point of relations with men.

There were no exceptions.

None at all.

Without realizing it, Ashta found herself standing before the entrance to the cubs training room. She stared up at the sword, shivering at simply being near it. But this time she realized the pressure on her mind was from the sword itself.

Shivering again, she reached up and touched the handle. The opal on the pommel shone bright, almost blinding Ashta as she was pulled into visions of memories that were not her own.

At first just flickers of images came through. A man turned away. A woman crying. A woman stepping off the boat, her dress cape pulled back to give a glimpse of a swollen belly.

Scared, Ashta jerked her finger back from the blade shocked. How was it possible? It couldn't be. But the last image, the one of the pregnant woman, had clawed into Ashta's mind. Was this unknown woman the answer to saving Ceerie's life? The woman had also been wearing lioness clothes. Clearly it had been known that she had lain with a man. And she had been free to walk about, despite how swollen her belly was.

Glancing up at the pommel, Ashta wondered if she held it, that then she could control the visions. The idea of some strange power seeping into her mind set Ashta on edge. But the frustration from the past few days with no answers was worse. The scrolls had given her nothing. Maybe this sword of strange qualities had the answer she was looking for.

Mindset, Ashta forced herself to ignore the hairs standing on end on her neck. She reached up and touched the opal on the pommel.

This time, the opal flashed bright as its light seeped up the veins in Ashta's arm. She watched, her heart racing as the blue glow lit up the marks on her hand, then seeped down her arm and into her shoulder. Her brow was damp, but she refused to pull away. Before she could look down to see if the light had reached her neck, her mind was pulled out of her body and Ashta was transported into another time, in another body.

The cold spray from the ice rain pelted Remina, but she didn't pull her hood up. She craved the numbness. Anything to drown out the memories. She had been so close. Finally free. She had almost had everything she dreamed of within reach.

Her eyes involuntarily glanced at the spot in *that* boat. The red stain. Where his body had lain for days before his soul had given out.

Remina had kept on sailing, straight south as far away from Tripsia as possible. Her father had taught her the stars as a young girl. But when she had been stolen as a slave for Tripsia, she had thrown everything from her childhood away. There had been no purpose in thinking about things that could never be again.

And now, finally free, she allowed herself to sink back into the memories of the past. But she still refused to turn her boat home. No, home was no longer there, it hadn't been for years. It never would be again.

Again, she glanced at the stain. She had thought she had found her new home with Justus, but even that had been taken from her.

She forced her eyes to the horizon, looking out for any signs of movement. When she scanned behind her, she breathed out with relief that no telltale sails followed her. The king may have dissolved the tether Tripsia had on her, but the laws of when she had been a slave could still hurt her.

A kick in her gut reminded her of the very real consequences. She rubbed her swollen belly, soothing her small unborn child.

No, Tripsia would not look favorably on her situation. The king would have her charged under the old laws, free or not. He had known that something was going on between her and Justus, but there had been no proof.

None at the time.

It had been close; her freedom had come only weeks before her pregnancy showed. Even at thirty-five weeks, her belly had not swollen out, instead it was pulled close to her, her muscles from years of training hiding the pregnancy better than any dress could.

A black dot formed on the horizon.

Land.

Finally.

Remina hurried, turning the sails to the dot and tying the ropes down. Justus had been prepared to sail for a long time with enough provisions to last a month. But Remina knew that she needed to find people before the provisions ran out.

The babe would be here much sooner, and she knew nothing about having a baby. Nothing in her memories as a child or as lioness had prepared her for the journey of motherhood. She only hoped that someone would take pity on a young mother and show her the way.

As the black dot formed into an obvious coastline, Remina began pacing. There was nothing she could do in the boat. Her provisions were packed. Her only clothes were the cape Justus had worn the day he had been shot by the arrow. Remina could feel the slightest chill still stinging at the hole in the cape. But she did not know how to fix such things.

As the coast came closer, so did the cool air. She pulled her cloak tight around herself. Please let this land be anywhere but Tripsia, she fervently prayed to the sun god. He had listened to her last prayer, maybe he would listen again.

Once she was close enough, she took the sail down and began rowing. Her arms worked the oars, straining against the sea water. Her fingers clung like claws, frozen to the wood.

She did not stop rowing until she felt the gritty slide of sand underneath the hull.

Finally. She was here.

Where-ever here was.

She turned and was surprised to find a group of men standing on the beach. Each man was covered in fur, only their eyes visible in the cold afternoon light.

One man, the only one with no sword drawn, stepped forward. Remina knew that she could hold her own against two maybe three of the men without hurting herself. But the kick in her belly reminded her that both her and the babe would not survive against five.

Carefully she got up and jumped out of the boat. The wind caught her cape, billowing it out.

The man's eyes widened, taking in her swollen belly and strange bandage and skirt.

He had never seen a woman dressed in so little clothing. He looked behind her, waiting for her husband or a man to join her, but none came out. With a nod to his brothers, he approached the woman as two of the men pulled the boat further onto the sand before jumping inside.

His eyes appraised the strange hull, noting that the wood had a red quality to it. He had only seen such colour in a great trade ship that had come from the north lands. The Midloean kingdoms.

Again, his eyes took in the woman before him.

Her bright blue gaze was as clear and cold as the sea. Her hair like spun sun rays. Even her skin glowed, as if the sun goddess had kissed every inch of her body.

She looked up at him with no fear in her gaze. She should be fearful, he thought, frowning down at the slight woman.

"She looks like she would be a wild one in bed," his brother Toru joked. Lucifer glared at him until the man shut up.

He would make this strange woman his. He glanced at her body again. Yes, this woman would make strong children. And a strong countess.

Shivering again, Ashta pulled her hand away from the sword.

Voices.

Someone was coming.

Not sure what to do, Ashta ran a few steps and hid in another darkened doorway, adrenaline from her vision pushing her fast.

As she waited, she couldn't help but hear their words drifting towards her. Two distinctly feminine voices.

"He has been unbearable these last few months. And you can assure yourself the King will only get worse as his daughter ages."

"That may be true, but the daughter is different."

A snort.

"No. Like father like daughter. We will be feeling the wrath and pain of the Kritol family for decades. All are unreasonable and emotional, especially those two. Not what Tripsia needs. Tripsia needs a coolheaded leader."

"Maybe the princess will marry someone-"

"The only use the King and princess have is dead. Until then we must wait…"

Their voices drifted away as the two must have turned into a doorway of the cubs training.

What did this mean?

Too worried to think about the things she had heard, Ashta turned and almost ran the entire way back to the library. She knocked on the doorway hard, not stopping until it creaked open and Carien's pinched face looked up at her.

"Close it!" Ashta barked as she slipped through the opening.

Carien jumped before locking the door with shaking fingers.

Once it was locked, Ashta sighed, resting her head back against the wall. Her thoughts were a whirling mess. She wasn't sure what to think. Instead she focused on the one thing that had been driving her these past few days.

"Have you found anything?" she asked, her eyes still firmly closed.

When Carien didn't reply Ashta forced her eyes open and took in Carien's dejected form.

Anger burned in her veins, pushing her forward into Carien's face. Not able to pull herself back, she spat into Carien's face, "You did nothing when I asked for your help with my half-sister's execution. If you care at all about me, you will do something for Ceerie."

Carien's face paled but she did not back down. "I am trying," she bit out.

"Well it's not good enough," Ashta yelled. Shocked at her own voice she fell back into the wall and rubbed her eyes.

"Were you two close?" Carien whispered, her heart aching for her friend. She had not seen Darkling this upset since princess Lillian. This Ceerie, she must have meant a lot to Darkling. She did not recognize the name, so the woman had not been part of the lionesses that had come to Naankdoen.

"Closer than sisters," Ashta chocked out, rubbing a stray tear away. Had it all been for nothing?

Carien stayed quiet, slightly hurt at the comment. She had thought that her and Darkling had become quite close over the past year. Especially in the last month since they had escaped from Naankdoen.

But then, this other woman must have known Darkling as a cub. The bonds of time were strong. Carien knew this. Her own heart was still wrapped around Liam.

"Come on. We will find no more today. Let's go to the court instead. There are always people looking for answers from the king, even today."

Ashta nodded not really listening. Her mind was still trying to sort through all the thoughts and visions that weren't her own.

She followed the princess, numb to her own emotions. The strange vision had her wondering if there was any point looking, when the answer was already staring her back in the face.

CHAPTER FOURTEEN

⌘

The Coming War

THE MONTH SLOWLY crawled by, each day making Ashta's muscles tenser. Carien tried to help what she could, but she had read every tome and scroll related to the lionesses and the laws. What was still left to be read were just legends and histories of neighboring kingdoms. There wasn't even a hope of an answer in the rest of the tomes.

But she kept trying. She still felt the guilt over the death of the heir to Bbrski. For that alone she kept trying. But it seemed pointless.

Plus, her father demanded that she spend more time dealing with the public. He kept stating she would be queen one day and she needed to be ready to rule. She hadn't dared to tell her father that she did not want to be a princess. That all she wanted was to rejoin the Alpen people.

The only thing that kept her from leaving was Darkling. Carien knew her father would have had her friend, her sister, killed from the moment they returned to Tripsia. So, for her safety Carien stayed.

That is how Carien found herself day after day sitting in the public courtroom, sitting in her father's throne as she listened to grievances.

Ashta stood to her side, her blank gaze watching as each person was led into the room by a soldier.

All that Carien had learned so far was that many of her people were poor. So poor that the two men that stood before her now were fighting over the ownership of a lone chicken. Both men were dirty, their hair long and bedraggled. She could smell them from the top of her seat.

"You stole what was rightfully mine and you keep the eggs for yourself! That chicken was my only money. I sold her eggs at the market to help buy food stuffs for my wife and eight children!"

Carien wasn't sure how a single chicken could feed such a large family. But she could see that both of the men had gone red in the face and were prepared to argue for hours.

She held up her hand.

When the men did not turn to her or fall silent, the soldiers on either side of them pushed in their knees till both men were on the floor.

With a sigh, Carien stood. "You shall return the chicken to Maglon."

The first man lightened but before he could say anything, Carien continued. "When the chicken begins her brooding, Maglon will give one surviving chick to you Sermua."

With a wave of her hand, the soldiers picked each man up and dragged them out the door before returning with the next person.

Carien sat with sigh, staring longingly out the great windows where the luscious courtyard could be seen. Birds flew in and out of the emerald green foliage.

Darkling coughed, bringing Carien's attention back to the court room. With a sigh, she leaned back and listened to the woman.

Ashta on the other hand grew more perturbed from her station in the throne room. She had given up for the most part on finding an answer for Ceerie. But only because there was something else brewing. Something much more dangerous than losing her former lover.

Each passing day brought people through the throne room, glaring up at the young princess. Ashta could see as more disgruntled people came through, the more restless the soldiers became until they were no longer polite. The soldiers manhandled the people, feeling the same threat in the air as Ashta did.

This time Ashta wasn't worried about individuals acting out on their own. No. From the angry faces of the poor Ashta feared a rebellion would take place in the near future. And Ashta knew that something like that could break the young princess from her kind and just personality. Would she still be so trusting when her people turned on her?

She tuned back into the old fisherman that stood before them now. His young son stood beside him, not saying a word, just glared up at the princess. But the words he spoke, brought a chill across Ashta's skin.

"The fire can be seen from days away. We had gone closer because my son and I trade with the Naankdoena, our fish for their cloths and silks. But their were no ships in their bay. There were no ships in the sea around at all. Just a large smudge could be seen on land of what must be the Bbrskian army."

"Thank you kind sir. You will be paid for your information." Carien waved the two away.

A soldier took the two men aside before allowing the next person in.

A few days later a boy came into the courtroom. He was a goat herdsman near the border. His face was laced with fear as he reported that his entire herd of goats had been stolen from men in furs. Berserkers.

More and more reports trickled in of animals being raided. Some even said that they had daughters, sisters go missing in the night. Ashta's father's presence loomed over Tripsia as Ceerie's due date closed in.

A week before Ceerie was expected to give birth to her child, the King called a council meeting. This time he called for his daughter's presence. Carien looked at the messenger with shock before burning the short note in the fireplace.

"Come Ashta, we must hurry to the council's chamber."

Despite the late hour, many servants roamed the halls. Ashta worried at their interested glances at the princess. It was only a matter of time before the next attempt on Carien's life. Ashta had been lucky to go so long in peace.

They entered through another small unassuming door, no different than the library's. But this one had a soldier stationed on either side of the entry.

She nodded to the man as she made to follow the princess. But their spears came down blocking the way.

Carien looked back at the soldiers, annoyance flickering across her features.

"She comes with me."

"I apologize, your highness, but only council members may enter the room."

Color flushed up her neck and into her cheeks as Carien turned around and stared the soldier down. "Tell me, soldier, does my father have his personal guards with him?"

The man flushed, before stammering, "Well, uh, yes-"

"Then as his heir, my personal guard will follow me anywhere as well."

The man looked confused before pulling his spear back. Ashta followed the princess quickly before the soldiers changed their minds.

The room quieted as a dozen men turned and stared at Ashta. Carien ignored their looks, stalking towards her father.

The king glared at Ashta's presence but said nothing.

"You requested my presence, your majesty."

"Yes…" He pointedly stared at Ashta.

Sighing, Carien pointed to the wall behind her. Ashta took the hint and leaned against the wall, not looking at anyone, least of all the other two lionesses in the room.

"My personal guard cannot protect me if she is not allowed to follow me wherever I must go."

He grunted before turning away from Ashta and looking back down at the map laid out on the table.

Without meaning to Ashta could see it was a map of northern Bbrski, the sea, the Midloean kingdoms and parts of the southern pieces of the Northern kingdoms. There were carved blocks placed across the map, but Ashta was unsure of their meaning.

The men spoke quietly, forcing Ashta to look at them rather than listen. Two of the men present were generals. The other eight were council men making the last man the most dangerous in the group to Ashta. Besides the king.

The last man, with white hair and sun spotted skin had light coloured eyes that were hard with no emotion. He was the head of the lionesses. He was the one who upheld the laws in place and carried them out. Often, he was the executioner.

His pale eyes glanced up at Ashta, making her shiver with true fear. If she did not die from fighting, she would die from at the hands of this man.

She turned away, instead focusing her energy on listening. Ashta could only make out a few words but what she did hear had her worried for the safety of Tripsia.

The princess leaned in over the table, staring at the map.

"And the pieces?" Carien asked. General Hariim looked to her father before answering her.

"These are all the locations we have of reports of raids or attacks from Bbrskian berserkers."

Carien stared down at the spotted map, understanding slowly dawning on her. The entire east coast of Tripsia was under fire. That wasn't including the desert or the one road that lead from the palace to Naankdoen. Because if its disuse, they had no idea if an army was marching towards them or not.

"Have we sent a scout on the Royal Way?"

"Yes, but neither have returned. This morning we sent out ten soldiers as a group. Hopefully one of them will make it back to us alive with a report of what and where the Bbrskian men are."

That was worrying. Then she remembered one of the reports from a few days' past that she had heard in the courtroom.

"And the ships? The Bbrskian Fleet, the Black Death?"

The other General shook his head. "We have our own ships out there scouting but so far we have seen nothing. On top of that, the slaver boats are all busy in the far west in Kae ol and Malten. They won't be back for months."

But where could the southern king hide his fleet?

"We should start making plans incase an army does arrive by land."

The king snorted, "Not if, councilman, but when the army comes. Mark my words, King Alerik will come for Tripsia. He has been eyeing the Midloean kingdoms for sometime. What happened in Naankdoen was the justified spark he needed to start a war.

He will come to us, making demands, and we will need to be ready with answers. Or, at the very least, be able to hold off his army long enough for the slaver boats with Ennris and the older lionesses to return."

"Even if the army comes, we cannot rely on the just the lionesses. Maybe if we push the cubs in training now to full status, we can supplement our numbers."

Carien gasped. Cubs were anywhere from fourteen to seventeen years old. How could a fourteen-year-old fight against a hulking berserker? "The cubs are too young."

General Hariim stared at her as he leaned over the table. "We have men in our armies that are younger than the cubs. Fourteen is old enough."

"But you can't-"

"Enough!" The room went deafeningly silent after the king's outburst. General Hariim and the King stared at each for a long moment before the general finally broke off his gaze. "The cubs will remain in training, for now. Bbrski has not declared war on us, or even sent a messenger. We will wait to see what it is they want from us first. Until then, we need to begin preparing."

He turned to the other man in military attire. "General Ttaabit and your men will upgrade the outer palace walls and battlements. Get the men to dig trenches and lace them with oil. General Hariim and his men will round up as many of our trades men and have them commit ships to our own meager fleet. In the meanwhile, we need to take a recount of the provisions at the palace. Now. How long can we feed our own people and the outer area people as they flood the palace, before we run out."

The men continued their debate over provisions and housing the general public. But Carien no longer listened. She looked behind her into Darkling's black gaze, seeing her own horror mirrored in the other woman's.

Tripsia would not survive a siege. They were a husk of their kingdoms former glory. A broken city with a few coastline estates that still produced fruit and lumber. It would be simple for King Alerik to take control of the estates and wait out the city until its surrender. Carien fervently hoped that it was not the king's intention. As he seemed far more interested, and invested, in the destruction of Naankdoen. What interest was Tripsia to him?

Ashta knew her father. She understood his greed and his thirst for power. Now was the time to strike the Midloean kingdoms. Naankdoen was just one great city with no other lands or people. Tripsia was slightly larger but just as small of a military presence. And once her father had established control over the two kingdoms, he would slowly make his way through the rest until he was king of all the Midloean kingdoms.

It was only a matter of time before Tripsia realized the man's true intention. Ashta hoped they realized it soon, but her heart ached with the knowledge that these old men could not see that far ahead.

The king maybe, but not the rest of the men in the council room.

CHAPTER FIFTEEN

⌘

Dark Day

THAT NIGHT ASHTA slept fitfully. She tossed and turned despite the glow wein. It should have pulled her down into a deep sleep. But its hold didn't stand a chance against the powers of the night.

Ashta sat up suddenly, a cry stuck in her throat. At first, she was lost in the familiar dark features of her room that sat just off of Carien's. She stood and checked the servant's hall behind her one door. Nothing. No movement.

She then turned to Carien's room, checking behind the doors and curtains until she was satisfied that nothing was out of place. Taking one last glance at Carien's peaceful form, Ashta turned back to her own room.

Before she crossed the threshold, she felt a cold touch on her cheek. Shivers wracked her body as she took the last step over the threshold. A sharp spike of pain in her abdomen pulled her down to her knees.

Ashta crawled to her cot, climbing in as the pain radiated out further, until her whole body throbbed in heat and the pain of a thousand needles.

She fell back into a fitful sleep, the pain never quite leaving her abdomen.

The next morning, Ashta followed Carien through the halls and out of the palace. A twenty soldiers carried Carien in a litter down into the city. Ashta followed behind, noting the scores of people lining the ruined city's main road. Ahead of Carien was her father's litter. Behind her Ashta could see the council men and other heads of families.

Their party walked to the center of the old city of Trian where the largest of the lion pits stood, sinking below the sand dusted ground. A dais had been made recently, still smelling of fresh cut wood. Ashta took her place behind Carien's seat, right beside the Kings larger throne.

Slowly, the council filed in front of them. With a shiver, Ashta realized the head of the lionesses was not among them.

Rubbing her gut, she stared at the seats encompassing the pit. The public – young, old, wealthy, poor – all stood screaming and crying out their excitement. It was a blood thirsty crowd Ashta thought grimly. Nothing good could come of it.

The sand in the center of the pit began to sink before it opened up.

There, standing directly below Ashta was the head of the lionesses, and standing beside him, defeated and bound, was Ceerie.

Ceerie.

The baby.

Ashta took in a shaking breath. She had thought there was more time. It couldn't be. Even as she counted the weeks in her head, Ashta knew she was too late. That the time to do something had passed.

She watched in horror as rows on rows of lionesses walked down from the palace and took their place in the stands across the pit from the King. Even from the distance, Ashta recognized Kkaar's dark head and Luci not far behind.

She had failed them. But most importantly she had failed Ceerie.

Darkness started swirling at the corners of her vision. But before it went completely dark, a hand grabbed onto her wrist. Looking up, Ashta stared into one of the king's personal guards. "Keep your eyes open. No matter what," she warned quietly, glancing back at the kings rigid back.

Ashta nodded, ripping her wrist away. She forced in several breaths before looking back down into the sandy pit where this life, the life of a white lioness, had begun for her. And where this life would end for Ceerie.

"People of Tripsia!" the head of the lionesses called out, his voices ringing out to the very edges of crowd. The people screamed back in elation.

It was time to begin.

He raised his hands and waited until the crowd died down.

"Today I bring before you a slave who has broken the sacred trust of our lands."

People booed and began throwing dirt and rocks down into the pit. One caught Ceerie's forehead, slicing it open.

Ashta watched with her heart in throat as Ceerie just stood there, a shell of the proud woman Ashta knew.

"Ceerie the Light-footed, first of her name has been found guilty of lying with a man, resulting of a child. As such, she faces the ultimate punishment."

"DEATH!" the crowd screamed, chanting it over and over again. The only somber people in the crowd besides the King and princess, were the other lionesses. They sat quietly and watched the proceedings.

Ashta shivered.

Knowing that the lionesses sat there so the king and soldiers could point out any woman that had looked away. If she did, she would lose her hand, as was the punishment for these things.

Ashta forced her own eyes back into the sand pit, remembering the other lioness's words of warning. No doubt the king had several soldiers watching her. He would relish any opportunity to bring Ashta pain.

Clenching her jaw, Ashta refused to let him gain anything from her.

She watched as four more soldiers, each with a horse, climbed up out of the hole.

In horror, she watched as Ceerie was unbound then rebound, this time her arms attached to one horse and her legs attached to a second. With a fierce whip to both horses, the animals jumped and pulled in opposite directions.

Ashta flinched at Ceerie's screams of pain as her body was stretched apart. *There is nothing I can do, there is nothing I can do.* Ashta repeated the mantra in her head trying to drown out the screams of Ceerie and the bloodthirsty cries of the public.

Apparently satisfied, the executioner unbound Ceerie's limbs.

But then he rebound them, each arm and leg to a different horse. Ashta watched in horror as blood pooled below Ceerie's body. How could they torture a woman who had just given birth? She didn't understand it, couldn't understand it, but forced her eyes to stay on Ceerie's face.

The other woman had tears streaking across her cheeks, her hair a snarled white mess clouded around her face.

As the horses stretched her again, the executioner came to her head and none to gently cut off the mass of her hair, nicking her scalp. He held it up like a prize, and the crowd showered him with screams of adoration.

Even from this distance Ashta could see him soaking in the attention. If she had not seen how ancient the man was yesterday, she would not have believed it. He bounded around the arena like a spry twenty-year-old, his hands already covered in blood.

Again, he signaled the horses to give. But this time, two more soldiers came up, holding a wooden table between them.

Ashta ground her teeth as the men dropped Ceerie's body on top of the table, keeping her still tied to the horses.

Another signal and the horses stretched her out just enough that she couldn't move on the table.

The executioner jumped on the table. He waved about a large black knife, its edge glinting in the late morning sun.

With the crowds approval, he cut off all of Ceerie's coverings until she lay naked and bleeding on the table. With the precision of a healer, he sliced up and down Ceerie's ribs, making her bleed but not too deep for her to bleed out.

The morning wore on as the torture became more unbearable. He cut of all her fingers and toes, stretching her in between each. Eventually, servants came by the royal dais and brought platters of food. Ashta briefly glanced at the crowd and noted many were eating or drinking alcohol, the smell pungent in the blood and sweat soaked air. And through it all the ever-present heat of the sun pressed down on everyone.

The crowd never let up their cheers and jeers, only becoming more crowded as more and more people from the city and surrounding area came down to the pit.

Ashta's own stomach clenched with disgust. She took some comfort in the fact that Carien had not touched her food. She was not heartless.

The King on the other hand went through whole chicken wings and loaves of breads and cups of beer, seeming to thoroughly enjoy himself. It took everything in Ashta not to sneer at him.

She had to remind herself that the king had people watching her and the other lionesses. She would do Ceerie no good by gaining the wrath of the king on herself.

Even so, watching the executioner cut open her abdomen and pull out her guts left Ashta feeling more helpless than she had at Lilly's execution. Her half-sister's death had been just as painful, extreme in its sickening torture. But in Naankdoen the people that had watched had been grim-faced. No one had taken pleasure in the young princess's death. No. Not like this.

Finally, with her liver held out to the king, the executioner bowed and walked down into the hole disappearing from the view of the crowd.

Was it finally over? Ashta hoped so as she watched the flutter of Ceerie's lungs, open and bare to the sun.

The soldiers cut the ropes attached to the horses then they all disappeared into the hole. The door closed on itself leaving behind the even floor of the pit. Ceerie lay on the table, blood soaking the sand underneath and around it.

The King stood up from his throne and walked down to the edge of pit. The crowd screamed even louder, the air pulsing with need and energy like a live thing.

Finally, the king held up both of his hands.

The crowd quieted down instantly as people stood still in their spots.

"Let this day be a lesson for all. No one is free of the law. Not the king, not the council, not the people and not the slaves."

People screamed with glee, chanting *the law, the law, the law.*

Again, he quieted the crowd.

This time, he turned to Carien and held out his hand. Ashta winced at the tremors in Carien's hand as she stood and walked up beside her father. He took her hand and held it high above them. The crowd's cries surged with approval and elation at seeing their young princess's face.

He leaned down and whispered into his daughters' ear before standing straight once more.

Ashta's gut rolled at what the king had done. There was already murmurs of rebellion against the king. To bring Carien in like this, to paint her with the same harsh brush as him, would only make it worse. But he didn't seem to care.

"The law is final," Carien's clear voice rang across the stadium, echoing out over the ruined city of Trian. "And death is final."

At her last words, Ashta watched in horror as a different section of sand sunk down and opened up like a gaping mouth. Emerging from the depths of hell were several lions, their mane's mangy and full. Ashta could count their ribs from her spot on the dais.

They couldn't, she thought in horror, watching as the hungry lions growled and swatted at each other before catching the scent of blood.

They *could*.

The lions fell upon Ceerie's body, ripping and shredding it apart as they toyed with her limbs.

The king and princess took their seats once more, waiting until the last remains of Ceerie had been consumed by the starved lions.

It was no different than the slave tests. Except Ceerie had no chance the second time she faced the lion pit. The had cut away her strength, leaving her to the terror and pain of the animals' teeth.

Once it was done, the crowds slowly dissipated.

The lionesses stood as a group and marched back to the palace.

King Roman stood and walked down from the dais. When Carien passed Darkling, she reached out and squeezed her wrist, not daring to look Darkling in the eye with so many watching her.

Ashta stared down into the sand pit for one last moment. Her gaze caught on a male lion as he stared up at her. His golden eyes were sunken. Blood lined around his mouth.

She knew the lions had no more a choice in this than Ceerie did. And for that she forgave them. But she could never forgive the head of the lionesses, the executioner.

And she could never forgive the king.
He would pay for this one day.
She promised herself to it.

CHAPTER SIXTEEN

⌘

Face of the Future

THE WALK BACK to the palace was filled with cheering and noise, a complete opposite to the somber walk out to the pit.

Ashta walked behind Carien's litter, her face set as stone. Just get through this day, she reminded herself. Then get through tomorrow, and the day after, and the day after.

Any hope and happiness that had grown within her these last few years had shriveled and died. All that was left was the hollow stone shell that was her body.

The King sat in his litter, silks swaying in the wind around him as he laid back and hid in the shade. The soldiers around his litter had made a barrier all around so the people could barely get in viewing distance.

Carien's was similar, but her silks were tied back, and she waved at her people. She also spoke with the soldiers and they tightened their circle. Men, women, old and young stood watching her. It was a happy procession. The distrust of the people was palpable in the air despite the celebratory mood.

Ashta stayed close, staring each person in the eye who glared at the princess. They quickly looked away, not wanting to gain the attention of the Lion Tamer, the woman who had made it through Naankdoen and the desert.

The one who could kill in the blink of an eye.

When the party made it back within the palace walls the crowd dissipated, finding their own entrances or returning to their homes on the coastline, below the great cliffs.

Carien waited for her father to disappear within the palace before carefully disembarking her own litter. The soldiers bowed respectfully to their future queen before returning to their stations.

Carien nodded to Ashta, who followed one step behind the princess as they entered the great halls.

At first Ashta thought Carien would return to her chambers to dress for court. Instead she turned the opposite way from her rooms. Curious, Ashta said nothing as she followed. Finally, the halls twisted in a familiar way and Ashta realized they were headed to the infirmary.

Screams wrenched through the narrow halls as healers walked around quickly. No one paid them any attention as the pair entered the room.

Carien walked through the cots with purpose, her confidence steering everyone around her. When she pushed through into a separate room, this one with only women, Ashta began to piece together what was happening. She stared around herself. All the beds were filled with women. All were in similar late stages of pregnancy.

In the opposite corner of where they had entered was another entrance to the room. The door was occupied. Ashta started at seeing a lioness of such advanced age, her hair snow white. And yet she still wore the bandages and skirts that marked their position.

Carien spotted the woman as well and walked straight for her. But another woman got to the guard first. The healer held a bundle of cloth out to the guard.

"Stop!" Carien yelled, picking up her skirts and hurrying towards the pair.

Both women looked up, the healer paled as she recognized who had called out the command. The other women in the beds quieted, watching the princess with interest.

Carien rushed forward until she stood within arms distance of the guard.

"Is this the babe that was born to the lioness?" She didn't have to specify more, since it was rare for a lioness to have a baby.

The nurse, still pale, began shaking as she gave a quick nod.

The princess turned to the older lioness.

"Hand me the babe," she commanded, wrapping the power of her birth right around herself.

The guard made no movement, holding the babe close to her chest.

Carien growled, angry, taking one last menacing step forward, "Now." Her voice was deadly calm as she glared at the woman.

The lioness blinked and then carefully held the babe out to the princess, without looking away from the princess's eyes.

Ashta could see the war within the woman's eyes. Her orders were coming from above, but she could not ignore a direct command from the princess. In front of the princess.

Carien pulled the babe within her arms and took two steps back, turning her back to the guard. The woman understood the dismissal and hesitated on the threshold. Ashta stepped forward and glared at the woman. Finally, she stepped back and disappeared into the depths of the palace.

Meanwhile Carien spoke to the nurse, "Find me a suitable wet nurse immediately, and send the woman to my personal chambers."

She waited for the nurse to nod her understanding. The nurse dropped into a shaky curtsy before almost running out of the room.

The princess turned and exited out the second entrance that the guard had only moments earlier passed through. She hurried down the hall, the silks from her skirt and hair covering fluttering behind her.

But Ashta barely noticed it.

Instead her eyes were caught on the small face that peaked over the princess's shoulder. Ceerie's babe.

The soldiers guarding the door didn't comment on the princess carrying a babe. They stepped aside and let them all enter. The moment they were both standing in the sitting room, Carien came over to Ashta and placed the swaddled babe on her shoulder. Ashta's hands came up automatically and cradled the little head.

Ashta stood still, the heat from the babe warming her heart up where Ceerie had been before. A small snuffle had Ashta pulling the small babe close to her neck.

She breathed in the scent and filled up with love.

This babe, she would protect this babe till the day she died. She may not have been able to protect Ceerie from her fate, but she would do her best for Ceerie's child.

The princess shuffled in and out of doors, gathering supplies before finally returning to the sitting room. She placed a thin cushion into the bottom of the wash basin. Then she tucked a cloth under the cushion, spreading it around the metal edges. She stepped back and gazed at her handy work. With a big sigh she turned to Ashta.

"It will have to do for now, until I can get a crib made for our little one."

Ashta was so filled with emotion, so overcome with thanks and love to the woman standing across from her that all she could do was nod.

The babe gurgled, trying to move in the confines of the swaddled cloth.

Ashta gently rocked her as she walked around the room. Still the babe did not settle. Pulling on her memories as a child, her own mother lulling her to sleep, Ashta began to hum softly. As the melody picked up, the words began to flow off her tongue, filling the room with swirling dreams of the past.

Carien took a seat on the settee, her head falling back as she was lulled by her friends soothing voice. Even her soldiers listened, the door propped open.

Smiling, Carien shook her head.

She had always been struck by her dark-haired friends nature. So deadly and hard in front of danger and yet now, a babe in her arms, she all but melted as she sang to the babe.

A thought struck Carien as she watched the pair.

Darkling would have made a good princess.

She could be hard, making the decisions of war, yet temper it with the empathy as she cared for her people's wounds. Bbrski had a good queen stolen from their future, and they didn't understand what they had lost.

Carien blinked up into Darkling's black gaze, surprised by the sudden quiet.

"She is asleep now," Ashta murmured, carefully shifting the babe out of her arms and into Carien's.

Carien then transferred the babe into the makeshift bed. All the while the small babe stayed quiet, sleeping peacefully.

Ashta couldn't help but reach out a finger and trace her small cheek. Her armor cracked and she could feel her eyes filling with unshed tears.

Ceerie had not only lost her life but lost her child. She would never see her babe smile, never see her grow older. To walk, to run, to laugh. All these things had been taken from her when she had died.

But if Ashta was being honest, Ceerie – and all the lionesses – had lost all these things long ago, when they had been first sold to the Tripsian slavers.

A knock against the door had both women looking up past the soldiers. A small, round woman stood outside. Her head was covered with simple cotton, her dress giving away her mediocre means.

"Enter," Carien called out, not getting up from the settee. Darkling stood at her shoulder, her arms loose. But the princess knew the illusion of calm was just that, an illusion.

The woman entered and gave a deep curtsy to the princess.

Before Carien could begin introductions, they were interrupted by another knock. But this time, a familiar face stood outside. The princess smiled as she got up and crossed the room.

"Kkaar the strangler."

She pulled in the soft women for a hug, shocking the lioness and the soldiers that stood behind her.

"Your highness," Kkaar replied, pulling back a safe distance and bowing low.

Carien smiled, walking back to the settee. Kkaar followed, her breath hitching at the sight of the little babe.

"Is that…"

"This was the lioness's babe. I have decided to take her and raise her as my own."

Kkaar swallowed at the princess's statement sharing a look with Ashta. It was a dangerous thing to say, as babes were harder to protect and easier to kidnap than a full-grown woman.

"Who sent you?" Ashta asked, knowing the other woman could not freely leave the barracks and enter the rest of the palace.

Kkaar turned to the princess and dropped a quick bow before speaking. "The king requests your immediate presence in his chambers."

Carien smiled, not surprised.

She had known her father would hear about her taking the babe. He had sent the older lioness, Melda, to collect the babe from the infirmary for a reason. The woman was from a time before, had been her father's guard when he was a young boy and then a young man.

Carien was lucky that the older woman had such respect for the royal family. Especially since she had watched two generations grow up. Well most of two generation at least.

"I will go but you must stay to protect the babe," she turned to the wet nurse, "And your name is?"

"Brinley, your highness," she bobbed into another curtsy, never looking the princess in the eye.

"Brinley, this babe, *my babe*, is now your charge. You will feed him or her until they are of an age he or she no longer needs you. Do you understand?"

She waited for the woman to nod before turning for the door.

As Ashta passed Kkaar, Kkaar reached out and squeezed her arm. For a moment they shared a look, understanding and loss passing between them. To soon, they separated and Ashta walked out the door, a step behind the princess.

This time the soldiers at her father's door did not bother Ashta as they entered.

Her father was pacing in front of the fireplace.

"Father, you wanted to see me?"

The king softened at hearing the unfamiliar moniker on his daughter's tongue. But the he remembered himself, and ire washed through his face and clenched his hands.

"You took that whores daughter when it was not your right." His voice was deadly quiet.

Carien didn't bend, instead taking a seat on the settee, non plussed.

"I am the princess of Tripsia, future heir. I have a right to any person in this kingdom if it so pleases me."

The king's face was flushed but he turned back to the fire.

"You will get rid of that babe right now."

"I will not."

He twirled on her, stepping forward, anger making his movements choppy. "I am the king and I command it of you. You will obey me!"

Slowly, Carien stood, straightening her skirts before looking her father in the eye. "Careful, father. Your reign ends on my twenty-first birthday. And then you will be just another man within my kingdom. No power. No rights."

She walked past him and looked into the fire before turning back to her father again. "I am keeping this babe, and if you wish to not make yourself an enemy than you will leave me and the child alone."

"I don't like it."

"You don't have to. I don't need your approval or the kingdoms approval. Anyone may claim the child of a lioness as their own, and I have claimed this girl. Are you sure you want to break the law?" she said so softly that Ashta almost didn't catch the threat in her words.

The king, defeated, fell back into the settee, running his hands through his hair. He knew when he had been beaten into a corner. He knew the laws as well as his daughter, and in this he would not win. Not against the council and not against Enzol the head healer.

Without another word, Carien walked out of the room, her head held high. She had won this round. Now it was just a matter of keeping the babe alive.

Girl, she amended, remembering her father's slip up. Keeping the little *girl* alive.

CHAPTER SEVENTEEN

⌘

Fair Trade

A WEEK LATER, Carien sat back in the sitting room and watched the wet nurse feed her little girl. She hadn't wanted to name the babe because it didn't feel right. She had known her mother.

Darkling had taken to the girl immediately, burping her and rocking her. At night she was up at the first noise, often walking around the room all night as she sang to the babe.

Carien knew she had made the right decision.

In the back of her mind, she had known her father would have broken the law and had the child killed. But she had been at the execution. She had seen the looks of hate and disgust from the people. Now was not the time to give them an easy solution for ridding themselves of the king.

No man, not even a king, was above the law. Not in Tripsia at least.

As Brinley finished up, Darkling came over immediately to burp the child.

"We should name her," Carien said quietly, watching the pair.

Ashta said nothing. She rocked the little girl in her arms. Every time she looked down, she saw Ceerie's white hair, her long limbs, her smirk. It didn't feel right to take this moment away from Ceerie. But Ashta knew it wasn't practical to call her *Child* or *Babe* or *Little Girl*.

No, they needed a name.

And Ashta couldn't give her Ceerie's true name. Or even the name *Ceerie*. It was too dangerous. No, this little girl would grow up safe and loved. Protected.

And that's when the name came to her.

"Mina."

Carien stared at Darkling, her face filled with love as the tiny girl burped. "Are you sure?"

Ashta looked up and stared into Carien's wide caramel eyes. Yes. She would be loved. Ashta nodded. "It is a pet name my mother used. It means loved one."

Carien slowly nodded, walking over to the pair. She fingered the soft tufts of hair aside, looking down at the babe.

Yes. She may not have borne this babe, but she would love this little girl as if she had.

"Mina," she whispered, the name tasting right on her tongue. "From now on you will be known as Mina of the Kritol family."

A knock at the door interrupted them, the messenger walking through before being called upon. "Your presence is needed in the throne room. Immediately."

"I will be there momentarily."

The messenger turned and scuttled out. Ashta handed the babe to Brinley.

"Brinley, from now on, you will go where I go. Mina must never be out of reach from me."

The woman nodded.

Ashta gestured for her to follow behind the princess before bringing up the rear.

The woman was quiet, having lost her own child. She had been forced to live with her brother and family on the coast when the healer had called for her. Ashta still worried, not trusting the woman fully.

It wasn't Brinley herself that bothered Ashta, but the brother who Ashta had seen in the infirmary a few times since Brinley had taken on the babe.

To soon they were walking through the throne room. Carien took the seat beside her fathers. Ashta directed Brinley to stand at Carien's right shoulder while Ashta stood at the opposite. The moment they were settled, the doors opened once more and man in full furs was escorted into the room by ten soldiers.

A Bbrskian berserker.

His icy gaze glared up at Ashta before settling onto the King.

She shivered. Oh, he knew who Ashta was. Her father's men had always recognized her dead gaze. A mirror of her father's.

"I come bearing terms. Join Bbrski in the war against Naankdoen. Our king has been greatly insulted and asks for your forces to join his and bring down the impenetrable walls."

Ashta started at the last words. So, her father hadn't found a way into the city yet.

Before King Roman could reply, the messenger continued. "If you do not join us, then you are against us. King Alerik will reign fire and terror down on Tripsia until all of you surrender, or die."

The King sat back in his throne, rubbing his bristled chin as he stared down at the warrior. "And how long do we have before King Alerik needs a reply?"

The man shifted, his cockiness disappearing.

Ashta snorted quietly, distracting the princess and Brinley for a moment. She shook her head until they turned away.

The berserkers were known as cocky bastards spoiling for a fight. When it came to diplomacy that confidence disappeared. The man knew he was is a tight spot, with Ashta's father breathing down his neck, while currently surrounded by Tripsian soldiers.

Finally, with a cough, he said, "You have until the new moon."

The king glanced his soldiers who had encircled the warrior. "Until then, you will wait here for my response."

And with that the messenger was dismissed, the party of soldiers leading him further into the palace.

Without any preamble, the king walked down the dais, giving a brief nod to Carien. The princess followed behind him as the king walked directly to the council room. The rest of the men already sat around the table.

King Roman took his seat at the head, Carien at his left.

With a sigh, the king relayed the message to the rest of the council.

"We cannot join King Alerik. The moment our soldiers leave the palace he will turn on us."

Ashta agreed in her head. It was definitely something he would do.

"But we cannot outright not join," this was from general Hariim. "The Bbrskian soldiers are tough, and King Alerik is a renowned strategist. He doesn't need numbers to win. He will use games and tactics, leaving nothing off the table to bring the palace to its knees."

Ashta looked at the general with fresh eyes. She had not thought the man that shrewd but clearly, he knew her father's tactics well. Even with a sea separating Tripsia and Bbriski, the Tripsians would have heard of her father's complete takeover of his own kingdom. How he had killed off any rebellion or hope for one.

The men continued to discuss, circling around the two options. But no matter how much they talked; the men could not find a solution. At least no one that would keep Tripsia out of the oncoming war.

Ashta's eyes caught several times on the pale eyes of the leader of the white lionesses. The executioner. He sat at the table, an honorary council member with no power. The only male slave in Tripsia.

She shivered, recalling the tales of past executioners.

The doors creaked open, jolting Ashta out of her thoughts.

The meeting broke up for a few minutes with dinner. As the council sat and ate, Ashta tried to figure it out herself. But she could not see a way out of war. Her father had already crossed the sea once. The taste of victory and destruction was to fresh. He would continue crossing until the Midloean kingdoms were beneath him.

The only way she could see her father leaving was if all the Midloean kingdoms joined together against him. But the cities were separated by long stretches of coastline. It would be easy for King Alerik to raid their ships and cities, and pullback until the kingdoms were weak enough to pluck.

What they really needed was to cut the head off of the war. Bbrskian were not a blood thirsty people, contrary to the midlanders beliefs. They enjoyed hunting and killing, but the land made it impossible to grow grains. That left people to their own devices.

But before her father, the kingdom had been at war with itself. The different factions fighting for food and coastline. With land on the water, there was opportunity to trade and get food.

But power?

That had never been the driving force.

Until her father.

King Roman smacked both his hands on the table, his face flushed.

"Enough! We have been talking in circles and are nowhere closer. He needs an answer by the new moon. That is tomorrow night!"

The council quieted, not one of them speaking out a solution.

Finally, the king turned his eyes on Ashta. She could see the spark there, the tiny smirk at the corner of his mouth. She kept herself rigid even as she watched her worst nightmare unfold.

This was why she had kept her true identity a secret.

"We have been looking at this all wrong, men. We have the *heir* of Bbrski right here. A slave bound for life to Tripsia. King Alerik doesn't have enough time to wait and mold a new heir. He needs his first daughter. And *we* will give her to him."

The council still sat quiet but now the generals were smiling while the others gazed thoughtfully up at Ashta.

She shook her head.

Even after years of training, her heritage bubbled up and broke through the bonds. It was Carien's quick shake of the head that stopped Ashta from speaking out of turn.

No. She would hold herself together and let Carien fight her battles. They were sisters, thicker than blood.

King Roman dismissed the council as he went to lay the terms. The heir to Bbrski in return for neutrality through the coming war.

Days passed as the palace waited. Everything now depended on Ashta's value to her father. But Ashta knew it was useless. She had always been just another pawn in her father's machinations. There was no love lost between father and daughter.

Least of all between King and Heir.

Ashta tried to warn Carien, but the woman was defeated. "What can I do? The council will not listen to someone so young, and especially not a woman."

"But you must try. They don't understand. I am of no value to my father. He will only use this as an opportunity to sway you or your father."

Carien leaned against the hallway wall. The cool stones did nothing against her over-heated skin. The fall weather on the coast was still filled with hot breezes. But soon the winter winds would trap the boats onto the coastline.

"Even if my father does agree to the terms, he will change his mind when he takes down Naankdoen." Ashta paced in front of the princess.

"The walled city has never fallen," Carien murmured.

"That doesn't mean it won't in the future."

Carien frowned, but she had no hope for the small kingdom of Naankdoen. No, if King Alerik didn't burn them out of their walled city, he would surely starve them. The Naankdoena farmers had only gotten part way through their harvests. It would be enough to hold the city through the winter but not much longer.

It was all too much for the princess's young shoulders. A baby, a kingdom, and a war.

She was only one woman.

"Your highness?"

They both looked up at the wet nurse who was holding a fussing Mina. Carien took the babe in her arms and the little girl calmed instantly. With a sigh the princess straightened from the wall and continued on to the council chamber.

Another messenger from the Bbrskian army had arrived to the palace, but this time Carien's father hadn't sent for Carien to come to the throne room.

Carien knew her father wanted to be rid of Darkling. She also knew that her father didn't understand the price of being rid of the hardened warrior.

The council members said nothing as Carien took her seat, the babe still in her arms.

Speaking quietly, the king looked anywhere but at his daughter. "King Alerik has changed the terms. A trade. He captured some of the soldiers and lionesses from the raid on the princess's caravan. His daughter, the princess Svetlana, for our men and women."

The men nodded.

All except the executioner. His pale gaze stayed fixed on the babe.

Ashta knew it the trade work. Desperation her her breaking her training. She stepped forward and whispered into Carien's ear. "My father won't let any soldier live. No matter the terms."

Taking a step back, she accepted the heat of the glares from various council members. She kept her stare on the king. How could he not see through her father's machinations?

"General Hariim, you said yourself the Bbrskian king is a cunning man. Do you believe him to be an honorable man?" Carien's soft voice was laced with power, forcing the council members to look her in the eye. And away from Ashta.

"Well, I uh," he stuttered.

"Then why are we taking his word for the safe passage of our men and women? What good would come from his releasing them?"

"The Bbrskian would get their *heir* back," the head of the lionesses spoke up.

Ashta stared at the man in shock. It was unprecedented for the man to speak.

The other council members ignored it, to focused on the princess.

"Maybe, but would we get our men and women back? I don't believe so. They would know too much. A good leader would keep his word. A smart leader would kill hostages. Dead men can't speak."

Ashta could see some of the men were no longer conflicted. The princess may have swayed them. Hope surged through her.

The King spoke up, "I believe King Alerik to keep his word. He swore on his first wife's grave he would."

And with his words, Ashta's hope withered.

How could the king be so blind?

But the look of love he sent his daughter said everything to Ashta. King Roman had loved his wife. He didn't know that Ashta's own father couldn't have cared less about his wife. King Alerik didn't even know where the late queen's grave was, Ashta thought bitterly.

Without any ceremony, four soldiers piled into the room. They quickly captured Ashta's hands and tied them behind her back. She was forced to follow them out of the council chambers, not able to say anything to Carien.

Carien watched in helpless horror as her friend disappeared into the hallway. Her father stood up, followed by the other men around the table. He passed by Carien's seat without a glance, followed by everyone else. With shaking legs, Carien stood and trailed behind the procession.

The king led the way through the halls and down several sets of stairs. The procession slowed when they came to an unusually dark entrance. Ashta shivered as one of the soldiers pushed her forward onto the steps. The walls and ceiling still held the rough cuts into the stone from the palace's first builders.

As they descended, the rushing of the sea swirled grew louder. The smell of salt clung to the ceiling as lichen smoothed the walls. After Ashta's legs burned and sweat poured down her chest and pooled in her bandages, the procession finally slowed.

Several gates were pulled open by the soldiers as the King looked on. He had known about the path since he was a little boy. He had walked it only one time in his life. Long before he had been King, before he had power over his people. His father.

From the little light coming in from beyond the gates, Ashta could see the soldiers were weary of their surroundings. This was their first time this deep into the cliff.

The last gate opened up into a massive cave, water lapping against the stone floor.

And there, inside the great cave floated a single sail boat, its large sails giving it away for speed. But from the sides Ashta could see the tell-tale holes for oars. It was far smaller than the Tripsian slaver boats.

As the soldiers pulled Ashta into the ship, another sail boat appeared in the small cave. Two lionesses gently steered it behind the first boat. The king walked towards the second boat, followed by a worried looking Carien.

Blinking, Ashta realized that Brinley and the babe was nowhere in sight, or any of the council men. Instead, the procession transformed to two lines of Tripsian soldiers. The men divided up into even groups between the two sailboats.

The soldiers readied themselves, arrows in place on their back, bows at their feet. Then each man grabbed onto an oar, five per oar, and they pushed off the water.

Ashta stumbled at the sudden movement, her stomach rolling at the memories of her last boat ride. She had been a just a young girl, sold to Tripsia, when a sudden storm had swept her – and half the other girls and lionesses – into the belly of the sea. She had been lucky to make it then.

As they rounded the end of the cave and the open water greeted them, Ashta worried she would not be so lucky this time.

CHAPTER EIGHTEEN

⌘

Second Death

BLUE SKIES WITH bluer water greeted the sail boats as they made their way out of the cove and into deeper waters. Ashta blinked in the sudden light, her eyes taking a long moment to adjust. When she could see again, she glanced around at the cliff face. The entrance was well hidden from the sea. It was a small wonder that a boat of this size, let alone two could come out of the small crack.

Her boat moved quick, the soldiers rowing to the rhythm of the captains call. They were well ahead of the second boat containing the King, Carien and the rest of the Council.

Ashta stared at Carien's forlorn form, as the princess stood apart from the rest of the group. With a sigh, Ashta turned, her gaze flickering to the right where a long sandy beach was littered with fishermen's homes and boats.

A whistle from one of the soldiers had Ashta whipping around and cocking her head to get a better view.

Out in the still open water of the sea stood a lone boat. It's dark hull, and black sails making it unmistakable to recognize. Bbriskian.

At first, Ashta couldn't quite understand what was on the Galley. As the Tripsian soldiers rowed their boat closer, Ashta began to make out the forms of people on the other boat. And breast bands. The uniform of the White lionesses.

A shiver ran along Ashta's back despite the heat of the fall sun on her shoulders. So, her father had not killed the Tripsian soldiers at the surprise attack on the Tripsian caravan.

"Send a signal!" the King called out. Carien shuddered as the soldier beside her lifted his has hand. Another soldier on Darkling's boat lifted his hand moments later.

A soldier at the front of Darkling's boat raised the Tripsian flag up the main pole on the sails. The wind picked it up quickly, setting it dancing proudly in the clear blue sky.

After a few tense minutes the flag of Bbrski could be seen flying above the Tripsian men and women.

"Prepare the small boat!" Again, the soldier used a hand signal. The soldiers on Ashta's boat moved quickly. Ashta was amazed when a small boat with a single set of oars was pulled out of somewhere.

The soldier closest to her shoved her. Taking a deep breath, Ashta stepped into the tiny boat. One soldier held a sword to her throat as he stepped inside and took a seat on the only bench.

The rest of the men scurried to setup the small boat on the ropes and pulleys on the side of the boat facing the open sea. Ashta looked over at Carien, barely able to make out the other woman's features. She had many regrets over the past year, but she was thankful for having such a strong and loving friend in her life. How ever short her life would be. With a deep sigh, she turned slightly to stare at the imposing figure of the King. From the distance the man seemed larger and more substantial than the old man Ashta knew him to be.

"Ready to lower!" A shout from nearby had Ashta jumping and focusing on the men around her. The dingy shook as it was slowly raised in the air. Ashta lost her balance and fell forward, her face catching the bottom of the boat.

The soldier grunted, but said nothing else.

Ashta at him.

The men lowered the dingy, their voices growing faint as Ashta got closer and closer to the water.

She still had choices. She could jump in the water and let herself drown. Ashta stared at the water.

"Don't you dare," the soldier hissed.

Jerking up until she was awkwardly on her knees, she stared at the poor soul that was joining her on a fruitless mission.

The soldier had black hair that curled out from underneath his helmet. What she could see of his face and arms was dark from years under the harsh Tripsian sun. His eyes were the same red as their desert, that red just moments before it sunk under the horizon for the night.

This soldier meant nothing to her. The kernel of fear in his eyes did not sway her. She owed the soldier nothing.

But then she thought of Carien, and little Mina. No, taking her life now would not protect the princess and the babe. Ashta could not afford to be selfish in these last few moments. And she had no illusions that her father would let her live long.

With a sigh she, settled back and glared at the soldier. "Well, what are we waiting for?" she asked, pointedly looking at the oars. He watched her suspiciously for a long moment before taking up the heavy oars. They pushed off and away from the Tripsian sailboats.

Forced to keep her back to the Bbrskian ship, Ashta watched as the Soldier rowed hard. In moments, sweat dripped down his face. Ashta wondered if the man knew what was about to come. What the Bbrskian would do to him. Did he really believe that the Bbrskian soldiers would let him return to the Tripsian sailboats?

Glancing over his shoulder, she watched as the boats, and the people on them, grew hazy in the late morning heat.

She felt as if she wasn't just crossing this small stretch of water between two boats but the entirety of the sea between two kingdoms. She was leaving the heat of Tripsia and could feel the cool winds of Bbrski at her back.

Or the imagined cold winds.

"Tell your man to stop there, princess!"

Ashta shuddered at the guttural shout. She had not been a princess in years. Yet these past few months people kept trying to refer to her as just that.

She was a slave to Tripsia, not the crown princess to the Bbrskian throne and people.

"They said stop here," She quickly translated. The soldier stopped rowing immediately.

Someone from the ship threw a rope over. The heavy end swung just above her head. Ashta watched the soldier as he warily stared at the rope.

"You are going to have to release me." The man stared at her; the whites of his eyes visible around his iris. Irritated, she added snappily, "Unless you plan to carry me up that rope."

He muttered under his breath as he clumsily reached forward and cut through the ropes on her arms. She sighed in relief and quickly rubbed at her arms.

The soldier looked away as Ashta stood. She tested the rope in her hands, staring up at the ships side.

This was it.

This was the last moment.

She could still decide to jump into the water. Leave all this behind. Take her death into her own hands.

For a single breath she considered it.

But then she saw Mina in her mind's eye.

No. She would do anything to protect that babe. Even give her life.

Ashta slowly pulled herself up. The moment her feet left the boat floor, she heard the dip of the oars in the water.

Coward, she though bitterly.

Of course, she knew why the Bbrskian men had lowered a rope. They had wanted her to enter the ship completely unprepared, her hands busy. They weren't dumb. They knew she was as well trained as any lethal assassin.

But Ashta doubted the ship realized *how good* she really was.

Taking a quick glance back she noted the tide had brought the Tripsian boats and the Bbrskian ship closer. Though they were still outside of arrow range. She could just make out Carien's smaller shape right beside her fathers.

With grim determination Ashta pulled herself up with her bare hands, her legs wrapping around the end below her.

When she was near the top, thick arms reached over and pulled her the rest of the way up.

She tensed as cold steel kissed her neck. She couldn't see the solder at her back, but she felt his hot breath on the back of her neck. His hand gripped her arm painfully tight. His other handheld the lethal dagger.

Ashta blinked, moving her eyes while keeping still. She could make out the two sail boats from the corner of her eye. The dingy she had been in minutes before already halfway back to the sail boats.

A Bbrskian berserker stood in front of her. The soldier beside him held a cocked bow.

Ashta watched dispassionately as the soldier loosed the arrow. Only a moment later she heard the unmistakable thud. She could just make out the slumped form of the Tripsian soldier.

As the soldier stepped back, the line of soldiers and lionesses came into view.

But what the king and the Tripsian sailboats couldn't see was the soldiers behind each Tripsian man and woman. Their knives and daggers at the ready.

Ashta shuddered, the dagger at her own throat pushing slightly in until she felt a warm trickle down her neck.

She made out familiar faces of her fellow white lionesses; Trea, Kellu, Mintia, Serrs, and Ulla.

The only comfort in that moment was Ashta did not recognize Trice or the soldier Theo. They must have died in the raid.

The thought hurt, a sharp stab in her heart, but she had become use to the constant loss of friends over the past weeks. Ashta knew nothing good could happen in the next few moments, but it soothed her conscience knowing that these men and women had survived. She would not have to wonder, and worry, any longer on what had happened to them.

A man came up beside her, careful to be close enough that she could make out his whole face. He smiled.

If it could be called that.

It was more a cut across his grotesque face, not reaching his cold eyes. While she did not recognize him from her childhood, she knew this type of man well enough.

He was one of her fathers hand picked soldiers. The ones that the Bbrskian King had beaten into submission until there were no thoughts left inside the soldier's brain except her father's orders.

The man raised his hand.

Ashta focused back on the line of Tripsian men and women.

In a quick procession, the Bbrskian soldiers stepped forward and slit the throat of each Tripsian soldier and lioness's. The Tripsians' didn't even have time to cry out, already choking on their blood as their bodies slumped forward falling over into the sea.

Shouts from the Tripsian boats could be heard across the waters moments later.

But it was too late.

The men with the bloody daggars were replaced by a second wave of soldiers. These men quickly knocked their arrows in their longbows. A young boy ran with a torch ran down the line.

With the arrows lit, the man at her side once more raised his hands.

Arrows whistled through the air before thudding into the sides of the Tripsian boats. Even with their sails still folded, the damage was done.

Several arrows caught the surrounding wood on fire.

Screams soaked the air as the ocean bloomed bright red around them.

And all this could have been avoided, Ashta thought bitterly, if the king had listened to her. She could just make out the second boat that held the king, already turning back for the cliff face and the hidden entrance to safety.

A strange purr came from the man beside her, his eyes bright with the blood fever. But if Ashta hadn't turned she wouldn't have seen his glance to the far left of them.

There, in the distance, a dark cloud moved over the water towards them.

Before Ashta could shout a warning to the Tripsian boats a horn blew across the watery expanse. The men on the Bbrskian boat shuffled on their feet despite the familiar call.

Ashta would be worried to had she been one of the berserkers. Her father could turn on anyone without thought or reason. Even turning on his own men.

King Roman yelled, and to slowly, the soldiers rowed hard back to the cove. The flames quickly engulfed the one side of the ship of the slower boat, catching the ropes before climbing up the folded sail.

Ashta watched with her heart in her throat. The sails burned in fiery glory, the ship shuddering forward to the cove.

Fear must have put strength in the Tripsian soldiers' arms. The first sail boat, the one carrying Carien, disappeared before her father's fleet were upon them. Thank the gods, she thought.

The second boat was not so lucky.

Neither was she, Ashta worried, glancing around herself.

The grip on her arm was still tight, the dagger digging deeper into her skin. Dozens of soldiers stood before her, glaring across the ship.

Ashta knew death would not come swiftly for her. Far from it.

The ugly man snarled, turning and punching the wooden wall. Blood poured from his hands as splinters stuck out, but he didn't feel it.

He turned and glared at Ashta.

The man crossed the space in seconds, his grotesque face right in front of hers. She could even smell his rotting breath. After a moment, his mouth, or where his mouth should have been, quirked into an evil smirk.

"Welcome home, princess."

He laughed again as the soldier holding Ashta threw her to the ground.

CHAPTER NINETEEN

⌘

Shadow Island

BEFORE SHE COULD get up from the slippery floor, the men had grabbed her and hauled her against the mast. She hadn't tried to fight, the shock of the last few minutes had frozen her limbs.

But now that she had moment, forced against the mast, she realized the men had made one crucial mistake. She still had her weapons.

"Man the sails!"

The men around her moved in a flurry of motion as the sails were raised, catching the wind and billowing out. Soon the ship was slicing through the sea waters.

The rest of the fleet waited further out, slowly turning. Their own ship moved to join the side of the fleet. Ashta could just see the other boats, only eighty in total.

Grimacing, Ashta knew her father's fleet was four hundred strong. At least it had been before she had left for Naankdoen. Where were the rest of the ships? She doubted all of them would be at Naankdoen. No, he had them hidden somewhere on the coastline. And with the massive stretch of uninhabited land between the Tripsian palace and the Naankdoen city, it would be easy to hide an entire armada.

The sun slowly sank towards the west, leaving Ashta a red-faced mess tied to the mast. Her throat was parched but at least she wasn't hungry like she had been in the desert. But the papna wouldn't keep her full to tomorrow.

The Bbrskians must have been making good time with the favorable winds because many of the men retired from their positions and were sitting and drinking on the benches.

Bbrskian ships were filled with oars. But unlike the Tripsian boat, the Bbrski built it narrow, making their ships some of the fastest on the water. What they made up for speed they lost in space. The Tripsian boats were deeper, making them prime cargo ships for trade; whether that cargo was people or food.

Right now, it made the Bbrskian fleet more dangerous in sea warfare. They could slide onto land and sneak out, without getting caught by other ships.

Ashta leaned her head back against the mast, staring up at the blue sky. When the opportunity came, she knew she would sneak away back to Tripsia. The princess needed her, more than her father, King Roman, could ever understand.

"Have yah ever seen such skin on anything but a whore?"

Pretending to close her eyes, Ashta peeked out at the crowd. More than half the men sitting down were red faced from the whiskey kept on board for the cold winters. Nothing warmed the blood of an ice-frozen sailor than the whiskey of his homeland. It burned the whole way down.

"Well yah no the best whores come from Tripsia, them bought slaves."

"I wonder if our *princess* learned any new tricks in that whores land."

"I heard she was a fighter."

The men broke out in great guffaws, the last boy to speak blushed bright red.

"A fighter? Would yah look at those skinny arms, she probably couldn't even lift a great sword."

"But-But the lionesses of Tripsia are known as the best-"

"They're just a bunch of cunning bitches that know how to twirl a knife and slip some poison in your beer. Ain't true fighters."

Ashta held her breathing steady, trying not to snort at the comments. The group of men had no idea how dangerous she was.

She almost smiled.

Maybe this moment was her chance to get back to Tripsia. The small dingy was long left behind but all she needed was a good piece of wood and she could float her way back. In another day, she would need a small raft with a paddle.

She tuned back into the conversation.

"If you're so sure of her being a fighter, then why don't we untie her, and you'll see how weak a woman really is."

She sighed at the last comment.

One thing Bbrski had never learned was to have respect for women, and view of them as deadly weapons. A powerful witch was no laughing matter, but the idea of a woman that could fight, and fight well?

The jeers got louder and Ashta opened her eyes to over a dozen men crowded around the mast. One even spat on her face, the saliva slowly sliding down her cheek. But she didn't let her temper show. She saved her anger for the moment they would release her.

Then one jeering idiot did, loosening the ropes. The rest of hulking Bbrski men stepped back, forming a ring around her and the young boy who had made the comment.

He was little more than a child, not quite filled out. He had much left to grow into. He stared at her with grim determination, his hands shaking slightly. His face was pale as sweat began to bead on his brow.

Ashta carefully stepped away from the mast, stretching out her fingers then rising up onto her toes.

Once more than half the group was distracted by the skin showing around her middle, she reached into her hair and threw four of her knives.

Before the men had fallen to their knees, the knives deep in their throats, Ashta had already pulled out her two half swords and sliced through the middles of the next two men.

A shout rose from above the deck. Ashta tried to hurry through the last six, but the men had time to grab their own knives. She struggled fighting all six of them at once. The boy thankfully tripped on the blood and landed outside of the circle. But all she managed were gashes on arms and legs. Nothing stuck where it counted.

A flash of light off the ocean blinded her for a moment.

It was enough.

In the next moment a fist came from beside her and crushed her cheek. Her head bounced on the wooden deck as her vision blacked out.

When she came to, she was tied to the mast again, but this time no man dared look at her. The bodies of the six she had killed were noticeably gone from the deck. All that was left of them was the blood being mopped by the young boy.

"Bunch of idiots, the whole lot."

The gravelly voice came from above her shoulder. She looked up into her father's man, surprised at the disgust in his voice.

"They are your own men," she whispered.

"And yours, princess. Don't forget that when you cut them down like a doe."

She snorted.

These men were no more hers than she was the heir of Bbrski. Did no one else realize that her father was not that simple. He knew the laws of Tripsia and the slaves. She was bound by magik and law to another kingdom until the day she died.

What good was a princess who could not and did not serve her own kingdom first?

But then, as she felt the man's clammy finger swipe across her cheek, she realized her father didn't need her. The crown may go through the female heir.

But the kingdom served the king, not the queen.

It always had.

Knowing her father, he had already picked the man Lily was to marry. With her dead, he was left with only one living heir. With only one means to pass on the crown.

"If their mine, then don't forget who my father is," Ashta spat out, glaring up at the man.

He hesitated than pulled his hand back as if just making the connection between the girl and the father.

He walked away.

Ashta was left in silence for the rest of the evening. When the moon hung high above, the young boy came and forced water down her throat.

She gulped it down greedily, not caring at the rough treatment.

Several days passed in relative silence. The other men on the ship left her alone. Once in the morning and once in the evening, the boy would give her water and feed her some gruel.

They didn't allow her off the mast, forcing Ashta to pee in her spot. The smell was horrible even as she slowly grew use to it.

The men didn't dare take the chance of untying her. Not after the quick ease she had dispatched the last men.

The ships finally arrived at their destination. Ashta had been right, the rest of her father's armada was camped out somewhere else.

But this, where they were camped at, wasn't a coastline. The small mountain island stuck out harshly from the sea, trees never having floated out this far into the ocean. A short stretch of sand ringed around the island, as far as Ashta could see.

What horrified her the most was the mass of tents on the only flat section of the island. It was the same size as the city of Naankdoen, but she knew this city had only been around in the last year. And there were thousands of soldiers swarming around the rickety docks and the beach closest to the makeshift city.

"*Aishma.*"

Ashta glanced up at her father's man who had suddenly appeared beside her.

She shuddered at the word, meaning shadow island. In the Bbrski myth, it was where death lived. Death only crossed the ocean to harvest new soldiers, when the ice covered the water making it possible for him to walk across.

As their ship slid into place to unload its passengers, Ashta found herself cut free from her bindings. Her legs were weak, almost collapsing on her when she stood for the first time in days.

The men were none to careful as they dragged her across the thin gangplank and down onto the long dock.

The first thing Ashta noticed was the stench. And she knew it wasn't just herself. No, this was a smell that came from thousands of unwashed bodies pissing where the pleased and it all sitting and collecting around the docks.

She glanced down at the green murky water and wrinkled her nose. When it came time, she knew she would jump in that water with no hesitation.

The second thing that hit her as she stepped foot onto the rocky land, was the noise. The air was filled with yells, screams, and laughter. Yet it all held an evil note. At first, she didn't understand where the tingle of awareness came from, but the moment her small party was walking through the tents she knew.

Men were everywhere.

Some were half-dressed and others naked.

And the women – if one could call what was left of the bodies around that lay about the tents – were always naked.

Always.

No matter how dirt covered, how much dried blood was splattered the length of their bodies. They were naked.

And the men just took them, raping them with glee as the other men yelled their approval before they took the same woman themselves.

The revelry and rape continued around the small party as Ashta was led up the path. Her father's man led the way up the slanted land. Above his head one tent could be seen, larger than all the others. Its black cover giving it away for what it was. And who was inside.

The King.

"Please! Please!" a woman begged from nearby.

Ashta stared at her, thinking the girl was barely fifteen. Her hair was bedraggled. Blood dripped down her chest from shallow cuts that lined her neck.

She ran towards Ashta's party, but before she got close, one of the berserkers who held Ashta let go and slapped the girl hard.

She fell to the ground, but before she could get up, he was on her, his furs pushed aside.

Another man came from within the tent city, blood dripping down his knife. He saw the woman and smiled with as he pulled her head up and played the blade across her cheeks.

The remaining men of Ashta's party had continued moving, but the blood curdling screams ripped into Ashta's skull.

The worst part was Ashta knew the woman wasn't Bbrskian. Her golden skin gave her away.

With sudden clarity she realized the reports from the past few weeks of women gone missing were because her father had taken them. Or more precisely, *her father's men* had taken them. And they didn't look like they would be returning them to Tripsia.

The last few tents were quieter, the men huddled in groups. Some looked up at their party as they passed, glaring at Ashta. *These* men knew who she was. And they wanted nothing to do with their dirtied princess.

After the last tent disappeared behind them, all that was left to stare at her was the stark black tent of her father. For a moment she stood still just looking up, dreading the next moment to come.

The men then untied her and threw her body through the flap entrance. Her face skidded across the carpeted floor.

CHAPTER TWENTY

⌘

King Alerik

"YOU SURPRISE ME, Svetlana," said a deep voice that rumbled across Ashta's skin.

It had been years since she had last heard it and still not enough time had passed to dull the pain. The fear.

She carefully picked herself up, glancing around the tent. It had been furnished with sumptuous great-white-bear furs and a real wooden table with chairs. Torches ringed around the edges of the tent. A crystal chandelier hung from the center.

Seeing the candles, Ashta snorted at the waste. But she had expected nothing less.

King Alerik wanted everyone to know how powerful he was, even when he was commanding an army on a rock island.

"Father," Ashta stated, finally taking in the man who sat alone at the table.

He was eating a veritable feast of roasted meats, potatoes, breads and green beans. Ashta knew that the last item came from the Midloean kingdoms. Bbrski summers were short and any fresh vegetables never lasted long into the fall.

King Alerik pulled up a white napkin and gently dabbed at his mouth. When he finally glanced up at her, Ashta shivered. His dark grey eyes were still as cold as they had been in her childhood.

She was shocked to see his hair had gone completely silver and that he had grown a short silver beard. Despite the change of hair colour, his face was still as impassive as it had always been. His face was timeless, un-weathered from the harsh winters of her homeland.

His eyes lazily took in the details of her dress and her sun coloured skin. Her hardened muscles. Her scarred body.

"You were always so weak as a child. Like your mother. I was surprised to hear that you had become a white lioness."

The king continued eating, leaving Ashta to stew over his words.

How dare he say such comments when he had not known her as a child, she thought. Ashta had done her best to avoid her father as a child, forced in his company only when he wanted to teach her the hard lessons of ruling a kingdom. To this day she still thought they were not necessary lessons.

Forced to watch someone be slowly tortured and killed without reaction had been one. She still had not learned that lesson, Ashta thought, remembering the last year of deaths she had witnessed. Of Lily. Of Ceerie. Of the soldiers and lionesses only days before.

"You never knew me," Ashta finally stated, her voice devoid of all emotion.

The only way to fight her father was to be as cold as he was. That lesson had served her well through the years of slavery.

The king snorted, pushing back from the table and staring over at her. He didn't bother to invite her closer or to sit, wanting to maintain power over the conversation.

"You were as soft as your mother, crying over small kittens and kids who disappeared after they had disrespected you."

Her mind brought up images of childhood friend after childhood friend that she had made the mistake of tattling to her father. They always disappeared. And their parents to. Ashta had never been sure of what had happened to them. Now, she realized that her father would have taken only one action.

Death.

"You almost drowned as a toddler. There was nothing of me inside that frail excuse of body you had as a child." His eyes glittered, his mouth cut in a sneer.

A small boy came into the room and cleared off the table. The tent was completely silent as he worked, her father and her locked in a battle of stares.

The only thing her father couldn't break of Ashta's was her mind. He had tried as a child. But like her mother, there were things within Ashta that her father could never change.

Once the boy disappeared out of the tent again, her father stood and walked over to a side desk where he pulled out a large cigar.

Her nose wrinkled at the sight.

Another example of his power, since Kae ol cigars could not be traded for. He must have had his men raiding the eastern coastline as well, not just Tripsia and Naankdoen.

"That whole business in Naankdoen with Lillian…" He puffed out. The smoke curled around his head before going up into the ceiling. Ashta's mind flashed with blood soaked streets, a burning barrel, and then silence. "Thank you. I hadn't worked out a way to be rid of the girl."

Ashta froze, not believing the words coming out of his mouth.

"She was your daughter," she choked out on a breath.

He made no gesture, no apology, just took another puff.

"So are you."

His stare burned a hole into her soul.

Ashta shook her head. No, she refused to be his daughter. "Were."

It was such a quiet word, but the king paused, cigar halfway to his lips. Thinking better of it, he ground the end out and replaced it back in the desk. He stalked back to his table, taking the seat once more.

Ashta was surprised he hadn't stopped in front of her.

"Contrary to the Tripsian *ideas* of slavery, you will always be the heir to Tripsia. Crown princess Svetlana-"

"Svetlana is dead!"

Both of them leaned back, shocked at Ashta's outburst. It was outside of the limits of their game, and Ashta had given her hand away. She worried as her father allowed a rare smirk to cross his face.

"I took the necessary precautions to ensure that you can still be the crown princess, incase Lillian did not work out."

Ashta's shoulders itched to take action. But she knew that she needed to be more cautious in their conversation. She had already given to much away. Yet she also knew she could not leave this tent without some answers. Because she planned to never see her father again after today.

"I thought Lady Arja was to your liking."

A statement. A challenge.

"She ran her course of usefulness."

"Before or after her daughter was brutally killed?"

"Lillian knew the price. She paid for it. As for her mother, I'm sure you would be happy to know that she has … gone… since the day I sent Lillian off to the Midloean kingdoms."

"Why did you send Lillian?"

He stared at her shrewdly before spreading his hands out over the table.

Ignoring social protocols, Ashta stepped closer until she could see it better. It was then that she realized the tabletop was a map of the known kingdoms. The edges of the North and Bbrski were softened, their harsh weather and people allowed no cartographer to draw further.

As she stared down at the table, Ashta realized that the great cities of Each kingdom were raised. And Naankdoen and Tripsia had a small chess piece set on top. A great white bear.

"How long?" Ashta whispered. She did not need to add since her stepmother had disappeared. They both knew what she was asking.

Her father had ship pieces set out across the coastline. But there were other bear pieces moving west to Kae ol and the green kingdoms. How long had he been preparing for this takeover she wondered?

"Seven years."

She jerked up from the map, staring at him as the king still watched the map.

That was when she had been sold to Ennris and the slavers. Could it be that he had not known about it? That it had been one step to far for her power-grasping stepmother.

It also explained why her stepsister did not dress and act as a lady of Bbrski normally would. And for her to make such an obvious mistake, trying to assassinate another princess.

Ashta made no comment on the time frame. Her father would give no honest answer. Instead, she decided to ask a different question. One that had burned in her heart for years.

"Did you ever love her?"

She wasn't so naïve to believe all marriages were filled with love. But watching how completely obsessed her mother had been over her father had hurt. And the idea that he had never given as much to his young wife burned even more.

"Does it matter?"

She stiffened.

"Do you want a willing heir?" she threatened.

It was the only thing she could hold over him, even if she knew deep in her heart that she would never go back to that life.

Alerik stared into her black eyes for a long moment, lost in the memory of another pair of black eyes that once stared up at him. But those eyes had always been warm, pulling him deeper. His daughters were like glazed obsidian, cold and deadly. He knew what it took to become a white lioness. She was more like him than her mother, a deadly fighter that worked with logic rather than emotion.

Blinking slowly, he opened his mouth. "Your mother had her uses."

The words shimmered in the air.

At that moment Ashta realized how much she hated her father. It was a burning volcano, simmering inside her and ready to explode and kill at moment's notice. But like her homeland, she stood cold and waited him out.

"Augustos!" her father called, eyes never leaving her face.

A ruffle behind her announced her father's man. The one from the ship.

"Take the crown princess to the ship and bring her back to the palace in Bbrski." Looking at her for one last lingering moment, he stated with deadly intent, "I will deal with you after the war."

Ashta let Augustos pull her arm back and push her out of the tent. Her father's last words still rang in her head. He was really planning to take over the Midloean kingdoms. Nothing would stop him.

As she stumbled through the now dark path between the tents, her mind barely noticed the raping and screaming that surrounded her. She walked in a haze, her eyes stuck on the back of Augustos' neck.

Her father was starting a great war, the size of which the known kingdoms had never seen before. Would Tripsia be ready?

A whisper in her heart told her the dark truth. That she would see her friends and Carien burning soon enough. Her father couldn't afford to stay on the ocean through the winter. The water was choppy and storms made it impossible to cross safely. He would either have to start his war before or after winter.

As she stepped onto the deck of the ship, taking in the thousands of men that were only part of his great army in the tent city below, she knew that the war had already started.

"Tie her to the mast!" Augustos yelled, making a line towards for the wheel.

The men who surrounded her leered as they touched her arms, her breasts, making sure to tie her tightly to the wooden beam.

Her mind was still slow, as if watching from a distance as the men crowded in closer. One man, his black beard long giving away his advancing age, grabbed her breast harshly. She knew it would leave bruises, but she could not shake the fog over her mind.

No, instead she stared blankly at the man as he leaned down and roughly slanted his lips across her. His breath stank of rotting meat. His teeth flashed yellow and blackened, those that were still there. His other hand roughly pulled her skirt up, trying to find purchase in her black leggings.

She didn't hear the taunts. Didn't notice the hungry stares of the half dozen men surrounding her.

And then it all came to a stop.

The man's body was pulled back and she watched in confusion as her father's man began beating the black bearded man. Augustos' fists were quick with power, breaking through muscle and bone.

When the man fell down on the bloodied deck, Augustos shook his fist at those who stood and watched. He glared at Ashta for a moment before staring down each of the crewmen.

"You are not to touch her. You are not to look at her. And you sure as hell don't speak to her. This is the *Crown Princess*."

The crowd of men that had gathered around her bloodied assailant quieted at Augustos' last words.

"She will be *our Queen* one day."

The men sobered up. A few warily glanced at her before turning away and busying themselves on the deck.

"Clean him up. We set sail at first light."

With those parting words, Augustos walked away. The men were quiet at first, but the night stayed anything but.

Ashta closed her eyes trying to drown out the feminine screams, the sick sound of flesh being hit – of bones breaking – but it was no use.

She thanked all the gods and the ones not known as the first rays of morning brightened the clouded sky. It was over.

She would never see her father again.

CHAPTER TWENTY-ONE

⌘

Bbrskian Strong

THE SUN PEAKED over the edge of the sea as shouts filled the air. Ashta watched the men working around her, prepping the sales, pushing the oars out.

She carefully wiggled her hands until she reached one of the blades hidden in her bandages on her back. She slowly slid the knife out from her bandages, carefully watching the men with a hooded gaze.

Augustos was busy on the quarterdeck arguing with another man. The rest of the crew were in constant motion around her.

She winced at the bloody smears on some of the men's faces and clothes. They wore the blood like prized jewelry, and the other men stared enviously at the marks.

Only Ashta was left feeling guilty for the women. Even the Tripsian pleasure slaves were not treated so bad. They were protected by soldiers, any man moving out of turn being banned from the pleasure house forever.

Despite the barbarian love of blood and death and fighting, the Tripsians wanted their women willing and soft.

She winced as she sliced her thumb on the sharp blade. Carefully, she left her thumb underneath her bandage as she kept working the blade against the rope. Hopefully it wasn't too deep or the men would notice the blood soaked rope.

The men pushed out from the docks and rowed hard into the open water, straight south for the barren wastelands of Bbrski. Her home.

Ashta shook her head. Bbrski would *never* be home for her again. That time was past. Now she was loyal, willing or not, to Tripsia.

As the morning slowly passed to noon, Ashta worked through the ropes, careful to hold the ends so they didn't slacken. As much as she wanted to be off the boat as soon as possible, she knew that she would have to wait for darkness.

Her stomach grumbled as she remembered that the men had not fed her this morning, or last night. Not even a drop of water had been given to her. She searched the deck for the boy who usually fed her, but he was nowhere to seen.

Instead she was left in the hot sun. Sweat tickled her eyes, as she waited. At least I don't have to pee, she thought, trying not to gulp against the harsh dryness of her throat.

Time passed slowly as the men pulled in the oars and set up the sails once more. The wind picked up and billowed out the great black cloth, as the ship cut through the water with deadly speed.

Each hour that passed meant the closer they were to Bbrski. And the longer it would take her to get back to Tripsia.

Ashta spent her hours plotting her escape. She had thought to steal the paddle boat. But she knew the men would not sleep hard enough for her to drop it into the waters. She didn't want to waste her energy killing the night watch when she had at least a three-day row ahead of her back to Tripsia.

No, she would have to content herself with a piece of wood or something to float on. The currents would be in her favor since they stayed far west of the Old Sow.

She blocked out her fears of the deep sea, filled with predators. She knew the story of sea monsters that swallowed ships hole.

Of sharks that swam in packs.

Of Torash's that jumped out from the depths of hell and ripped a body apart.

No.

She would grab the wide paddle in the hull of the small dingy and jump into the water. From there she would swim. Once on shore, one look at her clothes and people would know who she was and point her in the right direction. They wouldn't dare try anything against her, too afraid of the legendary skills the lionesses portrayed with knives and swords.

Ashta only hoped they would give her some food or water before the night. Otherwise she would die in the ocean, no matter how strong her will was.

The sun hung low in the west when a young boy came towards her, balancing a mug and a bowl. This one was younger than the last, maybe twelve.

The boy set it down in front of her before disappearing again. Saliva dripped down her chin as she stared at the grey colored gruel. Her stomach rumbled and growled, starved as the lion in the pit had been.

Closing her eyes, she took deep breaths trying to calm her racing thoughts.

A clang on the ground had her squinting at the boy, now seated on the upside-down wash bucket. He placed the mug between his feet, steadying it, before picking up the bowl.

He slowly spooned the gruel into her waiting mouth. She took each gulp greedily, not caring how she looked.

The boy watched her, the sun glinting across his mouse brown hair. His face was still soft with childhood, his eyes still wide with wonder.

Ashta tried to ignore her heart as it went to the child that she had once been as well. No, the world would age him soon enough.

When she finished the gruel, he set it aside, not picking up the mug yet.

"You should probably wait before drinking or you'll just get sick."

Ashta nodded, leaning back against the mast once more.

The sounds of the ship's creaks, the crashing waves soothed her as the food settled like a lead weight in her stomach. The men's shouts were a faint chatter in the background, easily ignored.

"You're really pretty," the boy said softly.

Ashta glanced up at him as he played with the spoon.

"What's your name?" she asked softly.

He looked up, his eyes brightening before he glanced around himself.

Good. He wasn't totally unaware of the danger he was in.

"Derek." He smiled briefly before forcing himself to look down at the bowl again.

Ashta looked behind him and noted that Augustos was busy speaking with several men around him. He probably wouldn't notice Ashta and the boy speaking.

To be on the safe side, she relaxed her face, opening her mouth just slightly. Then, focusing and staying her lips, she replied. "You are very kind Derek."

His ears brightened as he peeked up at her. "The big guy said we weren't to talk to ya, but I know it can be very boring on the boat. No one really talks to me, especially not the other boys."

"Why not?"

He sighed before setting the bowl down. Derek picked up the mug and carefully poured sweet water into her mouth.

To soon, he pulled it away and waited.

"Some of the men, the berserkers, beat us up if they see us playing. One, Vlear, always watches us. I don't like him. He took Toma with him once, and I remember when he came back Toma just cried in his hammock. He could barely walk the next day. I always make sure to stay far away from Vlear."

He fell silent again, carefully feeding her the water.

Ashta was thankful for his gentleness, it allowed her to get every last drop of water. She felt bad for the boy, knowing her escape the coming night would bring him some harm. But her conscience would not stop her from going ahead with her plan.

"Do you have a knife Derek?" she asked.

He looked suspicious before shaking his head. "I wish…" he mumbled before putting the mug to her lips again.

Carefully, she worked the knife into her other hand. When she finished the last of the mug, he set it down into the bowl.

"Derek."

He stopped; his legs ready to stretch up. When he looked into her eyes, she nodded her head. "Reach behind my right side."

He paused, not moving.

Then, glancing around to make sure no one was paying attention, he leaned forward and grabbed onto the handle. His eyes widened and Ashta whispered, "Hide it in your boot. Quick!"

He did, but before he could stand, another sailor shouted. "Hey! Boy!"

Derek shuddered as he turned to the advancing figure. The man was large, his face one of the ones from last night. Ashta focused on keeping herself relaxed, holding the rope ends together with a death grip.

"Augustos said no talking to the princess."

Derek dropped his head, mumbling out an apology.

Before he could finish it, the sailor swung out and punched the kid in the stomach.

Derek dropped to the ground, barely able to cover his head as the man began kicking him.

All the while, Ashta stayed silent. She knew that saying anything would make it worse for the boy, just as it had been for her when she had been in the Nursery.

At least he has the knife, she consoled herself with. *The boy would be safer now.*

"Get up and get back to work boy!"

Derek stumbled to his feet, his nose crooked and blood dripping down his chin. He glanced up at her, flashing a smile before disappearing. The man left quickly, returning to his own work.

No one wanted to get caught near the princess.

The flash Derek's smile reminded Ashta of the strength of her people. Even the children held a natural power against the harsh weather and harsher people. Her half-sister, Lily, had had a streak of harsh power that shone through her fragile beauty.

The sun sunk below the horizon. Ashta waited. The torches were lit as the men at first ate and reveled before disappearing into the hull of the ship to sleep. A half a dozen men stayed awake, walking the deck and keeping an eye out for changes in the sails.

Ashta waited.

She pretended to doze against the solid wood mast. She kept track of their motions, noting the patterns.

When the next man walked to the left, she would take her chance. Ashta took a deep breath before stretching her legs out. She tensed her arms. Her heart beat fast in her chest. There was only one throwing knife left in her hair, the rest just half swords and the daggers in her boots.

She counted down.

Three.

Two.

One.

The man's head was facing the other way as he came into view. She dropped the rope and whipped the throwing knife straight across. The man gasped before stumbling and falling over the ships edge.

Ashta was already running towards him, towards the paddle boat.

She picked up a torch and ran to the keg of Bbrski whiskey. She desperately pulled open the cork on the started barrel.

A shout from the quarterdeck rose.

Hurrying she poured the barrel over the spare rope and the other barrels.

Another shout followed by thudding footsteps.

Ashta dropped the torch on the still leaking barrel, the alcohol catching flame and bursting to life. Ashta was already running back to the paddle boat.

The barrels exploded, pieces flying past her shoulder.

Ashta pushed harder.

Clanks and creaks from below deck rumbled.

She never slowed.

She reached the boat and picked up the paddle.

A whistle by her ear. She her glanced back.

One man was already reloading his bow as three more ran towards her, swords out.

They would never get the chance to swing them.

Ashta turned and dove straight into the dark waters.

She kicked hard. She aimed straight, wanting to get as far out from the boat as possible.

The paddle pulled her slowly up.

Ashta broke the surface, gasping for air.

Behind her the flames burst higher, having caught onto the sails. She grinned. The ship didn't need the sails to catch her, but it would distract the men long enough. By the time morning light would shine on the great blue sea she would be gone.

And the crew of Bbrskian seamen would be searching for a needle in a haystack.

Despite the confusion on deck, arrows rained down near her. Obviously one man still had an eye on her.

Ignoring the ship, she pushed hard and swam the other way. When her legs began to burn, she flipped on to her back, the paddle under her back and arms.

Slowly, the sun lightened the sky, but it didn't stay long. Clouds rolled in from the east and the waves began to pick up.

Ashta ignored it, continuing her steady pace. She had no idea if she was headed north or south or just in circles.

The sky opened up and began slashing rain into the furious sea. Lightning blazed above her as its thunder rumbled through the charged air. It was all Ashta could do but hold onto her paddle.

Her limbs dragged her down, forcing her to choose between her swords and daggers or floating.

She stripped her boots off, the daggers pulling them down. They were quickly swallowed by the roiling waters.

She wasn't sure how long her body was tossed about the waters.

Her eyes closed.

The next thing she remembered was coughing up water as gritty sand scratched her back.

"Are you okay?"

After coughing and puking out what felt like the entire sea, Ashta blinked up at a young boy. Barely six years old.

Ashta tried to crawl to him but her limbs were weak and gave out.

The next time she woke up, she could smell fish and something acrid burning. She opened her eyes but realized she was somewhere dark. Inside.

Pushing herself up from the hard board beneath her, she sat up and waited for her spinning head to settle.

A door at the front of the shack opened. Bright sun glared inside for a moment. A woman stepped in and gasped.

"You shouldn't be up!" she exclaimed as she tried to push Ashta back. Ashta caught the woman's wrist and squeezed, stopping her motions.

"W-W-wate-"

Her throat was raw and dry from the salty sea. But the woman understood, moving away to grab a bowl of water. Ashta lapped it all up not caring how heavy it made her belly feel. The woman held out a hard lump to her. Bread.

Biting off a dense chunk, Ashta noted the other woman's weathered face. Her body looked the same age as Ashta but the sea had aged her faster.

The woman busied herself around the small shack. The door opened once when the little boy entered with rope. He sat down in the corner and practiced knots.

Once Ashta's stomach had calmed and her mind settled, she pushed up onto her legs. Despite their quivering, she stayed upright. The woman opened her mouth but wisely kept quiet.

"Palace. I need to get to the palace."

The woman nodded glancing down at Ashta's ripped skirt and bare chest. The tattoo glared down at the woman, telling her all she needed to know.

The princess's famous white lioness.

"Follow me."

Ashta and the woman walked outside. The woman followed a small stone path before coming back down to the beach. She pointed to the west. "It's more than a day's walk," she warned.

Ashta nodded, walking away from her without another word. The woman wouldn't want her around. That's what Ashta told herself.

Instead she stumbled across the rocky strand, eyes focused on the cliffs in the distance. *Just a little further, Ashta.*

Just a little further.

CHAPTER TWENTY-TWO

⌘

Unwilling Heir

H ER LEGS SHOOK as she scrabbled up the rocky outcrop. Ashta been was thanking all the gods for her luck in helping Carien read through the old tomes.

In one she had come across an old map of the first palace. In the map were secret passages in and out of the palace, hidden from the outsiders. The cove passageway that King Roman had taken her and the council through had not been on that map. It must have been a later edition. But the original palace had another passage. One that bent off of the path from the pits.

Pushing off the cliff face, she stumbled to her knees and found herself staring down a small hole. It was just wider than her. This was it.

Wriggling her body, Ashta squeezed through with plenty of space around her shoulders. She found herself in complete darkness. She crawled through the entrance before slowly standing.

As she stood, she stretched her hands, feeling the rough stone above her. This wasn't a natural cave. No, this was man made. Feeling around herself, she kept her hand on the right wall and slowly stumbled forward.

The path was not easy, sometimes having random steps in the stone. Sometimes slippery from a smooth cut. But slowly it wound up towards where the palace would be.

Her only companion in the darkness was the dripping of water onto the rough stone floor.

Ashta's knees hurt, scratched open from falls. Warm blood dripped down her face from a gash on her forehead.

And yet she continued.

She needed to get back to Carien.

Finally, sounds of voices echoed down the pitch-black stone hall.

She pushed herself, not able to feel her limbs just a constant buzz of energy. Eventually the pitch black lightened, allowing her eyes to make out the rough edges of the walls.

Ashta doubted this entrance was used often. And yet it did not have that dank smell from disuse.

A glint from the opposite wall had her stumbling. Someone had dropped a knife on the long walk.

Her mind was to dazed to bend down and pick it up. Instead she tripped past it, barely glancing down. Ashta kept stumbling forward until the wall beside her ended and she stumbled into the main hall.

Falling forward, Ashta landed in a pile against the wall. Her ragged breathes echoed in the cavernous space, yet she could not slow them. Or open her eyes.

The voices grew louder.

Then they stopped.

"Hey! You there!"

Ashta lifted her head and forced her heavy eyelids open. The Tripsian soldier stood before her, another man just behind him. He brought his torch close, the light flickering across her bare, sweat, and dust covered skin.

But the moment his eyes caught on the tattoo, he stepped back.

"Help me lift her."

The second soldier came forward, balancing her arms over their shoulders. She swayed on her feet but kept her footing. She barely kept her eyes open on the long walk, not caring as the hall changed from stone to brick. More voices filled the halls.

Her mind tried to swallow her down into dark blissful oblivion, but she fought hard to stay awake.

"Will she make it?"

A pause.

"It's hard to say. Her body is badly dehydrated and very scraped up. I'm not sure if she has even eaten from the look of her lean body. But, if everything…"

The cry of a babe woke Ashta. She sat up before registering the pain in her side.

"Careful, you have a lot of cuts."

Blinking, Ashta turned to stare into a familiar pair of caramel eyes.

"Carien," she whispered, her body beginning to shake.

The princess's eyes filled with tears as she leaned forward and pulled Ashta into a hard hug. "I can't believe you're here," She choked out, her tears leaving wet streaks down Ashta's chest.

Ashta said nothing, reveling in the familiar sweet smell that wafted around the princess. She had made it. Until that moment Ashta had not allowed herself to worry about what-ifs.

Her body began to shake as the past few days crashed down on her. Through it all, Carien held her close. She gently rubbed Ashta's back as she murmured sweet reassurances.

After a long spell, Ashta felt her limbs warming. She pulled back from Carien and threw her legs over the cot.

A healer hurried over to the two women.

"Your highness," she said, dropping into a curtsy before turning to Ashta. She took off the bandages giving Ashta the chance to look at the scrapes.

"Your only stitches are on the cut across your forehead. You'll need to get those out in a couple of weeks. The rest should be fine to leave open."

"Thank you," Ashta whispered. The stitches would be fine this time. And she wouldn't need someone else to care for her. Carien would take the stitches out for her.

Thinking of Carien, and her likely newly appointed lioness, Ashta glanced around but saw no one. "Where is your lioness?"

Carien stiffened. "I left her with the babe."

Ashta glared at the princess. Before she could open her mouth Carien stood and motioned her to follow. Ashta stayed quiet, ignoring the stares from the various servants and soldiers as they passed.

The cool air felt strange on her unbound chest. The novelty wore off as they walked past the soldiers stationed at Carien's door.

Standing in the room was Kkaar, behind her was Brinley with little Mina in her arms. Kkaar took one look at the bedraggled woman before stepping forward and pulling her into a hug.

"Thank the gods you are alive," She whispered. Darkling quirked her brow before disappearing into the back room.

"How is she?" Kkaar asked the princess.

Carien pursed her lips as she watched the doorway. "I-I don't know. She's alive. But there's something in her eyes."

Kkaar nodded, having noticed the strange fire behind her friend's gaze as well. She opened her mouth to continue but Darkling stepped back into the room, her clothes fresh, breasts bound, and her hair braided again.

Darkling walked to Brinley and took the babe in her arms. She smiled down at the little girl, pulling her close. She swayed before widening her stance.

The babe gurgled as she tried to focus her eyes on the woman holding her.

"You should sit," Carien demanded before heading to the door. She sent one of the soldiers in search of Papna. Turning back, her heart warmed at the sight of her friend seated on the settee, babe in her arms.

The moment lasted until the soldier came back with a bowl in hand. Carien and Kkaar stood silent as Darkling ate everything. They both noted the strange cuts on her arms and knees.

Before Carien could ask, Darkling stood and passed Mina back to Brinley. Then she turned and glared at the princess.

"I warned you it was a trap. My father would never free a captive. Not alive at least." Her voice was low and deadly.

Carien straightened her back, the tension from the past week still sitting on her shoulders. "What was I supposed to do, my hands were tied."

"You are the *heir* to Tripsia. Do something!"

"I can't!" her voice echoed across the room.

Brinley disappeared into Carien's room as Kkaar stepped outside leaving the two alone.

"You *can't* or you *won't?*"

Her dark-haired friend glowed with anger and something else. But Carien couldn't define what. Instead she fell back into herself, defending her position.

"It's the same thing," she said, her shoulders deflating as she was suddenly left cold. She rubbed her arms staring past Darkling.

"It's not."

"As if you would know."

Carien's sharp words echoed and cut through Ashta's heart. Ashta felt the blood drain from her face but didn't back down. She didn't need a reminder of her heritage. The past few days had been enough.

"I was an heir once."

Her soft words surprised Carien to look up. Her friend looked so lost as she swayed on her feet, her eyes far away. Darkling had never spoken of her past and Carien tried not to ask. She knew the other woman would not give her answers.

Carien waited, desperate to know her more.

"My father never listened to me. I was too soft. To weak-minded. And yet, my only piece of power against him had been that I was his first born. Our royalty goes to the first-born daughter. And our kingdom loved its traditions. Father could do nothing but accept me."

Darkling paused, eyes still gone to far away places.

Carien prodded her on. "And now?"

Ashta's eyes cleared as she blinked hard, staring back at her friend. "And now it doesn't matter. Tripsia is my kingdom and you are my future queen."

Carien could see the metal trellis sliding back in place behind her friends eyes. She would gain nothing more from her tonight.

She stepped forward and tried to grip the other woman's shoulder. But Darkling stepped back, enough to let Carien's hand slide off.

"You had choices, Carien. More than one. And the one you took almost cost you, your father and my life. Will you make the same choice next time?" Ashta stared into her friend's eyes, waiting, hoping.

But no words came out of Carien's mouth.

Both women knew that she would not change.

And because of that, Ashta turned away and walked to her room, falling asleep on her small cot.

Carien stood in her sitting room still thinking over the words her friend had said and found herself falling on to the settee.

What had she done? All she had prayed for these past days was for Darkling's safety. She should be happy to see her friend. Instead Carien was reminded of her inability to take control.

In her heart Carien knew she could have made the council and her father listen. They were all stubborn men, but she knew them, knew what threats would get them to move.

And yet she hadn't.

At the time she had seen only two outcomes, but now she knew the truth. There had been many choices, and hers had been wrong.

She shuddered at the thought of how close it had come. She could have died.

She could have *died*.

At that morose though, she stood and walked dazedly to her bedroom, dismissing Mina's nursemaid. Cuddling the babe close, she lay on top of the blankets.

Watching her small breaths and feeling each small perfect finger calmed Carien.

If she had not had the baby, Carien would have been a mess the past week. But she had to pull it together for her little one. And she had to be stronger next time.

She had promised herself to fight for Ashta after the raid in the desert. And she had failed to save Ashta's friend from the lion pit. Failed to save Ashta from Carien's father and King Alerik. She could not fail her friend a third time.

She would not, Carien amended as she leaned down and kissed Mina on the forehead.

CHAPTER TWENTY-THREE

⌘

Cold Royals

ASHTA HAD BEEN watching Mina with the nursemaid when a messenger came into the sitting room the next morning.

"You are required in the council room, immediately."

Before he could run away, Carien stopped him. "Tell the council we will arrive after we have breakfasted."

The boy paled slightly before running away.

Carien felt only slightly guilty for the dressing down the boy would receive from her father. But she refused to allow Darkling to face the council and her father without Carien at her side.

Once she was dressed and the babe's napkin changed, the three women walked through the halls. Servants and nobles refused to look at Ashta, their faces pale as if having seen a ghost.

Carien ignored them, her head held high as she sailed past. Fear was good. She had heard her fair share of rumors from the people and their dislike of Carien.

It was good to have Darkling back, creating a silent barrier between Carien and the people. No one stepped out of line or glared openly at the princess.

Not when a lioness who should have been dead stood at the princess's side.

They entered the council room. Carien took the seat beside her father and Brinley behind her, leaning against the wall. Some councilmen still glared at the nursemaid's presence but kept their words to themselves. Now, they all turned and stared at the woman standing at the opposite end of the table.

"Ashta the Lion Tamer." Her father's voice gave away no emotion, just as Darkling's face stayed stone cold.

In that moment, Carien realized Darkling's birthright. She was a true princess, hiding her emotions. Allowing nothing past. Nothing that could be used as a weapon later.

Something Carien had never completely mastered.

"Why do you stand before us when we fairly traded you to the King of Bbrski?"

Ashta looked at each councilman, the two generals, before staring down at the king.

"The trade is no longer valid. King Alerik did not hold up his end. I felt no need to stay and so I returned to my position at the princess's side."

No one spoke. Her words rang with truth, and an underlying threat. Despite her slave status, she still had the will and mind of a highborn.

"Leaving the boat would not have taken a week's time."

"No," she agreed, "I was taken to my father's encampment and escaped from the boat that was headed to Bbrski."

The men leaned forward. The general's tipped their faces up towards the slave.

Pulling in a deep breath, Ashta maintained her blank face as she recanted the past week. "The bulk of King Alerik's fleet is docked on a small island in the sea. It lies south east of the palace, a few days sailing with favorable winds."

The generals glanced at each other. Winds did not matter to the Bbrski fleet.

"A small portion of his fleet sits on the coastline by Naankdoen while a few boats raid the rest of the coastline. He has over ten thousand men alone stationed on the island."

All of the councilmen leaned back at the number.

King Roman watched her, his eyes glittering with something else. Not disgust, not fear, but something close to respect. There was no reason for the dark-haired woman to lie. And he knew exactly which island she referred to. A long time ago, almost another lifetime, he had sailed often to Kijarhro. Always under the guise of night.

Ashta continued, "That number does not include the armies at Naankdoen, Kae ol and our own city."

"They are in Kae ol…" General Ttaabit gasped, his face paling. King Roman rubbed at his short beard. He had not heard anything from Kae ol in the last report he had received from his sister.

"As for the recent reports of missing women along the coast," Ashta hesitated, biting her lip. She took a deep breath before continuing, "I have seen at least a hundred on the island, not including the dead bodies that littered the encampment."

"What use are the women?" Carien asked, her innocence shining in-between the men.

The generals kept their faces straight while the councilmen looked away, their faces flushed. Even the king did not turn to look at his daughter. Brinley turned her face away, suddenly bouncing the already quite babe.

Ashta waited a long, tense moment, hoping for someone else to explain the ways of men and war. But no one dared open their mouth. With a sigh, she stared into the hard eyes of the king while replying to the princess. "The women keep the men from fighting and killing *each other*. Instead they rape and kill the woman for sport while they are kept waiting for their orders."

At first Carien said nothing. Then, her face drained of all color as her shaking fingers touched her lips. She looked at Ashta with disbelief. But Ashta could only nod, the women's screams still echoing through her head. *She* had almost been one of those women.

"You can't possibly know if these women are from Tripsia. You said yourself that King Alerik is also in Naankdoen and Kae ol." General Taatbit reasoned.

Ashta shook her head, "The Naankdoena people live in their city. The walls so far have been impenetrable. As for Kae ol, the army he sent into the jungle lands heart have not reached the cities yet. There would be few women from there as the tribes tend to migrate around the center of the forest. That leaves Tripsia with its many coastal villages and estates ripe for the picking."

"I say that we cannot be sure of these women's identities-" He argued, pleading to the rest of the table.

"They *are* Tripsian."

Carien's hollow voice caught everyone's attention at the table. She stared at Ashta blankly. They were both aware of the princess's court sessions, of the many grievances of missing daughters, sisters, mothers.

Carien stared each man in the eye before looking at her father. "You asked me to do more court hearings. In the past few weeks alone, every other person came to report a raid, or a missing daughter, a mother, a sister. Ashta's assumption that the women on the island being Tripsian is more than likely."

Then she turned to the councilmen, "How many of you have had similar reports from your estates of missing people?"

One by one, each man nodded or raised his hand.

With the shocking numbers staring them in the eye, Ashta knew that the missing women would come back to haunt the council and Tripsia in some way. Nothing her father did was completely selfless. He would not allow the abduction of women just to keep his men occupied. The act of stealing helpless women had more than one effect. But what was the second? What was the other consequence?

"Anything else to report, lioness?" King Roman's voice rumbled as he rubbed at his short beard again. Everything had changed in a few short weeks. There was much to think about.

Ashta shook her head. She didn't mention her father's comments about her, her mother, her stepmother, and her half-sister. It was of no importance to the king. And she knew he wouldn't understand the meaning of it.

Disturbed, the King dismissed Ashta. She bowed before walking out of the room without a backward glance. She paused at the hallway and waited. Moments later Carien and Brinley joined her in the hall.

Carien was still pale from the news but she did not speak. She led the way back to her rooms.

They both knew that she was needed at court, but the princess needed a short moment to herself. She couldn't have her people seeing any weakness. Not now with the Bbrski army waiting at the door, so to speak.

Once inside her rooms she dismissed Brinley and closed the doors to her inner chambers. Even then, she took Mina in her arms and sat as close to the fireplace as possible.

"Put more wood on," she quietly demanded, gently rocking Mina.

Ashta frowned.

It was always cool in the palace with most of it underground. But it was never cold. Not like the snow and ice of Bbrskian winters.

Deciding not to comment, Ashta walked over and threw in several large logs. The fire sparked and crackled loudly before it became a roaring flame. The heat was sweltering but Carien did not step back, only covered Mina to protect her from the heat.

She turned to Ashta, her mouth set in a straight line and her usually warm caramel eyes were hard slates.

"There was more," she mumbled low.

Ashta nodded.

Glancing at the doors, Carien gestured with her hand for Ashta to continue.

Sighing, Ashta allowed herself the luxury of sitting beside Carien. She kept her senses aware, making sure to speak low so the fire could drown out her words.

"When I was sold, I thought my father had known about it."

Carien's brows pulled together as she watched Darkling's black eyes.

"But I don't think he did," she mused.

"How can you be sure?" Carien asked. Mina gurgled, distracting them both as Carien gently rocked the child asleep again.

With a sigh Ashta rubbed her hands before glancing at the doors. With a nod she continued. "He had my stepsister sent to the Midloean kingdoms right after I disappeared." Before Carien could say anything, Ashta continued, "And he got rid of my stepmother."

The princess closed her mouth with a snap.

Mina gurgled her eyes wide as she stared up at the two women. Her innocent eyes did not understand the gravity of what passed between the adults.

"Maybe he does care for you?" Carien asked quietly, not looking at the other woman. Instead, she gave her finger to Mina who gripped it tightly.

Ashta shook her head. "No. He said so himself that I am just a piece in his great puzzle he has been building for years."

"But then why would he react?" Carien worried, rubbing at her temple. It made no sense. The Bbrskian king's cold persona was known across the known kingdoms. He never reacted with emotion.

Then why would he react so strongly, removing the new queen and the daughter?

"There's something else. Something he didn't say. I could see it in his movements," Carien angled herself so she could make out Ashta's profile. "I think his hold on Bbrski isn't as strong as we all believe."

"Are you sure?"

"No." Darkling glanced up at Carien, the fire dancing across her black gaze. "It's just a feeling I have."

Carien sighed, curling her hand around Mina's tiny face. The little girl looked so peaceful. It was hard to believe the world around her was not.

"The women you saw…" Carien started.

The words hung between them.

Darkling said nothing. Instead she linked her hand with Carien's, squeezing the princess's hand. Carien didn't look up. She pulled the little babe closer, as if to protect her from the world.

"Why?" the princess's voice cracked. A tear streaked down her cheek.

Ashta wished she could comfort the other woman, but she asked herself that very same question. Why?

Deep down Ashta knew why. If she let herself into that place inside of her, where her father had shaped and molded an emotionless and harsh princess. A woman of power. A woman of cold calculation.

A woman she had tried to push deep inside of herself, since the day her mother had died. Since the day she had been replaced by her half-sister.

And yet that part of herself had never died. Merely shrunk.

Carien pulled the other woman close, forcing Ashta within a breath of Carien's face. The two searched each other's eyes.

Carien saw a woman, full of life with a seed of cold deep in her eyes. It reminded her of the realization she had in the council room.

"You are a princess."

The words felt strange on her tongue, and yet they were true.

Ashta shook her head slowly, not accepting the words.

But Carien pushed forward. "Svetlana Anichka of the Broskla Family line. First born daughter of King Alerik and Queen Anichka. Crown princess of Bbrski."

"No." But it was just a whisper, barely heard over the roaring fire.

"You are more a princess than I ever will be." The words echoed in the small room, the truth ringing in the women's ears.

Ashta shook off Carien's hand and stood before the flame. The heat was oppressing, pushing and clawing its way between the chinks in her armor.

Yet she reveled in it, despite her birthright to an ice kingdom.

She turned and stared down at the young princess and babe. "Svetlana is dead, lost at sea. Now, Ashta lives."

Her words crackled as Carien stared up at her flaming figure. For a moment, Carien saw a different woman standing in front of her; not a princess, no longer a slave. Before she could fully catch the thought, Darkling walked out of the room.

Carien and Mina sat alone in the sitting room.

As the babe twisted in her swaddle, Carien pulled her close into her arms. She kissed her on her tiny nose and breathed in her newborn scent.

"You will be protected, little babe. Your aunt and I love you," she whispered. The little girl's clear blue eyes looked up at her, full of unspoken knowledge. Carien couldn't help but confess her worries to the small child. "I just don't know if your aunt will be able to protect you from herself."

Mina blinked slowly, staring on as if she had already known. And Carien worried if Mina did. She worried that the kingdom might be in bigger trouble than she and Darkling had ever realized.

CHAPTER TWENTY-FOUR

⌘

Ravaged Land

"GODS, IT'S GOOD to see your face."

Ashta smirked over at Kkaar's looming figure. The other woman waited in the doorway for a moment before coming further into the room.

Brinley was nursing Mina while Ashta quickly ate her Papna. Ashta kept one eye on the open doorway where the princess and her attendants were helping her dress for the day. Or more importantly, dress for court.

"You are just saying that because you want to go back to the reserves," Ashta joked quietly.

Kkaar laughed aloud, smacking Ashta on the shoulder.

Ashta winced as the blow jarred through her but said nothing.

"I can't deny it. I miss seeing Luci's face every day. This protecting the princess shite is lonely. Not even the other soldiers look me in the eye."

"And you have only been at it for a week."

Kkaar shuddered at the thought of her position continuing into the unending future. No. As much as she missed the dark-eyed woman who had become her friend, she missed human contact more.

The princess was pleasant enough. But having her entire world centered around just one person was hard on Kkaar. Even in her days before the Nursery, she had always been surrounded by people. Part of a larger group.

"Did the King mention anything in your meeting with him yesterday?" Kkaar asked.

Ashta shook her head. She had been surprised that King Roman had not refuted Ashta's claim as the princess's protector once more. But then, Carien's choice of protection was no longer up to the King.

Ashta glanced up in her friend's pale moon face. Ashta was aware that she was unique from their little group. She handled the loneliness far better than most of the other women did.

"Kkaar!"

Both women turned to take in Carien's elegant form draped in emerald green silks, diamonds flashing throughout her headscarf. A large broach, with an amber stone, flashed above her eyes. She dripped in stones looking every part of the crown princess.

Kkaar bowed low before glancing at Darkling. A moment of silence reigned between the three, before being broken by Carien's sigh.

"I had hoped to see you earlier this morning, but alas time got away from me. I want to thank you for your services as a reserve lioness." She glanced over at the nursemaids shadowed face before continuing in a formal tone. "With Ashta's return, I will no longer be requiring said services."

With a nod, she dismissed Kkaar.

Kkaar smiled broadly before bowing and walking with a new lightness out of the room.

Carien looked to Darkling and the two shared a smile. Both women had been aware of Kkaar's discomfort with the position.

"Come, we must be off," Carien said with a small wave of her hand.

Ashta waited a step, allowing Brinley with Mina in hand to follow behind the princess. Too quickly the women took their spots in the court room and Ashta felt a wave of dizziness at the scene. It felt as if the last week was but a mirage. Could she really have come face to face with her father not three days ago? It seemed impossible, but Ashta knew she had. And that everything had changed.

Including the way she how she heard the reports in the courtroom. This time she noticed that most who passed through the court doors were men.

Time and again, reports from displaced fishermen and villagers came in about missing women and ravaged houses. Ashta's father was laying waste to the coast.

From the downtrodden and hopeless people walking into the courtroom, Ashta though he might be winning.

It did not look good for Carien to be surrounded so removed from the war, sitting on her throne, clean and bored looking. Not to these survivors who had barely escaped from the raging war outside of the palace walls.

Ashta gritted her teeth. The court was not her place to say anything to Carien.

Before the court broke for dinner a harried Tripsian soldier came to the foot of the throne. Carien had already stood and grabbed Mina from Brinley's arm.

"Princess," Ashta hissed, trying to get the other woman's attention.

Carien looked up from Mina's gurgling face to look at Ashta before glancing down. But instead of retaking her seat, she stood before the soldier.

Ashta could smell the man's sweat from her spot beside the empty thrown. She was disgusted by the stink but knew his message was important.

"You may speak," Carien said, her voice carrying across the room. It stopped those courtiers who watched from the pillars from disappearing into the bowels of the palace.

The man, too tired to notice Carien's arched brow and thinned lips, wiped his brow before speaking. "Your highness, villagers and fisherman are pouring into the city. Many have said their homes are gone and they fear the oncoming Bbrskian army. We do not have the quarters or the supplies for them in the palace. What do you want us to tell the people?"

Carien gently rocked the babe as Mina fussed, staring down the man. "Tell our people we have enough bread for all to eat at the table."

"But your highn-"

Carien turned away from the man and looked to the soldiers working the door. "Have half your men take out the military tents. I will meet them outside and oversee their placement."

No one moved.

Mina began crying loudly, her face re. Carien brought her up to her shoulder and kept rocking her.

"Well?" she asked, her tone deadly, "What are you waiting for?"

Ashta watched the men's throats as they swallowed before rushing out of the courtroom. Then Carien turned back to the first soldier. She didn't say anything, just raised her brow. The man fell to his knees, bowing, before scrambling out of the courtroom.

With the drama done, the people dissipated leaving Ashta, Carien and Brinley alone in the courtroom.

"Are you sure it is wise?" Ashta asked.

Their supplies were tight. Tripsia's neighbors had not been able to trade with the threat of Bbrski the last few months. The harvest had been plenty, but not bountiful enough to support the palace, the army *and* the Tripsian people. Ashta had no doubt it was more than just the local fishermen who came seeking aid. Tripsians from all estates came to the capitol, seeking the protection of the wall and the army. Even the councilmen had left their estates behind and now hid in the depths of the palace.

Carien looked up at her with fire in her eyes. "They are *my* people. I cannot abandon them. Especially not now. You know that."

Ashta did.

She knew who tenuous King Roman's hold was over his people. Carien needed to sway them to follow her father for a bit longer, until she was crowned queen.

Ashta nodded, keeping her head bowed.

Carien turned to Brinley. "Take Mina to the rooms."

"Yes, your highness."

With a quick curtsy, the nursemaid left the court room and disappeared into Tripsia's depths.

"Shall we begin?" Carien asked, looking back to Darkling. She needed the other woman's support. She needed her strength. As Carien had found out in the past week, the people did not respect or even fear her. But all, even her own father, feared the dark haired lioness.

"Lead the way, your highness."

Flushing at the words, Carien walked past her lioness and down the steps of the throne. She felt eyes on her the entire way, but she kept her back straight and her eyes forward. She would not shrink before them. She was *their* princess.

The great doors were opened for her. Carien was left blinking in the sudden light. It was still daytime outside of the palace and the sun burned over the palace grounds. Though not as hot as the midday.

Once her eyes adjusted, Carien's heart clenched at the sight before her. Children huddled around their mothers. Men were pulled away from there women. And everywhere ran soldiers with no feeling for the people around them.

Taking a deep breath, Carien waded into the mess of people and animals. She searched for someone that looked like they might be in charge.

There.

Finally, she caught sight of a tall man barking out orders. General Ttaabit.

She pushed through until she stood before him.

"What?" he yelled before looking at who he addressed. Panic crossed his face as he recognized the crown princess.

Carien held her hand up, cutting off his apology before he could spew it.

"I need forty of your men to go into the supplies and grab the campaign tents. We will have them setup against the outer walls of the grounds to afford the people some safety from the heat of the day. Good?"

He stared down at her in silence, shocked, before blinking back into himself. He turned to the nearest soldier and repeated the princess's commands to him. He turned back to Carien and asked, "Anything else your highness?"

"Yes."

She began walking towards a large group of citizens, their dirtied clothes covered in the red dust of the desert. General Ttaabit followed behind her, briefly nodding to the lioness. He didn't dare look the other woman in the eye, having heard of her skill with a sword. And her fists.

"How many are in your family?" Carien asked once she was within hearing distance. The older man looked at her, his face suspicious.

"Fifteen." A boy from the back yelled.

"I need you to organize into groups of forty. Once the tents are setup along the wall, you will go with the soldiers to set up pallets."

The older man still watched the princess but no longer glared at the young woman. Instead he watched her with a thoughtful gaze.

As the evening light waned and the torches glowed into the early night, Ashta kept watch over Carien. Again, and again, she watched the peoples suspicious and wary gazes shift to those of wonder and wary hope. Through it all, Carien kept her head high. She never complained as the cold air began to nip at her bared skin along her face and hands. Not once did she raise her voice or bark an order. She demanded respect with an even tone.

And the people gave it to her.

It was late into the night before Carien was satisfied with the comfort of her people. Weary, she stumbled up the steps of the palace. Ashta stayed quiet.

Once they were inside, Ashta lifted the princess into her arms.

"You don't have to," Carien protested.

"You have done enough. Let me take care of you now."

Nodding she leaned into Darkling's shoulder and reveled in the warmth. She would never admit it aloud, but she missed the closeness afforded to her when she was just an unknown girl.

Touch.

It was something so small, yet as an isolated princess it became the one barrier too great, too large, to break. And the one she wished to overcome the most.

It had abetted since Carien had taken Mina into her care. The small child broke through the rules, being the only person Carien could hold and touch in public. And in private.

It was enough most days.

But it was nothing like the warm embrace of another person.

"Thank you," she whispered into Darkling's shoulder.

The other woman tightened her grip for a moment, letting Carien know she had heard.

Once back in the room, Darkling set Carien down on the settee in her room before disappearing. When she came back, Darkling held her bowl of Papna.

"Eat. You missed dinner."

Carien didn't even protest, forcing herself to eat over half the bowl. She no longer felt hungry from the afternoon. The pains had disappeared with the rising moon. But the memory of the desert and constant hunger still scared her.

As she sat and chewed, exhaustion set into her shoulders. The day had been long. Much had to be done. And everywhere people had looked to her for strength.

What would she do when the war truly started? When the arrows rained down over the Tripsian walls and children's blood soaked the courtyard? Would she be able to be strong then?

Carien wasn't sure. And at that moment, she did not want to consider or worry about it.

Darkling pulled the bowl away from her and finished the rest herself.

For a long minute, two women sat in silence. Both lost to their thoughts as exhaustion lay heavy on their shoulders.

With a sigh, Carien stood. She passed Darkling without a word being spoken. In moments, she fell into her bed and fell into a deep dreamless sleep.

CHAPTER TWENTY-FIVE

⌘

Come in Peace

A WEEK PASSED and the tents become over full of people. Refugees streamed from across the coasts, through the ancient city and past the inner walls of the Tripsian palace. A small group of pale skinned travelers together were noticed by the soldiers immediately. The soldiers separated the travelers from the rest of refugees and pulled them aside.

Carien worried about the numbers but she could not say no to the onslaught of refuge seekers. They were her people. She *had* to help them. Somehow.

Each evening she went up into the old city and helped the army place new tents and latrines. Carien could not sit still knowing how much there was to be done. Every little bit counted.

A food tent was set up to help feed the masses. Carien set up a ration system, making sure one of the few servants who could write stood by the tent, taking names and tallying numbers. Almost three thousand to date. And still growing.

She rolled her shoulders as she adjusted her seat. The throne had gotten no more comfortable in the last few weeks. Carien tried not to let it show how it bothered her. At least her mornings were spent in comfort with little Mina, smiling and babbling.

"Your Highness."

Carien blinked, zoning into the soldier who stood before her. Behind him stood a group of strangely dressed men. Their faces were covered, their mantles fluttering down to the tops of their boots. Squinting, Carien felt a tickle of recognition.

"These men were seen walking into the city with the other refuge seekers. When asked from where they came, they refused to answer."

The soldier bowed before leaving the courtroom.

Carien waited, her hands stretching over the ends of the throne's armrests. Court was over soon, and she wanted to speak with one of the generals about the bathing pools and how to safely escort the people back and forth in the twisting maze of palace halls.

"Your highness."

Carien's back straightened at the familiar baritone voice.

Darkling took a step closer to the throne, but otherwise made no other move.

One man stepped forward from the group and lifted his face covering up to rest over his hair. Carien was not surprised to be met by a familiar gaze.

Violet and Blue.

Ashta winced internally, before looking past zHavier to the men that stood at the ready behind him. She recognized Trom, but not the other four men. A small party for a prince to travel in. Ashta mulled over it, wondering what else Naankdoen had planned.

"We come here to Tripsia looking for peace and friendship," his eyes never strayed from Ashta's face. He drank in the sight of her. He tried to speak with her mind but was met by nothingness. "Naankdoen is in a time of great need. Our enemies from the south have ravaged our coastline and barraged our walls for the past few months."

He tried again to mind speak but was still met by nothing. Had he lost her already? zHavier grimaced as he finally focused his eyes on the young princess. Her usually warm eyes were shaded. The trust that had once shined in them was darkened.

Are you still sure they will help?

zHavier didn't bother to reply to Trom because he could not even consider the possibility that Tripsia would not come to their aid.

"Tripsia is still at peace with Naankdoen as far as I am aware," Carien replied, her voice purposefully dead of emotion. She arched a brow, daring zHavier to correct her.

He bowed his head slightly before taking another step closer to the throne.

All of the soldiers in the room, as well as Ashta, stepped toward him. Their hands at the ready on their swords.

He paused, lifting his hands to show he held nothing. No one stepped back.

"Go on," the princess urged him from her throne, making no move to tell her soldiers to step back.

zHavier glanced at Ashta's face, looking for even a flicker of the woman he knew. Dead eyes stared back at him. He turned away and looked back at Carien, who was tapping her fingers against the armrest.

"Naankdoen would like to forge a stronger bond with Tripsia."

Carien waved her hand for him to continue. Taking another deep breath, he prayed this would work. "We come in friendship, pledging ourselves to Tripsia's aid in her times of need from now until the end of time. In return, we ask the same of Tripsia."

"And what is it exactly that you ask of Tripsia."

"Men. With a more sizeable army, we would be able to beat back the berserkers. As it stands, we do not have enough weapons or food to make a larger army." He stood and waited for a reply.

The princess's hand stilled as she watched him and his men thoughtfully. Her thoughts sped and twirled, flashing to quickly for him to grasp anything concrete.

Carien glanced over at Darkling. The prince's offer was what she had hoped to get from her initial stay in Naankdoen. And they did need support against Bbrski in the coming war. She also knew that the Naankdoen did not have a sizeable army compared to Tripsia.

But right now, Tripsia was engaged in her own battles. Who knew how long it would be before the Naankdoena soldiers were freed up to come to Tripsia's aid? Even so, it was something to consider. And at the very least bring up to her father.

Mind made up she turned back to the prince, his unnatural gaze never wavering from hers. Getting up, she stood tall before all that were present in the room; the courtiers, Ashta and Brinley, the zHavier and his men, her own soldiers.

Her voice carried her decree through the room. "Tripsia welcomes it's visitors with open arms. You all must be weary from your travels. My men will show you to your chambers and evening meals."

With a nod, her men closed around the Naankdoena and carefully herded them out the far entrance. Instead of sitting down to continue the sitting period, she turned to the soldier attending her. "Court is adjourned for the evening."

He nodded, trailing behind the other soldiers.

With a sigh, Carien stepped to the side. Brinley was quiet as a dozing Mina laid on Brinley's shoulder.

Ashta stepped up beside the princess as they left the courtroom and began down the hall. She was amazed at how well Carien held her power. Even in the face of an equal, she came across strong and unbending. Ashta was reminded again and again why she chose to follow her young friend.

"Where to now?" she asked, noting their direction was away from the palace entrance and the refugees.

"We must speak to my father."

They walked on in silence for a moment before Ashta asked the question they both were thinking about. "Do you really believe Naankdoen can help us?"

Sighing, Carien stopped and looked up into her friend's dark eyes. "I don't know. But we can't afford another enemy right now. No matter my father's answer, we will have to tread carefully."

Ashta nodded. There was no obvious win in the situation. They continued the rest of the way to the council room in silence. The quiet pad of Ashta's leather boots and the swish of Carien and Brinley's skirts the only sound in the barren halls.

The soldiers in front moved aside with a quick bow to their princess. Ashta smirked. The soldiers finally showed their princess the respect she deserved as a future leader. Especially now that she had proven herself as formidable leader, taking charge in the ancient city, setting up the refugees.

Ashta stayed silent behind the princess, noting the pained expressions on several councilmen. The king did not even bother to look up from the map where he and General Hariim were arguing. Loudly.

Carien stood at the head of the table and waited. Slowly her silence seeped into the closest councilmen as they turned and watched her, having also fallen silent. Finally, her father looked up. His mouth and eyes were lined with worry. Did he always look so tired, Carien wondered to herself?

Before he could continue speaking with the general, Carien stepped forward and interrupted.

"Father, the prince of Naankdoen has arrived within our city with a small party of soldiers. He comes seeking Tripsia's alliance against Bbrski."

His frown deepened as he stepped back from the table and straightened to his full height. "That is *all* he came asking for?"

Carien hesitated, not liking the sneer coming from Hariim directed at her. Glancing back at Darkling, she straightened her back as well and stared her father straight in the eye. "He also came asking for help from our army, against the attack on their city."

The King blinked once, twice before staring down at the map of the Midloean kingdoms. His hands were clenched in tight fists, but other than that he showed nothing outwardly.

With a deep sigh, he looked back up at his only child, "We cannot afford to pick a side in this war."

Carien frowned, "Has it not been picked already for us?"

"No," he hesitated, glancing at Hariim, "If we play our tiles right, we could stay outside of the influences of this fight and come out of it mostly unscathed."

Ashta snorted.

Everyone turned to look at her, but she just shrugged. As far as she could tell, there was no kingdom outside of her father's influence. He was a conqueror. He would never be satisfied with leaving any of the royals alive.

The room stood silent, filled with tension, as no one wanted to be the first to speak. Ashta wisely stayed quiet, knowing her voice was not welcome on the topic.

Carien took a deep breath and focused on calming her beating heart. She knew there was no changing her father's mind, not in front of all the other men.

"What will you have me say to the prince?"

He waved his hand already turning away from his daughter. "Lie. Tell him we do not have enough men and supplies to support them."

One of the councilmen near Carien coughed. She heard his quiet mutter clear as day, "It's not a lie."

The king turned and glared down at the man until the councilman shrunk into his seat.

Carien made no motion. She turned away from her father and the table full of men.

She was too angry to respond to her father. Did he not realize how precarious Tripsia's position stood right now against the other kingdoms? They needed every ally they could get. And Naankdoen, a well-known strong ally, would be an asset in the future. If not now then in the years to come. The prince's promise had been for time eternal. Tripsia would need them at some point. She had seen herself the power of their soldiers, the brutality of their mounts. They were a formidable foe and Carien knew that they would hold out against Bbrski long enough to tire the Southern army. And then the Naankdoena would strike and win.

Not coming to their aid was dangerous. The Naankdoena people would remember how their neighboring kingdoms had done nothing but sit back and watch as they suffered behind their walls.

And that animosity could start wars.

"Where to now?" Darkling asked, following silently behind Carien.

"To my chambers. The prince can wait another day for his response."

Carien heard nothing behind her. She did not know what her trusted guard thought of the situation. But her friend knew as well as she did that Carien had no power to make decisions. As long as her father was King, she would have to follow.

And right now, it looked like her father planned to take the kingdom down into the afterworld with him.

CHAPTER TWENTY-SIX

⌘

Paying the Price

THE NEXT DAY passed slowly as Carien avoided being near zHavier for too long. She would better able to hold the lie against him if she didn't have to defend herself at all. Besides, she had no power in the decision. As flattering as his attention was, she knew the truth of the situation and that she held no power.

She was the *future* ruler of Tripsia.

Not the current.

That is how she ended up spending the afternoon playing with Mina in the courtroom. Men and women mingled and moved around her, the stink of politics and power plays thick and cloying.

And it seemed the best deterrent of ungracious courtiers was a small babbling babe. Carien smiled down at the little girl. Her white hair gleamed in the candlelight, her eyes already grass green. Carien leaned down and blew hot kisses on Mina's belly, eliciting high pitched giggles and gurgles.

"Your highness, the prince is approaching."

Carien grimaced. She had hoped the babe would deter princes as well. Apparently not so. She nodded to Darkling, continuing to play with Mina.

zHavier approached the princess and Ashta alone. His men were spread out in the room. Trom was scouting to get a bearing of the size of Tripsia's army. A difficult thing when most of the ancient city was underground and under careful watch.

"Your highness," he called out quietly. He tried to catch Ashta's eye, but she stared past him, completely closed off. Not even a wisp of emotion came from the space from where she stood.

He swallowed. zHav knew he shouldn't let it get to him, that time had passed. That they were no longer as close and open to each other as they once had been.

He focused on Carien instead.

His eyes widened has he realized that a babe stared back at him. Bright green eyes like nothing he had seen before stared back at him.

Unlike Ashta, where he heard and felt nothing, the babe was a swirling mass of fog. Wispy, allowing the almost feeling to touch but before he could understand it was gone. He stepped away from the child, and inadvertently closer to Ashta.

"You wanted to speak with me?" Carien asked, her normally warm eyes now hard as slate.

"I…No."

She looked up at him confused as the babe gurgled in her arms. Deftly, as if she was a mother, she picked the child up and began bouncing her against her shoulder.

He took the moment to turn to Ashta. "I'm sorry. We have not had the chance to speak and I —"

Carien stood up roughly and pushed between him and Ashta.

He looked down at the princess with surprise, not understanding what was happening.

But Carien saw the slanted glances now directed at her guard. Darkling's position, and the respect she was owed, was precarious as it was. It wouldn't take more than a word to convince her father to have her executed. Even the hint of an illegal relationship would have her killed.

"Let me remind *you*, your highness, it is against the ancient laws to speak with our guards."

His mouth flapped as he kept glancing over at Ashta.

Carien pulled his arm into her own and pulled him with her to one of the many side doors hidden behind columns, and out into the courtyard.

And more importantly away from prying ears.

Ashta followed several steps behind, thankful for the princess's interference. She was also worried for the princess, as Ashta noted six men around the room slowly following and closing in on them. As they stepped out into one of the outer courtyards, she signaled to two Tripsian soldiers. They quickly fell in line behind her.

She had to be prepared for anything from the prince. His motivations at first seemed obvious. He acted the part of a lovesick prince well. But Ashta knew better now, that deep down inside the prince was a dark seed. His lack of reaction to having her half-sister killed brought it all into clarity.

Carien continued to pull the prince along, guiding them towards the Ashe-and-Roses labyrinth. "Tell your men to stay back," she said quietly, still gently bouncing Mina in her other arm.

The prince looked down at her with a blank look. Finally, he nodded. She pulled him to a stop in front of the labyrinth.

The princess glanced back, thankful Darkling was at least fifteen paces behind them. She turned to stare at zHavier's shoulder and spoke quickly, "Don't ever do that again. The laws are much stricter in Tripsia than when we were in Naankdoena. Here even the implication that the white lionesses speak to the people can have them executed." At her last word she stared him right in the eye, ignoring the dizzying effect of his lilac and blue eyes.

Instead she was haunted by the memory of Ceerie, the pale-haired lioness she did not know, being ripped apart by the lions. And there hadn't been a thing she, as a princess, could do to save the woman from her fate. From the laws placed and upheld by the people of Tripsia.

zHavier blinked several times. He couldn't leave it alone. The danger didn't stop him from grabbing Carien's other arm that was curled around the babe.

She looked past him, shaking her head in response to the feral looks that had come across the other two Tripsian soldiers fanned around them at a distance.

"I understand. I know that the white lionesses cannot have any relationship with a man. But *she* is different," He started, fiercely.

Carien did not rise to the bait, keeping her ground and replying with a steady voice. "You're right. She is different. She *chose* to be a slave. But the laws do not change for her. She is as much beholden to the ancient laws as I am. And nothing, not I, not the King, not the entire Midloean Kingdoms, the Northern Kingdoms, and the beyond, can change that."

He shook his head, letting go of her arm. "I don't believe that. She was born a princess. Your laws don't apply to her."

Carien laughed dryly. If only it were that simple.

"Tell me zHav, do they teach you the history of the Midloean kingdoms?"

He nodded slowly.

"Then you should be familiar with Tripsia's role in creating the peace for our lands. And the price it had on all the other kingdoms."

His eyes flashed. He ran his hands through his hair before turning away and pacing.

Carien let him work through it. Her kingdom had been the reason the humans had won the great war and were in the positions they were today. But it meant all the kingdoms had agreed to a price. Slaves could never return. Their families, their born kingdoms would hand them back over to Tripsia.

Over the centuries, slaves quit trying to run away. And now it was unheard of.

"There must be someway…" He muttered, just loud enough for Carien to hear.

She sighed. They would get nowhere with this argument.

"Why does it matter?" Carien asked.

She had to admit to herself she was more than curious, jealous of the attention the prince spent on Darkling. She knew nothing had happened in Naankdoen between the prince and her guard. Darkling would never endanger herself and Carien like that.

She had hidden her true heritage from all in order to protect Carien! No, it was something else that drove the prince to these lengths, she thought.

zHavier jerked to a stop and looked at her, his eyes ice cold. With another frustrated sigh, he came to stand beside the princess, leaning down to her ear so only she could hear. "I need to speak with her. About her half-sister."

Ah. And then it all made sense.

Lily.

The princess who had tried to kill Carien.

The first time Carien had seen Darkling break from her self-imposed prison as a slave. And yet Darkling's half-sister had still been punished.

Carien glanced over at Darkling who watched the perimeter, careful not to come any closer. Carien's heart ached for the pain her friend had been put through this last half year. She knew Darkling's half-sister's death still bothered her friend. Maybe talking about it would ease her mind. More than Carien had been able to ease her friend's heart by saving Ceerie's babe.

She nodded almost imperceptible and then whispered to zHavier. "Meet here later tonight, make sure no one follows you or sees you."

Then she stepped past him and walked briskly back towards Darkling. They had already been gone far to long from the court room. Tongues would wag. Hopefully the gossip of the Tripsian princess and Naankdoen prince was more valuable than the prince addressing a white lioness.

Darkling fell behind Carien and the babe and followed without a word. Even as they settled back in the room, Carien could still feel the eyes pointed towards her guard.

They would have to be careful tonight. Her eyes caught with the prince's as he re-entered the room, this time staying to the edges near the courtiers.

Soon enough the sun began to set, and the courtiers dispersed to prepare for the evening meal and festivities. Carien took Mina and began walking the way back to her rooms. But instead she took a turn early and doubled back to the courtyard, making sure no one saw her.

Ashta didn't say anything to her friend, but she knew she was being led to a confrontation she did not want. She had hoped that she would never see the prince again.

To soon they stood before the labyrinth. Moments after, zHavier appeared out of the evening mist.

The princess nodded, gesturing for them both to follow her into the brush. One of the few remaining ancient brush from Tripsia's time as a luscious rainforest. This specific type could be only found in the palaces many courtyards.

As they walked deeper in, the warmth from the sun was leeched out of the air, leaving the three cold. The shadows grew higher until the brush had grown to trees above them, intertwining their branches and leaving the three in the dark.

Sound was leeched into the bushes, leaving Ashta in an eerie silence. She had never felt so unsettled. Not even in the presence of the ageless tattoo artist.

"I will leave you two here to speak," Carien's voice broke through the silence, crisp and close.

"Your highness!" Ashta whisper yelled but was only met with silence. She did not know if the princess had left them or only stood silent.

"She's gone."

Ashta jumped at the hot breath on her neck. She whipped around, crushing his windpipe in her hands as she pulled a dagger and jerked it close to his side.

"Don't move or I *will* kill you."

His throat vibrated as his hands came and scratched at her grip. She loosened enough for him to breath but did on let go. Better to be in the arms of the enemy than caught unaware.

"I know you set this up. Now talk." She was terse, her hackles up with unnatural silence that surrounded them.

"I've missed you." His low voice rumbled across her skin and for a moment Ashta ached for something more.

But she shook herself and pushed the dagger blade a little further in. His gasp let her know that it had slid a little too cleanly in.

"Clearly you don't understand the situation." She twisted the blade slightly, satisfied from his grunt. "You are nothing to me. And you never will be for what you did to Lily."

"She tried to kill the-"

"She was my sister!" Ashta yelled. Her voice was swallowed up by the trees, leaving silence only silence behind.

"Half." He whispered.

Ashta ignored her burning eyes. "She was *still* my sister."

Her heavy breathing was unbearably loud in the small space, but Ashta couldn't control. She was lost in her memories. The emotions. And she couldn't claw her way out.

Instead she asked the question that had burned itself behind her eyes as she had watched him pull the drawstring back. "Why?"

She waited, her heart beating in her throat as the taste of salt on her lips distracted her.

Ashta felt his pulse, quick and strong, in his throat. It stuttered before picking up even faster.

"I had to. You know that," he begged. His whisper cracked and hissed in the air.

Ashta shook her head, denying her own part in it.

"No." Her voice broke and her breathing came out even harsher.

His hands wrapped around her wrist that held his throat. zHav's thumb gently stroked the skin. Her body craved that small bit of warmth. She wanted to fall into it. To quit seeing the blood on the cobbled streets.

Every moment she was awake, she was haunted by her decisions, and her hand in the deaths of those close to her. Her mother. Her grandfather. Lily.

Ceerie.

It was all too much.

She pulled her hands back and pulled up her knee hard, thankful when she heard his gasp of pain as his voice fell to the ground.

Ashta kneeled down to where she heard him cursing on the ground. Then she whispered, "We all have a choice."

And then she stood and walked back, her left hand along the edge. Her fingers touched and caressed the brush as she walked alone through the labyrinth out into the light.

Carien waited for her at the entrance. And in her arms, Mina giggled, her familiar green-eyes bright with life.

Without a word, Carien pulled Ashta into her arms, squishing the babe between them. And that was all Ashta could handle for those long moments as the last of the sun's rays stretched out from the horizon.

Her back stiffened at the familiar voice.

"I made the wrong choice. But I am here now. And I won't leave your side."

Ashta ignored zHav's words, pulling Carien into one last tight squeeze. Then her arms loosened and fell to her side.

Carien glanced back at zHavier's face, shivering at the cold depths of his gaze. Instead she turned and led her friend away from the prince.

Had she done the right thing? The princess asked herself this the whole way back to her rooms.

As she glanced at Darkling's paler than normal face, she wasn't so sure anymore.

CHAPTER TWENTY-SEVEN

⌘

Cloak of Night

ASHTA PACED THE floor in her small room. She had taken the glow wein over an hour ago. It was long past bedtime. And yet she couldn't sleep. Her skin crawled with tension and something else she couldn't name.

After the twentieth pass of the room, she sighed. There was no point trying to sleep. Even as she contemplated the cot, she knew her body wouldn't let her sleep.

Instead, she pushed the door back into Carien's room.

The silk curtains were drawn. Ashta hesitated. Maybe she shouldn't wake her friend. She walked over to the tiny crib that stood within reach of the princess's bed.

Looking in, Ashta couldn't help but smile. She caressed the babe's cheek, amazed at how impossibly soft it was. Her gut flipped as she wondered, how could she never want this?

But she had decided once and for all after leaving Naankdoen that motherhood was not in the future for her. Besides, there were other options for her. She had considered becoming one of the trainers for the cubs. Then she would be mothering many children that needed her.

"You can pick her up. She's a deep sleeper."

Ashta jumped, not having seen Carien pull the drape back.

"I'm sorry your highness, I thought you were asleep."

She rubbed at her eyes before standing. "I was. But ever since Mina, I've become quite the light sleeper." Carien smiled down at the babe dreamily. She slid a finger across the babe's small brows.

"Amazing isn't it?" she asked, still watching the perfectly formed little miracle.

"Yes," Ashta breathed out, in awe of the love she saw between the princess and the babe. She had assumed before that Carien had taken the babe in to try to appease her guilt with having failed Ashta. But now, Ashta wasn't so sure. The princess really did love Mina as her own.

"But that's not why you are here," Carien whispered.

In the night, the princess was almost unrecognizable with her hair down in a braid, uncovered.

Ashta shook her head in response to Carien. She took a step away from the crib, and the princess, settling herself into a resting stance. Ashta hesitated to say anything, but this was Carien, her friend, her chosen sister. Taking a deep breath, she let her angst out.

"I can't sleep. I…I was wondering if you wanted to walk the halls with me for a little while."

"Of course," Carien replied, pulling Ashta into a hard embrace. "Give me a moment to grab a cover."

Ashta walked out the room and waited for Carien by the fire. When her friend returned, a large silk cover tied around her middle, her long braid hanging past her hips, Ashta lead the way out.

At first, they stuck to the upper halls. But it only set Ashta's skin a blazing. She started to wind their way down into the bowels of the palace. Where the cubs trained, and the lions were held. Carien stayed quiet, only the swish of her silk robe making any noise as they traversed through the many halls. The deeper they went, the less soldiers they saw in front of doors.

Until finally there were none.

Just torches blazing on the wall, and the damp musk of cave and water filled the air.

"I remember the first time I came down here." Carien's words jarred at Ashta, pulling her mind back into her body. She slowed down her pace and walked beside the princess, giving her time to continue.

"I used to sneak down here early in the morning to get away from the court, and the maids and Ennris for a few hours." The princess's hand reached out to the wall, gliding across its rough rock surface. "At first I would hide in the doorways and watch the ripped-up bodies be pulled past. None of the girls ever moved. Some had their throats ripped open, others had their stomachs slashed. But always dead."

Her eyes watched into the past, seeing the bodies pass before her once more.

Ashta didn't know what to say.

She had known that not every girl survived the trial. But knowing and hearing about it were two completely different truths. One was impossible to ignore.

"One time, the girl that passed was alive, her arms ripped apart from the lion's claws. But her eyes were wide. I stopped that guard, not thinking, and told her to let me look at the body. I don't know what the lioness's name was, but I remember her laughing at me."

Carien chuckled humorously, before continuing in a deeper voice, "*Even if the girl heals, she will be too scarred to be of any use. Better to let her die from bleeding than for the king to have her executed.*

I couldn't believe her. And I pushed her back, standing tall for the first time since arriving to the palace. I wrapped up the girl's arms. Gave her some Ruutka."

She stopped at the edge of the torch light, her eyes staring unseeingly down at her hands.

Ashta stepped before her friend, trying to get her to look up. She gently prompted, "What happened to the girl?"

Carien looked up, her eyes hollow from doubt and the weight of so many lives. "I don't know," her voice broke halfway but she stared straight up at Ashta, her gaze unwavering even as the tears swam in her eyes.

Ashta opened her mouth to say something but glanced past Carien's shoulder.

And stared straight into a pale, scarred face, hair wet and plastered to the sides.

She didn't think.

She just reacted.

Ashta's hand reached into her hair and threw the blade into the man's throat.

He choked, falling back. His dagger falling from his hand and clattering onto the stone floor.

Carien began to turn but Ashta pulled the princess behind her.

"RUN!"

Carien did, not glancing back. Ashta followed behind.

To soon, the clatter of feet followed them.

Gods. There was more than one assassin.

Ashta rushed Carien to the nearest doorway, and was met face to face with the cubs entrance. The great sword gleamed above the archway. She stared up at it for a moment, hesitating as power thrummed from its eerie jewel at the hilt.

"ySsaa Esk!" Ashta shuddered at the familiar words from her homeland.

They were closing in.

She could discern at least four sets of feet. Anymore and she knew she would not be able to protect the princess. Staring straight into Carien's eyes, she whispered, "Hide behind the entrance. When I tell you to run, go straight down the hall then turn into the left hall where the cubs are."

Ashta didn't wait to see if Carien listened, she reached up and ripped the great sword from the wall. It creaked before falling into her grip. She was caught off guard by the weight and barely caught it from cracking against the floor.

She was just able to hold it up as the first assassin rounded the corner.

Swinging, Ashta felt the strange tingle of the something else racing up her arms and into her chest.

The first man fell to the ground his middle cleaved in half.

Ashta pulled back and readied the great sword.

The next two men ran into the torch light.

She swung and parried, moving faster than she ever had before. It felt like she wasn't even controlling her body. Like someone else had joined her inside and taken her limbs.

But she didn't have time to think or analyze.

Instead, she just felt.

And when the tingles reached her mind she didn't hesitate to open up. Fighting for her life, Ashta knew at an instinctual level that now was not the time to pause.

Now was the time to trust. Completely. Wholly.

And so, when her limbs reacted to thoughts that weren't hers, she went with it.

The bodies littered the hall as more men came running at her. They didn't stand a chance.

She swung down, cleanly slicing the head off one man.

As the next came at her, she pushed off the handle, her feet bouncing off the ceiling as she took the momentum around and landed behind the last man. With a flick of her wrist in midair, she sliced his throat open.

Her feet faltered on the blood-soaked floor, breaking her grip on the sword.

It skittered into the darkness.

Leaving Ashta frozen with shock, like cold water rushed through her veins. Suddenly her mind felt too big for one person's thoughts, her body to large.

Ashta blinked once before falling face first into the stone floor.

"Darkling?" The whisper reached into Ashta's darkened mind and pulled her close.

She blinked her eyes and found herself staring up at a stone ceiling, red footprints dripping down onto her.

"Wha…"

"Don't try to talk. Just take a moment to breathe."

Ashta blinked hard again, sitting up. Her legs were numb, her hands shook. She forced them to rub her eyes and immediately regretted the motion as something slick mashed into her skin and the taste of metal and something else filled her nose.

She groaned, the vibrations rumbling through her bones as she forced herself to stand on wobbly legs. Never had her body felt so beat up from a fight. Never had she felt so drained.

"Here, you dropped this." Carien held out the bloodied great sword to Ashta, its tip gleaming even as blood dripped of the edges.

Ashta shuddered, taking the sword in one hand. This time her body was ready for the weight. The blade was as familiar to her hand as a fingernail.

Gripping Carien's arm, Ashta checked the princess out. No wounds. But she had to make sure. "Are you-"

"I'm fine. I only came out when it was silent."

Before Ashta could say anything, she heard a scrabble from down the hall. She pulled the princess behind her as she quickly ran down the hall towards the sound. They reached the bend, where the side opened up into great holes to look out at the open sea.

The full moon bathed the stones in cold light as the torches fought to light the rest up.

Just as they reached the edge, a hand flew over the holes edge, and a head popped up.

Without thought Ashta reached into her hair and threw a blade at the man before his mouth could fall open in surprise.

She ran to the hole and looked down the length of the cliff, surprised to see several dark shapes clinging to the cliff.

Wordlessly, she handed the great sword to Carien.

Ashta pulled the rest of her daggers out and carefully picked off each of the shadows. Their screams of terror and splash of their falls filled Ashta with satisfaction. Nice try, father, she thought as she grabbed the great sword back from Carien.

"We need to warn the King of the breach."

Carien nodded and followed close behind Ashta, as they back tracked to the cubs' entrance. They ran straight into Ryce, Ashta's old training master.

"Assassins on the far hall that open to the cliffs."

The other woman swore, turning back to the arms room.

"Stay on the hall until we send a messenger!" Ashta yelled at Ryce, as she pulled Carien to the three forked hall. Without asking, she pulled Carien up the steps to the fourth hall entrance above.

"Don't let go," Ashta breathed out as she sped up the winding staircase, her lungs burning, her legs aching.

She didn't have time to think about how different using this hall was to the last time. All she could focus on was the dead assassins' bodies that littered the cubs' entrance. It had been to close. They should have known. Been more prepared. Something.

The darkness pressed down on the two as they ran towards chaos.

CHAPTER TWENTY-EIGHT

⌘

Bbrski is Here

AT THE SIGHT of the princess, the soldiers guarding the council room pulled apart. Ashta hustled the princess past and straight into pandemonium. Councilmen were shouting and standing. Several were missing. Carien pushed through until she stood beside her father. He glanced down at her, some of the tension around his eyes relaxing.

"Good. You are here."

He turned to the room, arms flying and tempers hot. "Quiet!"

No one paid him any attention. Carien went to step forward but stopped as a loud boom filled the room. Everyone froze.

Carien looked over and saw Darkling pull the pommel of the great sword out of the wall. Darkling nodded, before stepping back, the great sword pointed down as she rested her arms on the pommel.

How had the sword made that-? The princess shook her head and focused instead on the now quiet room.

"Everyone take there seats. Now," Carien called out, her soft voice awakening the men as they shook their heads and took a seat. The king did as well. Carien was the last to sit. She turned to her father to begin.

As she did, she noted General Hariim was missing. Ttaabit shook his head tersely at the princesses questioning gaze.

"I have called on you all at this late hour for a-" The King began, when his daughter cut him off.

"Father can I speak first."

He turned to her with an icy glare, but she did not back down. After a tense moment between the two, he finally relented, leaning back in his seat.

Carien stood, and stared each councilman and general in the eye, ending on Darkling. With a deep breath she recounted the attack. "My guard and I were walking the halls as I could not sleep," Darkling shared a look with her. Carien grimaced. She didn't want to lie, but her father didn't need more reasons to distrust her guard. "We were attacked by six men-"

"Eight," Darkling corrected. Her gaze never straying from the far wall.

Carien nodded and continued, "Eight men. My guard was able to dispatch all of the men. We then discovered more men grappling up the cliff side and entering the palace from the sea views along the old halls of the original palace."

The councilmen all gasped. Fear showed through the whites of their eyes as many unconsciously patted their hair and bodies down.

Carien didn't dare look at her father. She continued, keeping her gaze Ttaabit.

"Ashta the Lion Tamer was able to dispatch all the men we saw. But I do not know if there are more coming, or how many are already roaming the halls. We must be careful of these soldiers."

She sat down and waited for her father to comment.

King Roman sat still for a long moment, rubbing his chin. This changed everything. He turned to general Ttaabit. "We will graduate the cubs immediately."

"No!" Carien shouted, jumping to her feet again.

The other men stayed quiet, shocked at the princesses vehement response.

The king raised his brow as he stared up at his only daughter. Her cheeks were red, and a fire burned behind her eyes. In that moment, she looked exactly like her mother. And he had almost lost her tonight, he thought, fear gripping his stomach.

"They are just children. They do not have the skills to take on an assassin let alone a soldier," Carien spat, leaning closer to her father. Trying to plead with him to reconsider.

He turned to his personal white lionesses, and asked them in a quiet and deadly voice, "What do you think of the skill level of the cubs?"

The two women exchanged glances before the taller one stepped forward. She kept her eyes down as she responded in an even tone. "The cubs are at different skill levels. Half of them would be more than capable to take on assassins. As for the young ones, what they lack in skill they make up in heart. Every child survived the test. And they will follow the king's orders to their death without question. Gladly."

Ashta glared at the woman as a smug expression crossed the king's face. He looked over at his daughter with almost glee.

"You are just throwing them straight to their deaths," Carien accused, her eyes blazing as a stray hair fell over her shoulder.

Ashta agreed with the princess. The cubs wouldn't stand a chance against battle hardened soldiers. The younger ones didn't have the necessary fighting skills or training with weapons. They would be nothing more than bodies to slow down the oncoming war.

It wasn't fair.

"What is the purpose of slaves that dedicate their bodies to our kingdom, if we don't use them in times of war. Do you want to throw away our young Tripsian boys instead? Is it fair to *them*?"

Carien grinded her teeth. There was nothing she could say against his argument. Neither slave or boy soldier should have to be thrown into a battle they weren't prepared for. But her heart ached more for the children that had just barely survived the lion pits. To now be thrown to soon at the Bbrskian army? It was inhumane.

"Soldier!" The king shouted. One of the guards from the door came inside and bent to the knee.

"Your majesty."

"Send a message to the Lioness Ryce to prepare all White Lionesses for war. Including the cubs. They should be on standby for the next message which will be more detailed."

The soldier nodded before turning and running out of the room as if his life depended on it.

In some ways it did, Ashta thought grimly. All their lives may depend on it.

Before the king could start on the next part of the emergency meeting, he was interrupted. Everyone turned again to a different soldier coming in. This one had blood splattered on his armor and his nose was bleeding.

He fell to his knees. "I have a message for his majesty, King Roman."

"Go on."

The soldier stood up and swallowed. Ashta watched as he tried to wrestle his breathing to slow down. Her spine tingled as she watched his shaking hands.

"General Hariim was found dead in his chambers. Throat slit."

The kings face tightened as his fist came down hard on the table. Several councilmen jumped in their seat.

"Damn it!"

The soldier paled but waited to be dismissed.

The king ignored him and turned to general Ttaabit. "Prepare the army now. I want men walking on all the ramparts. A continuous watch will be set up from now until further notice."

The general nodded grimly.

In fact, as Ashta glanced around the room, the table was filled with grim faces. Only Carien's held a hint of sympathy.

The King turned back to the soldier. "Let the soldiers stationed above in the outer courtyard of the palace know and return to your station."

With a hand, he dismissed the soldier.

All at once the councilmen spoke up, shouting at the king and each other. King Roman stood up and this time the room quieted at his stance.

He glared down at all the men. "You are all dismissed until further notice."

The reason for the meeting was no longer important right now. First, he needed to wrestle back control of the palace and the oncoming battle. He turned and walked out of the room, his guards close at his heels.

The room stood still for a moment before pandemonium let loose once more. Councilmen were scrambling over each other to get out the door and back to their rooms and their own guards.

Ashta pushed through the crowd easily until she stood by the princess. Carien looked down at the great sword with a lifted brow.

Ashta sighed. "I meant to put it back, but I don't think now is a good time."

Carien nodded. "I would feel better if you carried it with you always."

Taking the princesses arm, Ashta lead the way out of the room and down the noisy stone halls. "It's too large and bulky to carry around always. It would only get in the way. Even for you, princess, it is too great a hinder. Besides," Ashta added with a wink, "I have more than enough daggers hidden on my body to make up for it."

Carien stayed quiet, watching her friend stroke the pommel unwittingly. Even if it was bulky, she couldn't help but remember Darkling fighting the assassins with it. It had been an extension of her arm, more than just a great sword. But she knew her friend didn't want to hear it.

It did however leave Carien with many questions. How had she never seen or heard talk of such a well-crafted weapon. Not even her history books mentioned it. Before she could ask Darkling one of the many questions floating in her head, they were interrupted by a familiar voice.

"Your highness, are you all right!" Prince zHavier came to a stop before the pair, his hair disheveled and a cut glistening with blood across his chest. His silk pants were barely tied up. He held a short sword lightly in his right hand, even as he leaned over on his knees trying to catch his breath.

"The princess is safe, though it is none of your concern." Darkling replied coldly, straightening up and loosening her hold on the great sword.

At this, zHav straightened up, finally looking at both of the women. His eyes caught on the massive sword Ashta held in one hand. Impossible, he though, it looked far to heavy and long to be held so easily in one hand.

"Nice sword," he commented, quirking his brow up. "Where were you hiding that?"

Ashta blushed, remembering that the prince knew very well the various hiding places the lionesses had on their body for their many weapons. "On a wall. I happened to grab it."

Both his eyebrows raised in surprise and curiosity but Ashta stayed quiet. Instead she turned to the princess.

Carien watched the entire exchange, feeling an uneasy prickling on her skin. Something more was going on between them. Shaking her head, she caught zHavier's eyes and relayed the message. "You and your men should stay in your rooms until further notice. The palace is under attack."

"I would gladly, except for the part that some of my men are dead or injured and there are several bodies littering my rooms."

Carien grimaced. She had not really thought about how widespread the assassins attack had been on the palace. Who else was hurt, she wondered?

"Take the injured down in to the infirmary. Just ask a soldier or servant and they will point you in the right direction. As for rooms, there are several unused ones surrounding the nursery. None of which have sea windows. Take your pick."

"Than-"

"Until the morrow, prince," She cut him off, before adding, "if you're still alive then."

His mouth fell open as he stared at Ashta, who didn't regret her harsh words. Instead, she grabbed the princess's arm and pulled her passed the prince and down the hall.

There were no more unexpected stops as they reached the princess's rooms. The guards stood in front of the doors, unhurt and unbloodied. Ashta breathed in a sigh of relief seeing them. They pushed passed the guard and into the sitting room.

Inside stood Brinley rocking Mina by the fire. Ashta let go of the breath she hadn't realized she was even holding.

The princess took a seat beside Brinley. Ashta went into the bedroom and checked that no assassins were climbing the cliffside below them.

And so went the rest of her morning, shifting between the sitting room and watching the entry to checking the window. The princess and nursemaid never left the settee in the sitting room while Ashta paced between her stations.

The night was still, broken occasionally by screams.

As the sun rose above the horizon, a soldier, face sweat-soaked and hands bloody, ran into the room.

"Your highness," he said between gasps for air. "The city is under attack-"

The room suddenly shook as a loud thud reverberated through the walls. Cracks formed along the ceiling as everyone turned to one another, wide eyed.

What was that, Ashta wondered? Her heartbeat picked up speed as another thud reverberated through the room, this time followed by screams of death and pain.

CHAPTER TWENTY-NINE

⌘

Lit With Death

CARIEN SCRAMBLED off of the settee and ran straight for her room. Ashta followed right behind, the back of her neck tingling. At the princess's gasp, Ashta moved beside her and looked out the window as well.

There, below, suddenly, sat more than two hundred ships. At first, Ashta didn't understand what looked wrong about them.

Then one of the ships shook, the trebuchet releasing the large boulder straight into the cliff side to the right of their window. The room shook but this time no screams followed.

Realizing that all two hundred ships were equipped with trebuchets, Ashta fell to her knees.

What could they do against such an attack?

They could move the people further inside the cliff but that would leave the front of the palace facing the ocean completely open to more assassins.

Even as Ashta began to grasp the full extent of the navy below, she watched in horror as the ship that had unloaded the last stone rowed out of formation. It moved towards the far side of the cliff. Before it reached the edge, another ship came into view from behind the cliff.

How many ships were there, she now wondered? How many were just out of sight, waiting to take their place in the armada in front of her. She watched four more boulders launch.

Ashta turned to shout to the others in the sitting room "Move into the hall!"

Then Ashta was shook by the blast of the boulder that smashed through the wall into her former room. Stone sprayed them, smacking into Ashta's temple.

She fell to the ground, her eyes on the princess who huddled down behind the window.

Her ears rang. What…

The dust settled around them and Ashta found herself looking out at the ocean where a wall and the princess's bed had once stood. But how…

Shaking herself, Ashta crawled to the princess. "We need to inform the king. Everyone needs to be sent further into the palace."

Carien didn't look up, her head still between her knees.

Ashta blew out a frustrated breath as she kneeled before her friend and shook her. "Carien!"

Finally, warm caramel eyes looked up into hers.

"We need to move."

She nodded her head, still dazed.

"Now!" Ashta yelled, turning back to the entry to the sitting room. Once she stumbled to her feet, she ran out to the entry. No sight of Brinley, Mina or the soldiers.

Hopefully, they had made it further into the palace.

Ashta turned back to Carien, who had just stumbled to the entry. Her hair was an open curling mass, falling down to the her hips. Ashta frowned, wishing they could somehow put it back. But there was no time.

Another thud shook the walls, this time stone falling through the cracks above them.

"Come on!" Ashta yelled, gripping Carien's forearm and dragging her down the halls.

She didn't slow, even as Carien tripped and fumbled with her skirts. No time. They needed to get further from the cliff face.

If Ashta remembered the setup of the old palace, she knew the nursery and the lion pits were farthest from the cliff face. Then came the cubs eating room, which stood just below the kings court room.

Mind made up, Ashta ran towards the courtroom, sure that the rest of the nobles and lionesses would be there.

As they ran another thud shook through the hall, tripping Ashta as she fell on her palms, the great sword bouncing further down the hall. "Umpf!"

Glancing back, she was glad to see the princess had just fell on her butt.

Screams from up ahead distracted her from asking about the princess. They both turned ahead.

"Hurry, Princess," Ashta hissed, forcing herself up, grabbing for the great sword as she ran ahead. The princess followed close behind. The screams and shouting grew as they turned around a bend and were met by a wall of people and chaos.

Children were running around, blood dripping down foreheads. A man walked by missing an arm. A woman knelt over an unrecognizable body, screaming. And all around were people. Servants. Lionesses. Courtiers. Nobles. Soldiers.

Ashta panicked, not seeing a clear path through.

Instead, Carien pushed past and knelt beside the nearest person. A servant holding their arm.

"Let me see," She asked in a gentle voice, prodding the arm which was clearly broken.

"Darkling, knife." She barked, hand out.

Ashta followed the order without question, watching in shock as Carien cut a long strip of cloth from her skirt and made a sling for the woman.

"Thank you, your highness."

Carien smiled, clasping the women's arm for a moment before turning to the next person.

Ashta didn't rush her.

From what she could remember, this hall was far enough from the cliff face that they should be safe from boulders. As for collapsing ceilings, well only the nursery was deep enough to not be troubled by the trembles.

Staying close to the princess, Ashta kept an eye on the crowd. Slowly people began moving, it seemed further down towards the court room. Good. With a little time, hopefully, she and the princess would make it there as well.

Stopping in front the nearest soldier, she pulled the man close. His eyes widened in fear, but he didn't dare pull back. "I need you to give a message to the king, the princess is safe and secure. Do it. Now."

The man nodded, weaving through the crowd before disappearing amongst the mass of people.

Hopefully the King's chambers were not hit by one of the flying boulders.

Not giving herself a chance to worry, Ashta focused back on the princess and the people around them. That's when she noticed a familiar uneven gaze watching her from across the hall.

zHavier leaned against the wall, Trom standing before him, dressed and armed. It seemed the prince had found a bandage for his cut, and a shirt sometime for his bare chest, in the night.

She hoped his injured men had stayed near the nursery.

He pushed off the wall and started to push his way through the people, his gaze never wavering. Ashta shivered, still unnerved by how her body reacted to him.

Suddenly, Ashta was pulled down, staring straight into Carien's eyes. "Mina," she whispered, panic lacing through her voice.

Ashta shook her head, "We must assume that Brinley and Mina are safe in-"

Carien shook her, stopping the words, her eyes widened even further. She stood up on shaky legs, the realization that Mina was not nearby finally hitting her. "No. I need to see her. Have her in my arms. What if Brinley is pinned under a rock? Or more assassins have breached the palace?"

Ashta stopped her, pulling the princess's hands into her own. "The Bbrskian King would not risk his soldiers while he is still bombarding the wall. We are safe from the assassins for now." At least she hoped her father would not do that. It made far more sense to send the assassins in first. And maybe again after they ships were empty of projectiles.

"But Mina-"

"I will bring her to you." Ashta promised. She swallowed hard as her tongue stuck. She shouldn't have said that. Her priority was the princess.

As she watched the princess's shoulders relax, she argued with herself. Carien was more than likely to run down the halls herself searching for Mina. It was better that Ashta went alone, in case any halls collapsed.

Ashta stood and walked straight into a wall.

A hot, well defined wall.

Reaching up, she pushed off the very male chest and found herself staring straight into prince zHavier's lavender gaze.

In that hectic moment, time stood still as she stared into his eyes. Here heart gave a big thud and a shiver ran up her arms. Her hands tingled from where they rested against his expansive chest.

"Your highness," Trom called down to the princess.

The moment broken, Ashta pushed off his chest and took several steps back. She glanced around the room, avoiding the prince's gaze. But she didn't see lionesses or soldiers in the mass of civilians surrounding them. They must have cleared out of the hall and moved further in.

Frowning, Ashta forced herself to look up into zHav's eyes again.

"Watch the princess," she ordered, her voice terse and filled with power. She didn't trust him with her own heart. But

Ashta knew she could trust him with Carien's life. He needed the princess support. He needed her alive.

She turned to leave but was stopped by his hand. His touch zapped her, shocking her enough to rip her arm away from him.

"Where are you going," he asked, not allowing her to move past him.

"It's none of your business."

"If I am watching your princess for you, I think it very much makes it my business." He crossed his arms and stood before her like an impenetrable wall.

Ashta let out a frustrated sigh. The walls shook again, starting up screams from further up the hall. Shaking her head, she glared at zHavier. "I am retrieving the princess's babe. Then I am moving Carien and the babe further into the palace, where it is safer. In the meantime, I need you to watch over her. There are to many unfamiliar people here."

Slowly he nodded, letting his hands fall to his side.

Ashta turned without another word and jogged back down the hall they had run from. Passing the princess's room, she ran further until she could make out a baby's whimper. She smashed into an unknown room, likely the old queen's rooms, and was met by two swords.

Halting instantly, she looked up at the soldiers. They dropped their swords the moment they recognized her. Behind them sat Brinley, Mina settled in her arms.

Ashta knelt before Brinley reaching out for Mina. The other woman released the babe instantly, her body shaking in fear.

Cooing down at Mina's perfect little face, Ashta rocked the babe until she lay silently in her arms. She looked at Brinley.

"You did well." The woman barely nodded, not really seeing Ashta.

Pushing to her feet, Ashta held Mina in one arm and the great sword in the other. She turned to the soldiers. "Take this woman to the infirmary and stay stationed at its entrance. When the boulders quit coming, the soldiers will be crawling up that cliff and hacking at everyone. I need you to keep the injured and the women safe. Understood?"

Both of the men nodded. The one passed her and helped Brinley to her feet.

"What about you, lioness?" The second man asked.

"I will be with the princess."

And with that she left the room, jogging back to where she had left Carien and the prince. She was careful not to jostle Mina too much. For the most part the babe stayed quiet, only a small whimper leaving her tiny body. Yet each one squeezed at Ashta's heart.

Ashta would make her father pay for this. She wasn't sure how. Or when. But one day, he would stand before her and face all the crimes he had committed.

Up ahead, the murmur of the crowd got louder.

CHAPTER THIRTY

⌘

Unlikely Ally

ASHTA SCANNED THE crowd, much larger than it had been when she had gone in search of Mina and the nursemaid. She saw the princess's caramel hair halfway down the hall.

"Move!" She shouted, pushing the crowd aside.

Most watched the edge of the great sword wearily. Slowly, the hall quieted until Ashta stood before the princess. Silence laid like a damp blanket as onlookers watched the lioness, the princess and the prince with interest.

"Mina," Carien breathed, pushing up from where she had just finished wrapping a bandage around a child's head. She pulled Mina into her arms and breathed in her unique scent. Her heart calmed, now that her babe was in her arms. Panic's fingers loosened until they no longer held her mind in shock.

"Thank you," She breathed out, knowing her friend would have heard her.

"We need to move to the court room now. It's safe there."

Carien went to argue, seeing all the people around her that needed her. But Ashta stopped her, leaning close until her breath warmed Carien's lips. "You are no use to your people if you are dead. We move to safety. Now."

As Ashta pulled back she threw out, "You can help those in need in the courtroom."

Carien nodded slowly, her heart pulling her one way. But she knew she had to follow Darkling. For Mina's sake.

"Are you coming with us?" Carien asked looking up at zHav, who had not left her side since Darkling disappeared.

He nodded briskly, his eyes never leaving Darkling.

Something burned low in Carien's belly, and it felt to much like fear. Jealousy. The prince should be watching *her* not Darkling with lust filled eyes.

Carien tried to push the emotion deep down, knowing this was not the place.

"Let's hurry then."

Ashta led the way, the sword parting through the rest of the crowd as everyone watched the blade with awe and suspicion. For a moment Carien wondered if any of them knew what the sword was. It's history.

But Ashta never slowed.

And zHavier pushed her on from behind.

They walked into the court room, even louder than the hall, as the ceiling magnified the noise. Everywhere Carien looked were her people, some injured, some not. Many huddled in groups.

"Take Mina," Carien held out the babe. Ashta cradled her against her chest, following the princess as she knelt before the first injured person. Before Carien could say anything to the frightened girl holding her limp arm, another thud reverberated through the hall.

It's not possible, Ashta thought, they were too far inside the cliff face for the trebuchets to make a difference.

Carien stood and made her way to the front of the court room; Ashta, zHavier, and Trom close behind. The big doors smashed open before they reached the front. There, a harried soldier came running in, an arrow sticking out of his shoulder.

Ashta tightened her hold on Mina unconsciously, until the babe cried out. Loosening her grip, she leaned down and kissed the babe. That sixth sense inside of her quivered. Something very bad had happened. Somehow worse than the ships attacking the cliff face.

The man was about to run by the prince.

Ashta held out her great sword, flat side towards him. He stopped dead in his track. His eyes widened as he took in the disheveled appearance of the princess before dropping to his knees.

"Your highness."

"What news do you bring, soldier."

He shuddered as another thud trembled through the cavern, this one lighter than the last.

"The army is at the walls."

Not understanding what he said, Ashta held the edge of the blade against the man's neck. She watched his Adam's apple bob as he tried to swallow.

"Darkling," Carien whispered tersely, but Ashta did not pull the blade away.

The man stuttered before continuing.

"T-the Bbrskian army is inside the ruined city. Entire legions. And they have brought trebuchets and rams with them. Our walls won't hold them back for long. We don't have enough men," He begged, desperate as the fear poured off of him in waves.

Ashta moved the blade tip to his chin and gently lifted it. He stared straight into her eyes.

"It is not the count of men that matter but the men that count." Her words, though quiet, rang through the space.

He slowly nodded his eyes still wide as he shivered.

Carien stepped forward and gently pushed Darkling's hand until the sword hung limply towards the ground. She looked at the soldier and gave him a quick nod. "Leave and send your message to the King."

He nodded before scrambling back out of Darkling's reach. Once he had disappeared down the halls and into the depths of the palace Darkling turned to Carien.

"You are no longer safe here, princess. We must move you."

"There is nowhere safe in the palace Darkling," Carien despaired, her arms shaking.

The prince stepped closer and rubbed her arms. His touch soothed her.

Ashta glared at where his hands touched the princess. It was completely inappropriate. But no one in the court room paid them any attention. Shaking her head, Ashta focused on the real problem, how to keep the princess safe.

"I have an idea," Ashta whispered, not looking at either of them. "But Trom stays here."

zHavier glared down at Ashta. When her expression didn't change, he gave in and nodded to Trom.

Let me know what's happening up here.

Yes, your highness.

Without another moment of hesitation, Ashta back tracked out of the room and slightly down the hall before turning off. Carien and zHavier followed close behind.

Finally she stopped before a door. Nothing special about it.

She turned and made sure both the prince and princess listened. "Stay close to me, keep a hand on my shoulder. The room is laid with traps."

Carien shuddered, her mind conjuring up the hazy memory of running around and around in a staircase. It had all been dark and she had never let go of Ashta's hand.

Carien nodded, reaching out an gripping Darkling's shoulder. The prince hesitated before grasping Carien's shoulder.

They entered the secret hall that connected the palace with the cubs training room. She passed through the dark room until she made it to the top of the staircase. She turned, knowing neither of them could see her.

"Sit down and don't move until I come back for you."

She placed Mina back into Carien's arms. The babe sighed, otherwise making no noise.

"Where are you going?"

Ashta hesitated, her mind whirling on the soldier's words. The Bbrskian army was in the ruined city. It wouldn't take them long to find the pits. And then the palace would be split in three. If all the Tripsian armies had to worry about was the cliff face and the wall surrounding the palace then it wouldn't be so bad.

But Ashta didn't want to worry the princess.

She told the princess only part of the truth. "To find the King and make sure he is aware of the danger."

When Carien said nothing back, Ashta took it as assent. She walked past them and hurried to the door. She couldn't think about leaving the prince and princess together. It was a risk she had already taken once, and would have to take again.

Besides, she knew zHav was a trained a warrior, if the arrow shot that ended her half-sisters life was any indication of his skill.

Pushing everything in the past, Ashta focused on running through the halls. The king's chambers were empty, as was the library. With doubt clouding her judgment, she decided to run for the council room.

But he wouldn't go back there after early this morning, she reasoned with herself. Would he?

Her question was answered when she saw the two soldiers stationed before the entrance.

At first, the soldiers blocked the way with their spears. Ashta sliced through the wooden spears easily with the great sword before glaring at the men. "I am here to deliver a message to the king."

Doubt still filled their eyes, but they both carefully stepped aside and watched her pass warily.

Once inside she was hit by the cacophony from the few councilmen present with the King. This time no general sat present. Just a soldier standing to the side.

A messenger, Ashta realized.

Ashta stood still, not sure what to do. She didn't have the princess to hide behind this time. Before she was able to move, the decision was made for her.

Across the length of the table the King caught sight of her and leaned over the table. "Where is the princess!" He yelled.

Everyone stopped, staring at the king and his impassioned yell.

Ashta took a deep breath before stepping forward. "In a secure place, safe, your majesty."

"Liar! If she was safe you would be standing beside her."

"I had to leave her because of the lion pits."

Confusion rode his face as his brows came down over his eyes.

"Lion pits?" One of the councilmen at the front echoed.

Ashta nodded once, quickly, before continuing. "The palace right now has three entrance points as it stands. From above through the ruined city. From the ocean through the cliff face. Or, from below. The lion pits sit at the edge of the ruined city, but beneath each are rough halls that connect them back to the palace through the cubs training space."

No one moved, taking in what she had said. Then she laid down the last tile as she spoke one last time. "We cannot win a three-front battle, we would be spread too thin. That means we need to make sure the pits are secured."

The king didn't say anything, just kept watching her with shadowed eyes. Finally, the councilman from before spoke up again. "I'm not sure the pits are securable."

She looked at him before turning her gaze back to the king. "In my time with caring for your daughter, I learned that there are ancient gates above each hall that can be closed. They close the pits access to the palace and are said to be near impenetrable. Send someone to close them now, before the Bbrskian find their way inside."

The king nodded slowly, but when he spoke, his words chilled her. "The pits must be closed off. But you, Ashta the Lion Tamer, must do it as no one else from the lionesses or soldiers know where the ancient gates are."

And in his words, she heard the warning. She knew too much for being a simple lioness. And the king didn't like it. Not one bit.

CHAPTER THIRTY-ONE

⌘

Underground Tunnels

SHE TURNED AND left the room without another word. Time was of the essence. The army was already at the walls. It wouldn't take them long to find out and – more importantly – figure out the connection between the lion pits and the palace.

Ashta ran down the halls, barely noticing the weight of the sword still in her hand. She would need to find a holder for it. The thing was to dangerous and too valuable to just give to any soldier or lioness for safe keeping. No, she would just have to take it with her everywhere. For now.

She ran past the court room and out into the main courtyard where the barracks were attached.

If possible, it was even louder outside than the courtroom had been. All around her were screams of scared women and orders being shouted down the lines of soldiers.

She briefly glanced to her right. The wall still stood tall. It was built thick; the trebuchets would need time to whittle at them.

Time.

That's all they needed. Time to make a plan. To regroup and redirect men and women.

Ashta almost tripped over a peasant kid that had been running back to the white tents.

The refugees. Ashta stopped completely, watching the tents with horror. They couldn't keep the people out here. It was too dangerous. But there wasn't enough room in the palace. Not for the thousands that huddled along the wall, praying the boulders wouldn't come down near their piece of wall.

Not now, Ashta berated herself. They couldn't care for everyone right now. Once the palace was secure, then she would have to mention to the princess the issue of the refugees.

She picked up her pace again, not slowing inside the barracks. Women jumped and moved aside at her appearance.

"Luci!" she called out, continuing down the room. "Kkaar!"

At the end she saw a familiar dark head.

"Kkaar," she gasped, stopping in front of her friend. Kkaar was in the middle of strapping on leather armor on her chest. Ashta frowned at the strange piece.

"What…" She couldn't finish.

But Kkaar filled her in, understanding her confusion. "The general has ordered the reserve lionesses to suit up and patrol alongside the soldiers." She grimaced down at the leather plate.

"But our weapons?"

Kkaar sighed. "Apparently we will all be needing just a sword or a spear depending on which legion we are told to join." Kkaar's eyes flashed with frustration.

Ashta understood. The lionesses weren't common foot soldiers. They had special skills. But apparently that did not matter to General Ttaabit.

Ashta knew there was a reason she disliked the man. Now he had proven his lack of foresight.

"Where is Luci?" Ashta asked looking at the beds around her. None of them were occupied by the little sprite.

"She is still waiting at the armory, getting her armor and spear."

Ashta took a seat across from Kkaar.

Kkaar looked at her friend curiously but continued strapping on the leather.

"I need your help." Kkaar's hands stilled as she looked up into Darkling's black eyes. "Yours and Luci's. But I can't tell you what until we get further in the palace."

"Does the general know?"

Ashta shrugged. "Doesn't matter. It's King's orders."

Kkaar's face lightened as she ripped off the leather and threw it on the ground. "Damn glad I won't be needing that."

They shared a brief smile.

"What's *she* doing here?"

They both looked up into Luci's suspicious gaze. Kkaar stood and pulled Luci into a quick hug.

"Darkling has mission for us. Leave the leather."

Luci smiled tightly down at Ashta before dropping the armor. Her eyes brightened as she gazed up at her lover.

Ashta smiled, glad her friends had been able to maintain their relationship back in the city. They both deserved happiness.

Standing, she stretched, flashing the great sword.

Kkaar's eyes widened as she took in the opal pommel. "Is that from the-"

"Don't ask. We need to get a move on it."

Kkaar exchanged a quick glance with Luci before shrugging. "Lead the way, Darkling."

Ashta smiled, then walked out of the room. She quickly broke out into a jog. The lionesses milling around parted for her easily. The three women were able to run through the courtyard without issue.

Once inside the palace, Ashta veered off from the usual path as it ran along the cliff face. It was hard to know if it was still standing as the trebuchets could still be felt in the halls.

Kkaar and Luci followed close behind.

Finally, after long minutes, they halls around them began to darken. They became grittier. Less precise. The torches became less frequent. After running hard for what seemed like hours, they made it to the entrance of the first gate.

The wall was hewn out roughly, with no discernable pattern except the trench in the floor. The torches stood apart leaving long stretches in darkness.

"Now what." Kkaar's voice bounced down the hall. She shivered in the damp hall, recognizing it as one of many that led to the lion pits.

Ashta slowly walked down the hall, her hands sliding along the edge.

"Now we close these halls off."

"That's not possible, we don't have the weapons or the people."

Ashta ignored Luci's comment and kept feeling. Then her fingers slid across something cold, exactly between two torches in the darkest part. She moved closer and felt around the mechanism. Her fingers deciphered a number. Two.

"Kkaar, I need you to go ahead between this torch and the next. Stop when you feel metal along the wall."

Kkaar ran to do as Ashta said.

Ashta turned back to Luci. "I need you to do the same but the other side of me."

She waited until both women called out.

"Okay, once we unlock the mechanism, we have ten seconds before we are locked between the gates. Run hard back up the hall." Ashta felt along the metal till she found a hook. "Pull as hard as you can on the hook in three."

"One."

"Two."

"Three!"

Ashta grunted with effort, the rusted mechanism slowly creaked out until a shuddering click rang down the hall.

"Now run!" She yelled, not turning back to see if Kkaar followed. Just as she passed where Luci had stood, she heard the gate grinding down.

Kkaar ran past just as the metal slid out of the wall and crashed into the floor.

"Damn. What was that!" Kkaar yelled, turning back to place a hand on the big metal piece that cut out the view from the rest of the hall.

"That is some of the strongest steel, mined from deep in the Northern Kingdoms," Ashta whispered. She hadn't been sure if the books were true. Now she thanked the gods for the time spent pouring through books trying to save Ceerie. Because it may have saved Tripsia.

"One down," she said glancing at the gate before looking both women in the eyes, "Two more. Let's hurry."

Ashta turned and jogged back up the hall, feeling her way in the darkness for the fork into one of the other halls. Kkaar and Luci followed silently. The air was still with the mention of the north. And the memory of Trice and her home in the north.

Kkaar pushed the hot feeling down. It seemed impossible that two of her former roommates were dead. One tragically witnessed by all. The other taken from them to soon without resolution.

The next hall closed easily without any problems. The women ran to the third. But as they got into position, they heard a noise in the distance.

"Feet." Kkaar cursed, looking back at Ashta. Kkaar stood at the furthest gate again. But judging from the sound of the footsteps, whoever was coming was going to be there soon. And there was more than one. Many more.

"Ready!" Ashta hissed.

"One."

The clink of metal and armor was now unmistakable.

"Two."

A light could be seen, and with it Ashta made out the fuzzy shape of several men.

"Three!" She hissed, just as the group let out a shout. The man at the front began running toward them. Ashta ripped her hook and was about to run when she heard Kkaar cursing.

"It's stuck," Kkaar yelled, no longer bothering to be quiet.

Ashta didn't think, she just ran to her friend and put her hands around the other woman's.

"Pull!"

She felt her shoulders pop and her arms stretch as she pulled with her whole body. Every muscle in her arms strained, working against centuries of rust and dust.

Finally, the hook clicked.

Ashta turned down the hall and could make out the long beard of the man in the lead. His sword was drawn as he let loose a chilling cry.

Berserker.

"COME ON!" Ashta yelled.

She pulled Kkaar and pushed the other woman ahead of her. Ashta ran for all her worth to the other side of the final gate. The great sword shimmered, the opal almost glowing, where it leaned underneath the torch, just outside of reach.

The tell-tale clicks and screech sounded.

Ashta watched as the edge of the metal gate fell an inch. The spikes finally visible.

She dove hands first without thinking.

Shick!

Her hands burned from scraping against the badly hewn stone floor.

Silence rang through the hall, the imagined echo of the gates coming down still reverberating in her ears.

Did they make it, she wondered?

Ashta slowly got up, the hot feel of blood running down her arms and legs. She slowly brushed her hands against her skirt before trusting herself to turn. Ashta breathed out in relief seeing Kkaar beside her, on her back.

"That was close," Ashta breathed out. She winced at the burn in her palms and knees. The stinging was already going down to dull noise.

Luci opened her mouth to respond.

Bang.

BANG.

Bang.

The three women turned as one, towards the solid metal sheet. The so-called gate.

It stood still.

But obviously the men were still there.

Ashta shuddered. That had been to close.

She walked over and picked up the great sword, wincing at the weight of the pommel in her hand.

"Now what?" Luci echoed Kkaar's earlier question.

Ashta turned to the two women that she would trust her life with. Who she would trust the princess's life with.

She took a deep breath before giving them their next order.

"I need you both guarding the halls. If – and that's a big *if* – the berserkers do manage to break through, one of you need to run and warn the king of the breach while the other stays and fights the soldiers off."

They both stared at her. Then they glanced at eachother. Both women understood that if the worst were to happen, it was a guaranteed death for one of them.

"You two can pick for yourself who is the messenger." *And who dies.* It wasn't what Ashta wanted to say, after having witnessed the love between the two. But she knew her loyalty was first to the kingdom. And when it came down to it, Kkaar would follow as well.

Ashta walked up to Kkaar and clasped her on the arm hard. "Until we see each other again."

"Soon Darkling, soon," Kkaar promised.

Ashta turned to Luci and did the same. But the women said nothing back, just stared at Ashta with venom. Ashta couldn't blame her. They both knew Kkaar, would force Luci to run to the King. And that Luci would obey only because of her love for Kkaar.

"What about the sword?" Kkaar asked, glancing at the great sword that still leaned against the wall. It's opal glowed in the torch. For a moment, Kkaar swore she saw a face looking back at her.

She shook her head and turned to Ashta in question.

Ashta glanced at the sword as well. "Use it to keep the berserkers back," Ashta said.

Kkaar nodded and grabbed for the sword.

Turning away from her friends, Ashta ran the entire way back to the cub's entrance, the phantom sword she had left with Kkaar sat heavy in her hand as she passed its old post. Someone had cleaned up the bodies of the Bbrski assassins, she noted dispassionately.

Ashta kept running up the hidden fourth hall and took the stairs two at time.

Finally, she broke out of the entrance and stopped to try and slow her breathing. She slowly took the last steps to where she had left the prince and princess, her heartbeat thrumming in her throat. Ashta fell to her knees, trying to get a hold of her breathing.

"Ashta?" called a soft feminine voice out, hesitantly.

"Yah."

Silence. Then movement as something warm touched her head.

"Are we safe?" the princess whispered.

Ashta took the hand on her head and pulled herself up.

"As safe as we always are, princess."

zHavier said nothing but she could feel his presence near. "Come," Ashta beckoned, "Let's get down to the infirmary. It is the safest place in the palace for the night."

No one said anything as the prince and princess followed Ashta through the dark hall.

When the group finally stumbled out of the doorway, Carien gasped.

Ashta turned, worried there was an assassin. But instead, her friend stared down at Ashta's legs.

She glanced down her body and was surprised to see how much blood had dripped down into her leather boots. Ashta grimaced. That wouldn't heal easy, she worried. "I'm fine," she said tersely.

Before Carien could say anything more, Ashta started a quick pace down the hall and down to the infirmary. Carien, with Mina in her arms, followed behind with zHavier trailing.

When they finally burst into the infirmary, they were met with a much more controlled chaos than they had seen earlier in the day in the court room.

A woman came up to them. Ashta stopped her and spoke quickly and quietly. "I have princess Carien and prince zHavier with me. They will both be needing cots, near a wall preferably."

The woman's eyes widened but she said nothing. The three followed the woman further into the room and finally stopped at two small cots by the wall. Carien sank into the one by the wall without a thought. zHavier stayed standing, frowning.

"What about you?" He asked Ashta, glancing at the second cot.

Ashta leaned against the wall before sliding down until she sat. It felt so good to be off her feet that she almost sighed aloud.

"I'm fine here."

He opened his mouth to argue but Carien stopped him with a touch on his arm and firm shake of her head. He looked around and realized several curious eyes watched the three.

Rubbing his hair, he finally lay down on the second cot, uncomfortable but knowing there was nothing he could do. If they were in Naankdoen it would be different. But then, he remembered grimly that if they were in Naankdoen, they would be starving soon enough.

Ashta rubbed her eyes, taking one last glance around the room. Nothing suspicious. Most of the other occupants near them were already asleep in their cots, or on the floor. The silence was broken by the occasional cough or moan.

Closing her eyes, Ashta focused on keeping her ears sharp. They hadn't failed to wake her before. Hopefully, despite her wariness, they would still work tonight.

And then she dozed off.

CHAPTER THIRTY-TWO

⌘

Love and Lust

WOMEN, WITH ME!" Remina screamed out, ten lionesses falling in behind her. Everywhere she looked flames licked up into the now lightening sky. They needed to hurry, before the berserkers boats made it off the beach.

As she ran, her women close behind her, she ignored the screams of death and whistling of metal around her. She could not allow herself a moment of distraction. A flutter in her belly reminded her what all was at stake.

A fur covered body ran at her, blood dripping down his heavily marked chest. She didn't pause as her blade arced up and sliced through the soft skin of his neck. His clear blue eyes widened for a moment before rolling back.

Not pausing, Remina kept running through the still burning courtyard to the far wall, one of many access points to the ocean.

Even as she ran down the beach towards the boats, she knew she was too late. By now, most of Justus's estate would be lost to fire, and the rest hidden away on the Bbrski raiding boats which had already reached the open water.

It didn't stop her from slicing down the nearest berserker.

The rest of the early morning was spent in blood. It was past noon before she and her women had gone through and stabbed each body through the heart, taking out valuables and weapons from the berserkers bodies for the king to use.

Four boats.

That's how many had made it out into the night. It didn't matter that Remina and her lionesses had killed a half battalion and made sure another two boats never made it back into the ocean water.

She had failed Justus.

Even as she glanced up at the blackened façade of the main building, she knew she had never truly had a chance at a life here with Justus, at his estate. All her gentle prodding over the summer to convince the King that she should be allowed to work with baron Attel over the winter, was now for nothing.

All it had done was agitate the king more and more, until Atticus had repossessed Justus's summer residence and told him to never return to the city again.

Or risk his head.

It had been hard watching Justus leave while she was forced to stand there, beside the king, and not show any emotion. Even harder as the small flutter in her belly reminded her of what was between her and the baron.

As soon as the call had come from the city of the fire signal from the west coast, Remina had jumped onto a horse. The other women in the barracks had barely stumbled out into the courtyards while she had ridden past them.

"Mina." His voice rasped as the smoke in the air curled its foggy fingers around them.

She shivered standing in the smoldering courtyard. Blood dripped down her arms. Her great sword flashed in the afternoon light, its power keeping it clean.

Remina felt the warm pressure of his hand on her shoulder. She knew Justus would go no further. Even as the grief washed through her from his thoughts, he was still mindful of all the watching eyes.

"I'm sorry, Justus." More than she could ever say. But for now, it would have to be enough.

His grief lightened briefly at her words. It warmed her, knowing their love still held true. Even with the king and the entire kingdom coming between them.

"Master!"

They both turned as one of the servants from the house came running towards them where Remina and Justus stood in the middle of the courtyard.

Remina grimaced before the man could say another word.

Justus's parents were dead.

She had never even had the chance to meet them, and now she never would. Remina straightened her shoulders and walked away from Justus. The latest news would be too much, and she could not afford to break the law. Not now, in front of so many watching eyes.

Instead, she walked over to Arlia. The older woman looked up from cleaning her throwing blade. She tucked it into her hair before nodding to Remina.

"Prepare the women," Remina commanded, glancing around at the other lionesses. Some were still cleaning through bodies. Others stood around, not talking.

Arlia hesitated, her mouth opening and closing.

Remina quirked a brow.

"Should we not help dispose of the bodies?"

It was a fair question, and in the past, it was part of their duties. But Remina knew that her position of favor with the king right now was tenuous at best. She could not push it now. No.

Everything would have to change after today. She could not afford to wait any longer. But to manipulate the king, she would need to be in his good graces.

With a terse jerk of her head, Remina left Arlia to round up the other lionesses. She jumped up on to her own mount and carefully guided the mare through the still smoldering remains of the main buildings.

Remina did not turn back to Justus, even as his frantic thoughts called to her.

She pushed her mount hard, wanting to reach the palace before nightfall. As she reached the outer walls of the city, she pushed harder. The men on the wall opened up the gates as she barreled past them.

Remina jumped off her mount and ran up the palace steps, not bothering to put the horse back in the stable. Her mount knew the way and eventually someone would grab it.

The last ray of day caressed her shoulder as she stepped into the darkened palace. Only her hard breathing echoed through the barren halls.

She didn't slow until she stood before the king's personal chambers.

The soldiers stood silently, tension holding their shoulders high.

Neither man wanted to fight her but they knew they could not allow anyone to pass. Remina sighed, turning to the one on the left, Leo.

"Can you tell the king that the lionesses have arrived back from Baron Attel's estate?"

She didn't wait for him, instead turning away and walking back down the hall.

Remina ducked into an empty doorway and leaned against the wooden door, trying to calm her heart. She listened hard and found the kings mind, skipping over it to the soldier's.

Now where am I supposed to find her? Should have just told her to wait...

Good. He wanted to speak.

Taking in another deep cleansing breath, she returned back to the entrance.

How did she..?

She pushed a wall up from her mind, not allowing anymore thoughts to wash over her. Normally she could ignore the thoughts that washed through her, but with the king close by, she had to be careful. She didn't want her disgust to become visible.

Remina walked past the soldier and into the antechamber, and then through to the main room.

The king sat before the great fireplace; his round belly exposed to the firelight from his loosened shirt.

Remina locked her jaw. She had to do this. For Justus's sake. And for hers.

"You asked for me, your highness?"

He jumped before turning his greedy eyes on her. His gaze caught on her bandages, where her breasts were, before coming back up to her own eyes.

"Report to me."

She nodded, taking a step closer. The hairs along her arms raised even as she pushed herself closer to the vile man. "The estate as well as much of the orchards has been burned. Four ships with materials made it to sea…" She paused, her throat closing at the memory of Justus's grief before continuing, "The late baron and baroness were caught in the flames."

"And the son?" His cold gaze watched her shrewdly. No matter how careful she had been these last five years, Atticus knew there was something going on between her and Justus.

"Alive."

The king rubbed his chin before absently reaching out to her and tracing her belly. Remina pushed down the shudder as cold fear washed through her.

Could he feel it?

She let her careful wall down enough to taste the edges of his thoughts.

Lust hung heavy on his mind and Remina quickly pulled her mind back.

You have to do this, she reminded herself as she steeled her spine. It was the only way.

His other hand came up and traced the edge of her skirt where it met the sun darkened skin of her waist. Softer now.

"Remina," he gasped as he tried to pull her closer.

She carefully stepped outside of his grasp.

Before anger clouded his feature, she knelt down before him and pulled his hand to her cheek.

"We can't, your highness."

His eyes blazed with lust.

This was it.

This was the moment she had been waiting for.

"We can. I am King. And you are mine."

She shook her head, averting her eyes as words spilled out of her mouth, "It is against the law, even for you to be with a slave. I couldn't bare anything happening to you because of me, your highness."

His hand stilled against her cheek and she forced herself to look up into his caramel eyes. She watched as his thoughts battled inside him, but she did not dare listen to them. His mind was a dark place she could not allow herself to fall into.

He licked his lips, staring down at Remina's body. A shudder racked through her body. She hoped he couldn't feel it.

"If…If I released you from being a slave, then you could be mine."

She glanced away, forcing herself to breath quietly.

"But," he continued. She waited for the condition that would decide her life. "You must marry me."

Her heart stilled at the thought.

Never!

Yet even as she thought it, she could see the smallest slice of freedom. After years of coming to terms with being a slave, the almost taste of freedom was too sweet for her to ignore.

She licked her lips before glancing up at the king through her eyelashes, demurely, "Yes. I accept."

Before he could surge towards her, she continued, "But you cannot tell anyone until after I am free that we are to be married. If anyone suspects something between us before I am free, I fear for your safety from your own councilmen."

"I can handle them," he said off handedly. But Remina could feel doubt edging its way around his thoughts. Good.

With a jerk, he stood and walked to the soldiers, expecting her to follow behind, as was her duty. She did, but Remina couldn't hide the slight smirk pulling at her lips.

It had been almost too easy.

But then, she though grimly as she gently rubbed her belly, he hadn't freed her yet.

CHAPTER THIRTY-THREE

⌘

Gone

ASHTA SHIVERED, her hand drawing a dagger out before her eyes were even open.

When she did open them, she wasn't surprised to see Carien half out of her bed. "Where are you going?"

Carien glanced over to the nurses who were rushing around the room, clearly overworked.

"No."

Carien turned back to Ashta and glared. "Why not? I will be in one room and I will be helping my people."

Ashta kept shaking her head. "To many people."

Carien threw her hands up in frustration before turning to watch the nurses again.

Seeing the yearning on Carien's face softened Ashta's resolve. She replaced the dagger and rubbed at her eyes, wiping away the last of the dream's hold on her.

Ashta sighed, stretching her neck. Sleeping against the wall did not help relieve the tension in her muscles. Carien was right, Ashta thought, the room was no worse than when the princess was in the throne room. There were the same number of unknowns.

"You will have to cover your hair," she finally conceded in a quiet voice.

Carien turned back in shock, her eyes wide as she sat still for a long moment. Then she jumped off the cot and pulled Ashta up off the ground and into her arms. Ashta squirmed in the hug until Carien finally dropped her arms.

Looking past Carien, Ashta saw Brinley, the nursemaid, in one of the cots, an old man in the cot beside her.

Nudging Carien aside, Ashta leaned over the caught and gently picked up the sleeping babe. Carien followed Ashta, as Ashta led the way to Brinley. The other woman looked up in shock, holding her arms out automatically for the babe.

Brinley didn't say anything, her face blank, as she adjusted her dress to feed the babe.

"The princess will be in the nursery all day. You must stay here with Mina," Ashta commanded. She rubbed her arms, strangely uneasy. Taking a quick look around the room, she noticed nothing strange or out of place. Ashta focused back on the nursemaid.

Brinley nodded, not looking up at either Ashta or Carien.

The poor woman, thought Carien, the nursemaid was so pale and almost shaking. The attack last night had definitely shot the woman's nerves. Carien wanted to take Brinley into her arms and calm her. But she couldn't. Not in front of so many people. Instead, Carien nodded down at the woman before turning away and finding the nearest nurse.

Soon enough the princess had tracked down a clean dress and head scarf that was appropriate for a nurse. The itchy dress sent a thrill down her spine. She had loved the anonymity and power the dress afforded her back before Darkling had become her lioness. The princess had spend many years helping others. It felt right to be back in the dress and helping her people now.

Ashta stationed herself at the entrance and watched over the room, keeping an eye on Carien. If only she had another lioness here to help her. The room was filled with too many uncertainties. There were multiple entrances and a steady stream of injured, and not injured, citizens moving in and out of the room. It would be safer for the princess if she had one lioness on her person and another at the door. But Carien had neither. Ashta would have to do, from her position on the wall.

zHavier sidled up beside Ashta, copying her pose, leaned against the wall. He didn't say anything at first, just watched the princess as she helped wrap a bandage around a man's head who had lost an eye.

Finally, without turning towards or looking at Ashta, the prince spoke. "If I had not seen the princess before, I would not have recognized her now."

Ashta said nothing. What he said was true.

zHavier scoped out the room, making a point to look at all the corners and entrances as well as the people in the room. "I imagine protecting a princess in this room would be a nightmare."

Sighing, Ashta glared up at the high stone ceiling before resting her gaze back on the princess. "It is, but I can't exactly leave my post to get more lionesses."

"Why not? She is there princess. Should she not be the priority to your people?"

Ashta nibbled at her bottom lip. Yes, Carien was the priority. But leaving her unguarded went against everything Ashta had been trained for. Especially leaving her unguarded when there had been witnesses that watched her come into the room as a princess.

"I can guard her for you."

Ashta jerked away from the wall, facing him for the first time. He still kept his gaze on the princess.

Before she could argue or say anything, zHav continued, "You have left me to guard her before. You know I am more than capable, and nothing has happened to her before."

Her mind urged at her to trust the prince. She knew logically that he had done all those things. But there was still something in her heart, a small shiver that told her not to trust him. That she should stay here. She should watch the princess herself.

Glancing, over at Carien, Ashta watched as a man grabbed onto the princess's arm. Before Ashta could take a step, Carien had extricated herself from his hold.

To close.

Decision made, Ashta turned to the prince, looking at his ear. "Watch the babe and the princess. I will return by evening meal at the latest with two more guards."

Before she stepped past him, she reached down and grabbed his crotch in a vice grip. He grunted, tense but not daring to move for fear of excruciating pain.

Ashta leaned into his ear and whispered, "If anything happens to her, zHav, I will kill you, prince or not."

Releasing her hold, she left the nursery and ran up to the courtyard, her face split by a wide grin. Men. So predictable.

As she ran through the courtyard, her grin dissipated amidst the shouts and screams. Nowhere could she see lionesses. Kkaar had said earlier that the lionesses were being sent to General Driet.

Ashta grabbed the nearest soldier by the throat and pulled him close to her. The man's pale face and he visibly began to shake. His fear disgusted her.

She wasn't a monster.

And if she was, it was *his* kingdom that had made her one.

"Where can I find general Driet?" she asked, tightening her grip slightly.

The man stuttered before finally pointing to the far walls where the soldiers' barracks were.

Ashta dropped him, not watching him as he scrambled away. Instead she focused on the barracks she could see in the distance. She slowly wound her way between tents, soldiers, catapults, sheep. Her pace never slowed, and her aim never faltered. The war raged from behind the wall with the occasional arrow making its way into the courtyard.

Just as she reached the barracks, the outer wall shook with a bang as something from the other side smashed it. Ashta looked up at the men on the wall, there screams and shouts impossible to ignore. Shuddering, Ashta turned away from the carnage and walked into the barracks.

Silence descended on the room as men – naked to dressed – shut up and turned to watch the lioness. Some had fear in their eyes. A few had respect. One man, standing a head taller than anyone in the room glared at her with burning hatred. The scars on his chest told a tale of a slave. Ashta paused on him, shocked to see a male slave. They were quite rare. Unlike the women, Tripsia didn't give its male slaves a choice. They all became soldiers for her wars. And if they were lucky, survived, they might one day sit on the council as the leader of the white lionesses.

Ashta glared back at the man before taking in the rest of the room with a cool stare. "I am looking for General Driet."

The man standing closest to her, his hands covering his nakedness, spoke up, "He's on the wall in the third watch tower."

Ashta nodded, leaving the barracks without another word.

Since her time being Carien's white lioness, she had never seen so many men in one space. Not even in Naankdoen, when their party had been made up one third lionesses and two thirds soldiers.

Ashta entered the bottom of the closest watch tower, a sweat breaking across her skin. She didn't want to be on the wall. She had seen enough carnage when her father's men had massacred their party. The shock still echoed through her body and her scar pulsed with the memory of the pain. Yet she forced herself to take each step up, closer to where she could she the fighting. And see her father's people.

Men passed her on the stairs without pause, making her take comfort in her invisibleness as a lioness. Just as she had been trained to not engage any people, the soldiers and the people of Tripsia had been trained to ignore lionesses.

Finally, she stepped out onto the top of the wall, and the sight stole her breath. Below her lay a burning wall of molten fire. Behind the smoke wall she could see the hazy image of the Bbrski army. Thousands of men. At least a hundred trebuchets. Men on horses. And off way in the distance, bright from the sun lay the unending Tripsian desert.

Taking a deep breath, Ashta took a step back and made her way to the tall black figure she could see in the distance.

General Driet.

Stopping before the watch tower, Ashta noted lionesses milling about the wall before her. The women nodded to her. But they looked foreign. Gone was the hair, the bandages and the leather skirts. They looked nothing more than a man, with armor and short hair.

Ashta worried her lips. When the war ended – because it *would end* – what would be left of the famed white lionesses?

She lengthened her stride until she stood right before the general. She could feel him purposefully ignoring her. He kept his eyes on the wall and on the trebuchets that were just within reach of the Tripsian long bow men. He never let his eyes, or attention waver towards Ashta. Ashta knew the game well. And she was better at it.

She stood just to the side of him, barely in his view, and waited. And waited some more.

"What?" He finally barked at her, looking into her eyes for the first time.

Straightening, Ashta spoke in an even and authoritative voice. "The princess needs two guards on her –"

"Ask someone else." He began walking away from her.

Ashta frowned for a moment before chasing after the man. "Sir, I don't think you understand-"

He whipped around cutting her off. His eyes were blazing with anger and something else. "No, it's you who doesn't understand. We are at war. Even with all the lionesses and our own soldiers, we will barely survive this fight. We can't spare a single man, woman or child on the wall. So, I advice you to do *your* job. Guard the princess."

Then he whipped back around and began shouting orders to the nearest lionesses on the wall. The women straightened and saluted him.

Shivering, Ashta took a deep breath. So he had recognized her as the princess's white lioness. Deep down she had known asking for support was a futile attempt. But she had to try.

Besides, what was the point of saving the kingdom without ensuring its future?

Shaking her head, Ashta turned and jogged back down the yard, through the stone halls. All around her people milled around busily. Fear and desperation hung over the castle like a dark cloud.

She didn't stop until she was inside the infirmary. Somehow in the short time she had gone up looking for help, the infirmary and filled up even more. There was barely any standing room as nurses yelled and threw elbows to get to their patients.

Ashta pushed through, trying to catch a glimpse of caramel eyes. Instead she saw a familiar dark head above the crowds.

She angled straight for zHavier, ignoring the bodies that pushed and jostled her around. At least there were no fingers gliding over her. Otherwise she might consider pulling her half swords out to clear a path.

As she came up beside zHavier, she glanced around, surprised Carien wasn't right beside him. The hairs on the back of her neck stood up. She tried to calm herself, rubbing at the spot.

"Your Highness."

zHavier continued helping the man leaned against the wall beside him, wrapping the bandage around bearded man's arm.

Impatient, Ashta grabbed his shoulder. "zHavier."

"What?" He asked, irritation flooding his features. As he looked up the long, lean body into a familiar pair of black eyes, his irritation shifted to embarrassment. Darkling.

Coughing, he straightened up, rubbing his elbow.

"Where is the princess?" she asked, glaring up at him.

He turned to point over at the bed beside him. "She's just…"

Stopping, he stared at the empty bedside. She had just been there a minute ago when he had turned to help the bearded man with his arm.

Turning back to Ashta, he tried to open his mouth and say something. But his mind was blank. No words came.

Darkling's face flooded red as anger flashed in her eyes. "You lost the princess?" She asked in a deadly, quiet voice.

Before he could defend himself, she turned and disappeared into the crowd. He tried to follow her, but there was no way through the people. And even as his mind searched the room for the princess's familiar mind, he knew that she was already gone.

Ashta pushed through the crowd, towards the back entrance that led down to the to the room where not three years ago she had received her tattoo. As she marched, Ashta caught pieces of conversations.

"He shouldn't have forced her…"

"...Did you see how sweet the babe was?"

"...Brinley sure ran quick with the princess and that man, must have..."

"...did wonder why she worked for them royals, all considerin'."

Whipping around to the last man that spoke, Ashta reached up and pulled his face down to hers by the collar of his shirt. His hair was greasy, and dirt and blood speckled his face.

"Tell me everything." When he didn't speak immediately, she shook him. "Now."

As he spoke, her anger rolled tighter in on itself as she glared across towards the area where the man who she had trusted still was. She had stupidly trusted him even though a piece of her heart said not to.

Never again would she make that mistake.

CHAPTER THIRTY-FOUR

⌘

Into the Sun

ASHTA LET GO of the man. He fell on his back, crawling away from her as quick as possible. She ignored him and pushed her way back to the infirmary main entrance. The one that connected to the palace. She needed to inform the King. Before anyone else did.

She ignored the stares and whispers as people slowly moved aside and made a path for her. Maybe they could feel her anger, Ashta thought. It felt like a vicious animal curling around her, ready to strike at any moment.

As soon as she entered the cold hall Ashta let herself fall back against the stone wall. Truth be told, she wasn't ready to face the King. She still had not regained his trust. First from the attack on the princess when they had been traveling back to Tripsia. And second when she had spoken against the trade with her father. Which, incidentally, she had been right about. Sometimes it was better to be wrong and to remain unseen.

Losing Carien right now would further push the King against her. The only reason she was still alive in the palace was because Carien had chosen her. Had fought for her, *against* the king. To go to him now would be his perfect excuse to rid himself of her.

Shivering, Ashta straightened up from the wall and pushed the dark thoughts deep down. Now was not the time to let fear make decisions for her. Cariens safety, her *life*, depended on Ashta having a clear head and being decisive.

"Darkling."

Ashta gasped.

Somehow the prince had snuck into the hall and now stood across from her. How had she not seen him?

Shame coursed through her veins, even as she jabbed him in the chest with her finger. She glared up into his familiar uneven eyes, the lavender sparkling down at her.

"You!" She spat.

All of her problems seemed to circle back to zHavier. And it needed to stop now. For good

"I trusted you to watch the princess!"

His hands came up, but he made no other moves. "I know, and I think I know where-"

"I don't need your help. Ever. You have done enough."

"Let me fix this," he pleaded.

This time Ashta used her hands and shoved him against the far wall. The thud from his head echoed through the near empty hall. Voices whispered out from the infirmary entrance but otherwise they were alone.

"I don't think you understand," she said on a low whisper. Ashta pulled his face down to her height, staring him down as she let loose her anger. "You are the problem. You are the reason my friend is dead. You are why Lilly is dead. And now it's you, surprise, surprise, who is the reason for the princess being gone." She took a deep breath before spewing out her anger. "I don't care if you die or if your kingdom burns to ashes. You have screwed everything up for me. So, stay the hell away from me, or so help me goddess, I will kill you myself."

With a final shove, she stomped down the hall straight to the council room. For once, no one is inside. Ashta turned and made her way to the King's chambers instead. Spotting the soldiers outside, she smiled with grim determination.

Now for the hard part. A sliver of fear pricked her heart, but she had a duty to do.

This time, the soldiers recognized her and let her pass without comment.

The King sat in front of the fire, one of his lionesses standing at his side while the other stood on the other side of the room. Both women looked her in the eye before briefly nodding.

Taking a deep breath, Ashta walked forward until she stood before the King. He looked up at her, a scowl already forming. His silk clothes were as neat as ever despite the war raging on two fronts just outside his rooms.

She spoke up before he asked her the obvious question. "The princess has been kidnapped."

There was a long pause.

King Roman stared up at her a moment before he stood up and exploded.

Ashta couldn't make out any words as he screamed obscenities, his hands pulling at his hair.

Just as suddenly as he exploded, he quieted and glared up at her. Ashta couldn't help but note that the King of Tripsia, a man his people feared, came barely up to her chin. The throne added height to a man that may not always be deserving.

"Who?" He asked in a deceptively calm voice.

Ashta breathed through her nose before replying, "The wet nurse and her father as far as I can tell."

"I knew that babe should have been given up to the Nursery! Now look what happened!"

Her cheeks heated as Ashta took another step forward. The distinct slick of a sword being pulled from a scabbard stopped everyone.

Ashta glared at the lioness before turning back to the king. "The *babe* is not to blame for this. Why do you think a Tripsian Civilian, one of *your* people, would try to harm their princess?" She continued before he could try to answer. "Because *your own people* hate you, hate your actions, and they believe that your daughter will rule with the same ruthless hand. They didn't care about trading their own princess for their own safety."

"How do you know they traded her?"

She sighed. Of course, he hadn't listened. "Because the wet nurse lost her sister, babe, and husband to a raid to the berserkers. They hope to trade princess Carien for the sister."

Then she muttered quieter, "But it won't work."

The king didn't hear the last part, already yelling orders to his own white lionesses.

Ashta interrupted, "I can help with the search, your majesty, I've been to the camp my father has made-"

"You have done enough," he cut her off. His voice was low, his eyes flashing. "Why don't you do something useful and join the other lionesses on the wall."

And with that she had been dismissed.

Angry with the king and with herself, Ashta left the chamber in a haze. Her feet automatically took her down into the depths of the palace. Her vision didn't clear until she looked down at the familiar flashing opal. Her gaze tracked up its length and for a moment she stared at Kkaar. Kkaar stared back.

"Darkling?" She asked, hesitant, glancing at Luci who sat against the wall. A knife flashed in the torchlight as the other woman deftly cleaned under her nails.

Ashta held a finger to her mouth as she glanced behind her. Straining her ears, she caught nothing, not a breath out of place.

She nodded to both women before pacing the width of the hall.

Kkaar and Luci exchanged a glance, but neither women said a word aloud

Suddenly, Ashta stopped and stared straight into Kkaar's eyes. "The princess was kidnapped."

Kkaar nodded carefully, unsure of what else had gone on above ground.

"I'm going to get her back."

Luci snorted. "You and what army?"

Whipping around to glare down at Luci, Ashta barely reined her anger in. "I don't need an army for where she is. My father's camp is crawling with people. It is better to go it alone."

"What of the babe?"

"Also gone."

"Some lioness you are," Luci muttered, flicking her blade up carelessly Ashta.

Before Ashta could step forward, Kkaar grabbed onto her forearm. "What is it you need from us?"

After a moment Ashta took a deep breath. "There is a secret exit from the palace that goes down to the beach."

"You mean the dock?" Luci asked sarcastically, "Because that's the other way."

"No." Even as she said it, a thought in the back of her head wondered how Luci knew about the King's path to the hidden cove.

Shaking her head, she took a deep breath. Ashta walked down the hall into the shadow. Her hand grazed the wall on the right rather then the left. Her hand ran over a bump. Stopping she felt around until her hand pushed in a stone and a breeze of dank air filled the hall. All three women shivered as they stared into the darkness.

"This secret exit."

"Are you sure you should go alone?" Kkar asked as she rubbed the pommel thoughtlessly. Warmth spread from it up into her heart and lay over her like a blanket of comfort.

"I must." Ashta stared off into the darkness. "I failed the princess. And *I* will save her. You understand."

Kkaar was slow to nod but agreed.

"If you must we will not stop you. But I am going with you to the beach," the other woman said, the thought coming to her unbidden. As soon as she said it, the rest of her mind caught up and agreed to the action.

Kkaar cut Darkling off before the other woman could argue. Instead Kkaar stepped around the dark haired woman and began cautiously walking down the dark hall. Her right hand, still gripping the great sword, trailed the wall as her left extended ahead of her.

Before she disappeared, she glanced back at Luci who watched her with caution in her eyes. "I'll be back soon," Kkaar promised. Her lover nodded but made no move otherwise.

Satisfied, Kkaar took a step and began the long journey to the beach.

Ashta waited a heartbeat before joining her friend in the dark. She kept one hand on Kkaar's shoulder as they descended into the depths of hell. After a while she began to make out the hushed rush of water breaking.

With each step they came closer to the beach.

Kkaar was stopped by a hard wall. Feeling around herself, she found a small crevice just big enough to squeeze her body through. She checked her blades to make sure they were secure. Then with the great sword extended ahead of her, she began shimmying sideways.

Finally, sunlight cut through the darkness, momentarily blinding Kkaar.

"Oomph!"

Kkaar fell forward as Ashta landed on top of her. Both women laid there letting their eyes adjust. Sand scratched their palms, warm on their skin. Around them was a narrow strip of beach with the hard cliff face of Tripsia and her palace at their back.

Kkaar looked back at the unassuming rock, a part of the rocky face of the cliff. If she had not fallen through the crevice, she would never have believed a tunnel to be situated right there.

Ashta smirked, glad that the readings from when Ceerie was locked up had paid off more than once now. Her last time in the hall had been a hazy memory and she hadn't been sure she would find the other side of the passage.

"Now what?" Kkaar's voice pulled Ashta back into the moment. She jumped to her feet before helping her friend up.

"Now we say goodbye. If you do not see me in one week's time, tell King Roman that I went to the island where King Alerik has set up his base."

Kkaar nodded before pulling Ashta into a hard hug. "Be careful my friend."

Ashta breathed in the familiar scent of Kkaar, washed in the feeling of home and safety. She hugged her friend back before clapping her on the shoulder. "You to, my friend, you to."

And with that Kkaar turned back to the crevice, the great sword leading the way once more and disappeared back into the depths of the palace.

Ashta stared after her for a long moment.

She took a deep shuddering breath before straightening her shoulders and turning away. It was time for her to fix her mistakes. It was time to be the white lioness she had trained to be.

CHAPTER THIRTY-FIVE

⌘

A Woman's Pain

THE SUN SHONE from the horizon on the west, spraying the beach with golds and umbers and oranges. Ashta surveyed the thin stretch of beach for a boat or anything she could use to get in the water. The rocky outcropping hid the length of the beach from Ashta's view.

Sighing with frustration, she pushed through the hot sand. Her feet sank down with each step. She could feel the grittiness catching on her leather boots.

Ashta ignored the sand as she stumbled across the beach. Most of the Tripsian people, the peasants, lived along the cost. Fishing was not only done for trade, but for survival. She scoured the sands and large rocks for any hints of a lost fishing boat.

Surely a fisherman had pulled his boat up on this stretch of beach. It was so close to the palace, making it prime spot to come in and trade in the small market of the ruined city. Or to get help from the palace infirmary.

The sun sunk lower, forcing Ashta to move faster. A quick glance at the sky confirmed her fears. There would be no moon to guide her tonight.

She needed to find a boat. Now.

Ahead she spotted a promising dark spot in the cliff face. She trudged up the beach. Her progress was slow in the soft sand that pulled her down. A shiver of worry ran down her spine. Maybe there was another reason for the bare beach. Something much more sinister. Quicksand was not unheard of in Tripsia, the land with many deserts.

Finally, after an hour of walking and the Tripsian cliff long behind her, Ashta was rewarded with the sight of canvas.

Hurrying, she fell to her knees and pulled off the canvas. She prayed to all the gods and goddesses for good luck and thanked each one as her hands ran over a smooth hull. A fishing boat.

No obvious holes. Hopefully her luck would hold.

Using her legs, Ashta was able to push the boat over. She stored the canvas under the lone seat. Spying the well used set of oars, Ashta placed them also inside the boat. She walked around to the back of the boat and carefully wiped her hands against each other.

She stared at the thin stretch of sand between her and the water. It looked deceivingly short. Maybe twenty paces. Her calves ached already from having pushed through soft sand.

With a sigh, she wiped her brow and braced herself against the boat.

Ashta pushed the boat at unforgiving sand until it finally began to slide. She kept pushing, her feet sinking and slipping. The twenty paces seemed to drag on as she strained in the last light of the day.

"Please!" she begged on mumble, her teeth clenched in determination.

The sand became cooler and began sqelching as it clung to her boots. The boat lightened as it began to float on the water.

Ashta kept pushing, making sure to grip the boats edge. When she was far enough out that she could row, she pulled herself up and crawled into the back of the small boat. She fell back into it. Her heaving breaths broke the silence as sweat streamed down her skin and dripped to the hull. She took a moment for herself, just breathing.

Then her body was washed by cold as the last of the fading daylight disappeared behind the horizon.

Ashta sat up and placed the oars in their holds. Carefully aiming northeast, she began the long row back to the island of hell where her father waited.

She rowed through the night, until the next midday. When the sun was at its highest, she pulled the canvas over her and tried to catch an hour or two of sleep. The fisherman who had left the boat had also stored some dried fish and a canvas of sour wine underneath the bench.

Ashta chewed slowly, using the wine to wash everything down. Now wasn't the time to complain. Or ignore the gift she had been given. Carien needed her at her best.

Soon enough she stored the canvas and continued rowing. Her cheeks burned and her lips blistered by the late evening.

She caught sight of the dark spot on the horizon as the sun began its descent.

The island her father was on.

She could not make out any ships from his navy. Hopefully they were all occupied at the cliff face of the Tripsian palace.

Ashta sat and waited in the slowly drifting boat, watching as the sun sank lower. Only when she was sure that she would no longer be spotted did she take up the oars. This time she rowed hard, not wanting to lose a single moment.

It was easy to navigate towards the island, as fires were lit up its length. She easily maneuvered the boat to shore, a good mile upwards from the main fires.

For a long a moment she hesitated on the beach. Should she bring the boat ashore, or push it off? The tide would take it back out if she did push it off. But what if she needed it later to get off the island?

She glanced at the fires and the dark outlines of ships along the coast. Most would be trade boats with supplies from the mainland. They would likely have a dingy on board.

Nodding to herself, she turned back to the fisherman's boat. She said a quick thanks to whoever had left the boat on the beach for her. Then she pushed the boat off again, not wanting the strange boat to be sighted by an sentry.

With the cloak of night, Ashta snuck into the tent city. She skulked between canvases, listening carefully to the drunk exploits of the Bbrski men.

She had almost wound her way up to where her father's tent stood, when she finally heard what she was searching for.

Four men were seated around a fire. One had a crying woman in his lap, her pain muffled by the man's hand over her mouth. The other three held great steins filled with beer. They spoke to each other loudly, ignoring the fourth man with the woman in his lap and his misadventures.

"...I don't see why we can't all have a go at her."

"She's ripe for the picking, begging for a rough tumble."

"That poor bastard stuck watching her all night."

"You don't think Giandor will take his share?"

The man in the middle glared at the man to his right before bending closer, his voice becoming hushed.

Ashta strained but couldn't make out their words. She tried to sneak closer, but was careful of the fourth man. He could easily spot her if she weren't careful. She ducked down and crawled as close as she dared.

"... Not worth losing your dick over."

The other man murmured his assent. Ashta waited as a brief pause filled the conversation. Then they spoke again.

"A drink, men, to Giandor!"

"To Giandor!"

"For his sake, I hope that woman and her babe die quietly in the night on that ship. Otherwise the king will burn the docks looking for them..."

Having heard enough, Ashta carefully backed away from the fire and the men. Carien was on the island. And Mina as well. Somewhere on a ship. Her heart beat fast at the confirmation. Now to find them.

Her heart tore as the woman across from the fire began screaming in earnest. It wasn't her place, Ashta reminded herself, despite her fingers itching to throw one of her knives hidden in her hair. There was nothing she could do for the other woman, except save the princess and maybe end the war.

Saving Carien would not help this woman but might it would save thousands of other women from suffering the same fate. The Bbrski Berserkers were famed for their raping and pillaging. Ashta doubted if her father won the war, that he would stop his men from ransacking the people and the kingdom.

She carefully wound her way through the tents, avoiding torches and flames. The occasional feminine scream tore through the night. Each time she would hesitate until she was certain it was not Carien or Mina.

The noise of the tents and their nefarious activities was dampened near the docks. Few men walked about. Only the occasional drunk stumbled through the night as Ashta methodically searched each boat.

As the night wore on, her frustrations mounted.

She needed to find Carien. *Now.* Or she would have to somehow hide an entire day on the island. Ashta had her doubts at escaping notice for an entire day, in the light of day.

A cry broke the quiet night air. Ashta paused. This scream was a familiar one, that of a hungry babe. Ashta hurried down the dock and stopped before a large black vessel, its mermaid figurehead screaming in horror from the bow.

Another cry filled the night air. This time Ashta knew it came from the vessel before her. She walked around to the gang plank. A small fire burned at the ships entrance. She counted five men seated it, drinking and laughing quietly in the night.

Even for her, it was to many men to kill silently. She could not risk any of them making a noise. Or escaping to the other tents.

She would have to board the boat a different way.

Mind made up, she spared one last glance at the black ship. Somewhere on its deck was the princess and the babe. Ashta turned back to the tent city. She needed to gather a few things first. And quickly, as the horizon would soon lighten with the morning light.

She would need a rope to start off with. And maybe a sword. And a Bbrski bear pelt.

CHAPTER THIRTY-SIX

⌘

Light the Night

"SHH, IT'S OKAY, shh, little Mina," Carien crooned as she gently bounced the squirming bundle. The princess paced the short length of the captains quarters. She had been trying to soothe the crying babe since the late afternoon to no avail.

The small babe kept crying, her face red with exertion. Carien understood, her own stomach empty from the lack of food since King Alerik of Bbrski had come by in the morning.

She shivered at the memory of his dark gaze, familiar yet so different. Where Darkling's gaze was sometimes warm, especially when she watched Mina, there were other times when it was not. Staring into her father's cold slate eyes had been like staring at still waters. Cold. Unyielding. And yet, Carien could feel the edge of something darker behind them.

Movement from near the door had Carien glancing up. The guards unnerving gaze never wavered from her body. Carien shivered. If she hadn't seen the king threaten the man by knife point, she would be far more worried about her safety.

Even so, these Bbrski warriors seemed to fear nothing. Ignoring a King's order wouldn't be unheard of among the warriors. At least so she had heard from the men when they had first taken Carien to the King's tents.

Hopefully the threat would hold. Otherwise, the small knife that she carried in her cleavage, neatly held by her binds, would have to be enough to protect her.

She had taken to wearing the small blade since she had returned from Naankdoena. Carien never wanted to feel so helpless again. The men that had kidnapped her at the ball had been far stronger than her. But if she had had some sort of weapon, Carien was sure she could have saved herself.

Maybe.

She fervently hoped so.

Especially as she now relied only her wits and the short blade.

"*Wahh!*" Mina screamed. Her hands were balled up into tight fists as tears leaked down her cheeks. Carien sighed and continued rocking her.

"If you don't shut that thing up, I will!" The man growled from his spot near the only door in the small room.

Tired, hungry, and irritated had Carien whipping around to face him. She screamed back, "She's hungry!"

The berserkers face darkened as he stood and took a menacing step towards her. The man towered over her, his shoulders twice as broad as she was. "Then feed it!"

Before Carien could reply, or edge away from the man, an audible thump sounded through the galley. She felt her legs sway a bit from the motion of the boat. *Had they moved out of the dock*, she wondered?

The berserker held a finger to his mouth as they both stood frozen.

After a long moment of silence, the man glared down at her. His eyes glanced down at her cleavage once more, and lust filled his face. He adjusted his pants with one hand befre taking a menacing step towards her.

Carien gripped Mina close, her heartbeat in her throat. Her eyes darted around the room, looking for something.

He grabbed her by the shoulders and pushed her towards the bed.

She fell across it, her arms shielding Mina from the worst of the tumble.

The berserker roughly grabbed her one wrist and wrenched it towards the headboard.

Carien tried to squirm, but with Mina cradled in her other arm, she didn't dare move too much. The babe had begun screaming even louder now that it was being slightly crushed. Carien tried to keep her weight off the babe but it was no use.

Shock kept her mouth closed as she watched in horror as the man wrapped a rope around her hand.

The berserker surveyed the quickly knotted rope around her wrist before turning back to the only exit. He pulled his sword out and carefully opened the door before gently closing it behind him, without even a click of noise.

For a moment, Carien stayed tense over the baby. She had believed in that moment that the worst would happen. She wanted to scream, or cry.

Instead she curled her free arm tighter around Mina and gently rocked her. She sang a soft lullaby and slowly, the little babe calmed before her eyes fell into fitful sleep.

The princess didn't dare try to grab her small knife for fear the jostling would wake the babe. Frustration and fear kept her muscles tense as she stared at the door, waiting.

Please let someone save me, Carien prayed fervently, please.

Ashta waited beside the exit of the galley, picking up the slight creaks of someone coming up the stairs. She adjusted her grip on her short sword and carefully let out a slow breath.

The door creaked open.

Before the man had taken one step out onto the deck, Ashta slit his throat. He didn't even have a chance to cry out in shock. She carefully let his body down to the floor. Then she dragged him to the side. She checked his pulse. Nothing.

Not letting herself get pulled into the moment, Ashta cleaned her short sword on his pelt. Mina's crying had dissipated. Hopefully it was only to sleep, and not worse, Ashta worried.

She carefully went down the stairs, pausing at the bottom. Her instincts told her it was safe. But just to be sure she checked the galley over. Thoroughly.

Finally, in front of the last door, the door to the captain's quarters, Ashta paused. She listened hard and heard nothing. Not even a creak. She slowly turned the doorknob.

She took a quick deep breath before slamming it open and jumping into the room.

Carien jumped on the bed with a squeak, but thankfully did not scream. Mina grumbled at being jostled. Carien looked away from Ashta and quickly soothed the babe before she began screaming again.

Ashta surveyed the room, and upon seeing it was empty of enemies, she ran to the bed. She cut the rope around the princess's wrist easily. After putting her sword away, she pulled Mina into her arms.

"Are you okay?" Ashta whispered, "Did anyone touch you?"

Carien shook her head, knowing that what Ashta really wanted to know had not happened. Yet. Thank the gods.

Relief flooded Ashta's eyes as she took a deep breath and relaxed. In the next moment she straightened, the tension returning to her shoulders.

"Come on," she whispered, already walked to the door. "We have to be quick and quiet."

Carien followed, ignoring the gnawing emptiness of her stomach. In moments, they stood out on the deck beneath the black empty sky. Carien took in a deep clear breath, pausing at the door. Her prayers had been answered.

"Carien," Ashta hissed.

Jerking her eyes open, Carien quickly ran to where Ashta was carefully untying a dinghy.

"Jump in."

Carien took Mina in her arms and settled in one of the seats. Ashta pushed the boat over the side and gently lowered it with the pulleys. Every creak and squeak had Ashta wincing. She had gotten distracted the guards in front of the black ship.

But soon enough, they would return to their post. And by then hopefully the princess and her would be long gone.

Once the boat was just above the water, Ashta stopped and ran back to the pile of bodies. She grabbed the Bbrskian whiskey and poured it over the body and the length of the ship. Grabbing the lantern, she smashed it against the man.

The flames burst across the bodies and up into the night sky in a plume of oranges and heat. Ashta covered her eyes before running back to the boat and the princess. Hopefully the burning boat would give the two enough of a lead on the waters. The small dinghy was no match to full sized ship.

Ashta lowered the boat the rest of the way.

"I've unhooked it," Carien shouted on a whisper up to Darkling.

Snuggling Mina in her lap, Carien lifted an oar and pushed off of the great black ship. She was able to get a grip on the second oar and pulled as hard as she could through the water. The small boat moved quietly in the still night waters.

Ashta took the pelt that she had stolen from the tents and ran inside the ship despite the growing flames. She doused the captains quarters with whiskey and threw the pelt on the bed. After it was doused she grabbed the small lantern in the room and smashed it against the floor.

The room burst into flame, barely giving Ashta enough time to escape. She slammed the door behind her before rushing up the stairs.

This time she did not care if her steps made noise, time was of the essence.

At the top of the step she was stopped by a wall of heat.

The flames had spread and were now licking up the mast and tearing at the bound sails.

Covering her face, Ashta pushed through the flames and ran blindly to the edge where she had lowered Carien. She jumped over.

The shock of the cold sea on her blistered skin brought a scream from Ashta's throat. Instead of noise, water poured into her mouth, almost drowning her. She paddled her arms, breaking through to the surface, sputtering and coughing.

An oar pushed at her back. Ashta blindly reached for it. She blinked several times and could make out Carien's shadowed face. The flames behind them barely illuminated the dark moonless night.

Carien pulled her into the side of the dinghy. Ashta reached up and hauled herself over the boat edge and fell into the hall, a soaked lump.

She couldn't help but laugh aloud at herself. It was the second time she was out of breath from crawling into a boat. Hopefully by the third time she would be able to get into a boat with more grace and poise.

Shouts began filling the night.

Then the eerie blow horn of the Rviun Tribe.

Ashta shivered, but not from the cold. She scrambled onto the seat and gently pushed Carien aside. Ashta grabbed the oars and began rowing in earnest, fear giving her strength.

It was time to get out of here.

CHAPTER THIRTY-SEVEN

⌘

Legacy

"Now stay close, Mina."

Svetlana smiled up at grandfather from where she sat on her own horse. They had taken their mounts out of the fenced-in paddock and out onto the path that lead to the waters.

"Don't worry grandpa, I won't fall off."

He smiled down at her indulgently, as his eyes checked that she hadn't let go of the hair at the nape of the horse's neck. She tightened her hold as her mount tripped on the rocky path. It caught itself before continuing on the narrow path.

The skin around grandfather's eyes tightened but he made no move to take over. His hands still held on loosely to the lunch basket the cook had packed for the two.

Svetlana leaned back as they hit a steep section, biting her lip hard. She was determined to show her grandfather that she was good enough. That she was a Broskla. Just like her mother.

"Take it slow Mina, there is no race today."

She ignored him but did not urge the mount faster. Besides, it wasn't a fair race if grandfather was in front of her on the path. She was smart enough to know that going off the path wasn't safe for the horse or for her and her grandfather.

No, instead she held on to the mane as she felt her body slide along the bare back of the young mare.

Finally, the rocks gave way to sand as they reached the thin stretch of beach. Svetlana turned and looked up at the jagged cliffs, the dark trees lining its edges were tall and imposing. Svetlana smiled.

"What's the happiness for, my little one?" her grandfather asked, his raspy voice finally familiar to her young ears.

She turned and urged her mare until they walked beside her grandfather and his own mount. She flipped her leg over, staying seated on the horse, but now she completely faced him.

"Isn't it beautiful?"

He quirked a dark bushy brow, but said nothing. His dark gaze took in the black sand of the beach and the blacker cliffs. It was a harsh kingdom, theirs. Little life could be seen.

As his gaze took in the view, he halted the horse and asked his mount to kneel down. He slid off. His feet were no longer fast enough to catch him as he stumbled across the sand.

"Grandfather!" Svetlana called in worry.

She jumped off her horse and ran over to the tall man who had become as important to her as her own mother.

Before she could touch him, he had straightened himself, shaking his shoulders. She held back, not sure what to do as she watched his body harden up.

He turned slightly and reached his hand back. The little girl slid her hand in his easily. She stayed quiet beside him as they walked to the small outcropping of rocks. Many a fires had been made there with his men, his daughter, and now his granddaughter.

The sting from losing his wife so early in their marriage had lessened, but her image haunted him. Especially every time he saw his daughter.

He tightened his hand around his granddaughters. Ten years had passed before he had been allowed to see his daughter. To finally meet his only grandchild.

It had been a long time. And he had held on as long as he could.

"Are you going to build a fire, grandfather?"

He smiled down at her, her black eyes sparkling just like his wife's had. "Of course. Can you help me gather some branches?"

She pulled away from him immediately and began skipping to the bottom of the cliffs edge. He chuckled at her energy. The girl was filled with life. If only her mother had the same desire to live.

Placing the basket aside, he took to the task of setting the already collected driftwood. His land was one of the few areas where trees had grown taller than a man's height. And the only reason the wood stayed was because of the power of his family. He worried if the forest would stay once he had passed on. Would Anichka come back to raise her daughter here?

Svetlana's giggle's twinkled through the air, filling the beach with life and wonder. It had been so long since a child's laugh had been heard on his land.

He frowned. No. His daughter's husband would never allow Anichka that much power over herself.

If only he could stay on this land a little longer and help his granddaughter along. She needed someone steady in her life. Someone good. Someone to show her her own strength.

Shaking his head, he took the sticks and rubbed them until smoke lifted up from the small pile of wood. Svetlana had finally settled beside him, shivering with energy.

"Now blow carefully, Mina," he coaxed. "Enough wind for the fire to breathe. But not to much or it will drown."

She nodded even as she blew down at the small pile of smoke.

Eventually the fire's flames grew until it crackled with heat. He sat back, his granddaughter seated beside him. She watched the fire with big eyes.

"Let's see what cook has packed for us today," he said as he began rummaging through the basket.

Svetlana shook herself free from the flames grip and watched her grandfather eagerly.

"Bread. Some pieces of cheese. Apples. And…A wine skin!" His eyes lit up as he unscrewed the top and took a quick swig. The wine burned its way down his throat, and he smiled at the fire inside and outside of him.

He passed the wine skin to Svetlana while he prepared the bread, slicing cheese and apple pieces onto it. Svetlana took several swigs, never grimacing at the burn. She didn't want to admit to grandfather that she didn't like the taste. Instead, she sat still as her entire being vibrated with focus on the food.

He almost laughed when she ripped the first sandwich out of his hand. His Lyudmila had been the same.

A horrible scream ripped through the air, setting all the hairs on Svetlana's arms and neck up. Before she could say anything, another scream ripped through the air.

The horses, which had been standing off to the side of the fire, bucked and screamed. They broke into a run towards rocky outcropping at full tilt. Svetlana turned away from her grandfather and her mounts, which were escaping.

She turned towards where the sound had come from. There, further down the beach was another horse.

She opened her mouth to ask grandfather about it but his hand on her arm stilled the thought.

She watched with wide eyes as a different horse moved down the black sand, towards them.

Not a horse. But *like* a horse. The thing had long black teeth and red eyes. Its breathing was heavy as it galloped towards them.

"Stay still," her Grandfather warned, his voice barely quieter than a whisper.

The creature stopped before them, rearing up on its back legs. Its sharp hooves glinted in the mid day sun.

Svetlana's heart raced as she watched it.

Finally, the thing fell onto its feet and chuffed at them.

Without thinking, Svetlana reached her sandwich out towards the thing. It came closer, sniffing at the sandwich before pulling it completely out of her hands. It sniffed at her palm. Then bunted it.

Svetlana giggled as she caressed its muzzle. It was softer than she had expected. It's sharp black teeth glinted along its lips. She leaned forward and kissed the creature on its nose. For a moment it stayed still.

Then it jerked its head back and let out another ear-splitting scream, before racing straight into the ocean.

The water swallowed it up, leaving a deafening silence behind.

Svetlana turned to her grandfather, questions bubbling up from inside of her. But her grandfather stopped her by pulling her into his arms. He held her tight, forcing her to listen to his quick beating heart.

"What's wrong grandpa?" she asked, squirming at his tight hold.

A shuddering sigh ruffled her hair, but he didn't let go.

"Promise me Mina, you will never speak of this. Not to anyone. Not even your mother."

She pulled back and looked up into his pale eyes, fear having left them wide and his pupils dilated.

Slowly, she nodded.

He let out another sigh, as his shoulders relaxed by just a fraction.

"Come, let's return home. It will be a long walk," he said, his hunger forgotten.

She nodded again, jumping off his knee. He quickly replaced everything in the basket and stood. She reached for his hand and they walked up the beach.

They walked in silence, slowly picking their way up the steep path. Rocks cut and scratched at Svetlana's legs, but she ignored them. Something was wrong with grandfather. She could feel it in his wheezing breath and the tremble in his hands. But he said nothing. Once they finally got to the top of the cliff, Svetlana let go of his hand to go ahead.

She only made it four steps before realizing that grandfather was not following her. She turned in time to watch him stagger to his knees. He just barely caught himself on his hands, air barely winding into his haggard lungs.

"Grandfather?" When he said nothing, Svetlana rushed back to his side. "Grandfather!"

Grandfather!

A shiver whispered through the air and shook the pine needles. But no one paid it any attention. Moments, or hours, passed before the sound of branches broke through the constant wheezing.

Their mounts stopped before Svetlana, nuzzling her hair. She reached up blindly and called the first one she touched to kneel.

Her mare immediately dropped to the rough ground.

Together, with Svetlana pulling and the other horse pushing its head against grandfathers butt and legs, they were able to wrestle him over the back of the mare.

Again, she patted its neck and the young horse stood and began picking its way along the path back to the estate. Svetlana walked behind, watching her grandfather breathe. His old mount nuzzled Svetlana's neck, her hair, kissing her with warmth.

But she did not feel anything.

Not when they reached the estate. Not when the men pulled her grandfathers still body off the mare. Not when her mother came screaming out of the stables, falling to her knees and sobbing before his body.

She stood in the grass, alone, no one seeing the small girl.

The horses came out and stood behind her, nipping and nuzzling her cold body. But nothing helped as she watched her grandfather's last shuddering breath leave him.

And then everything was still.

CHAPTER THIRTY-EIGHT

⌘

With Blood

ASHTA PULLED THE oars hard, ignoring the shouts and the crackle of the flame in front of her.

"Darkling?" Carien whispered, still gently rocking Mina.

Ashta looked at Carien but couldn't make out the princess's expression in the shadowed silhouette of the burning ship.

Before Ashta could ask, she saw the glistening of water on the hull of their small dinghy. She tried to dismiss it as water from when she had hauled herself on.

But it kept rising.

Damn it.

The boat had a leak.

"I need you-" Ashta was cut off by a hungry cry from Mina.

Her eyes widened. Carien leaned over and tried to gentle the babe. Instead, Mina squirmed and began screaming and crying in earnest.

"There!" called a male voice from the docks. Others joined it.

Looking beyond Carien's shoulder, Ashta could make out dark shapes on the black ship. The men had spotted the dinghy. She glanced back down at the water in the boat.

Mind made up, Ashta pulled Mina out of Carien's grasp.

"Give me your head scarf."

Carien did, with shaking hands. Ashta in the meantime stood up and stomped on the bench. She broke through easily. Still holding the now quiet Mina, Ashta ripped the rest of the bench off the boat wall.

"H-here," the princess said on a shaky breath.

Ashta took the silk scarf and carefully wrapped Mina around the board.

The shouts of the men on shore grew louder. They didn't have much time.

Ashta forced her heart to slow and calm to settle over her limbs. She pushed her *sleep* thoughts onto the babe until she saw Mina's eyes flicker closed.

"We have to jump into the water. Are you ready?" Ashta asked Carien. Not glancing at the other woman, Ashta checked that all of her knives and swords were well strapped down. Swimming would be difficult, but not impossible.

Carien nodded before standing as well.

"Now!" Ashta hissed, holding Mina's swaddled body above her head. Both woman jumped over the boat edge.

The cold of the ocean wrapped its fingers once more around Ashta, trying to drag her further down. But she didn't let it. Not today.

She kicked to the surface.

Carien was beside her, barely staying above the water.

"Here, hold onto Mina," she said, passing the princess the babe.

Carien grabbed onto the ends of the board and the slightly damp, but still sleeping babe. Ashta gripped the other side of the board and began to stroke her arms and kick her legs for the both of them.

The men from shore must not have seen them jump from the boat. As the shout to find the boat rang along the docks.

Ashta didn't count on it staying that way. Soon enough the men would know the women had jumped. Ashta aimed for a ship near the end of the docks, far from the flames of the black ship and the tent city. In the distance she could see the horizon slowly begin to lighten. The day was coming. They were losing their advantage.

Ashta didn't let it discourage her. Right now, she couldn't let herself think about any of it. Instead she focused on reaching the ship and finding them another boat. Preferably one that didn't leak.

Why had the boat leaked? She wondered without giving anymore room to think about the strange coincidence.

The shouts of men and clang of swords could be heard in the near distance.

Changing her direction, Ashta instead made for the beach. Hopefully there would be a boat near its edge. Maybe even the fisherman's boat she had taken to the island earlier. It could have beached itself.

The gods had helped her a few days ago with the last boat. Maybe they would answer her prayers again.

With that hope close in her heart, she kept swimming, never letting Carien know of the plan, or its changes.

Carien didn't worry. Darkling had come for her. And just like in Naankdoena, Darkling would save her one way or another. She had complete faith in her lioness. She tried to help the other woman swim by kicking as well. Carien wasn't sure if it was making a difference, her long skirt wrapping around her legs and slowing her down, but she had to try something.

"Be...Ready to...run," Ashta panted quietly as she made out the white sand of the beach. The princess said nothing, but Ashta didn't have time for her to reply. A few more strokes and they would be there.

The tickle of sea grass on the back of Ashta's knees had her fighting to stand. She walked Carien and Mina as close to the beach as she could.

"It's shallow enough...to stand here," Ashta panted, looking back down the beach to the dock and the tents east of them. The sky had lightened quite a bit, showing the dark billowing smoke from the black ship, now high in the sky. And at the end of the dock she could just make out several dark figures.

The men would easily see them out here on the beach. Ashta had to risk it. Especially as she glanced the other way down the stretch of sand. She saw the familiar hull of the fishing boat.

"Run!" Ashta whisper screamed, taking Mina into her arms. Carien lifted her skirts as high as she could and ran. Her skirts weighed her down, but she didn't slow.

Then a shout rose up from behind them.

Ashta risked a glance behind them. The berserkers had seen them and now a small party ran at them, the morning sun glinting off their brandished swords.

"Keep running," Ashta urged, shouting, now that they had been seen.

Just a little more and they would be at the boat, she thought. Just a little further.

Carien ran, then her foot slipped in the sand and she stumbled to her knees. Ashta turned just in time to see her fall. Ashta turned back and reached down, pulling Carien up easily. Behind her, the men were closing in. It wouldn't be enough time to push the boat out.

Steeling herself, she pushed Mina into Carien's arms and stepped in front of her.

"Stay behind me," Ashta warned as she pulled out her half swords.

The lioness waited in tense silence as the berserkers fanned out into a half circle around her. There were five of them in total. It would be hard, but she knew that she could take them. This time she did not need to worry about being silent. It was too late for that.

One of the men stepped closer with his broad sword and swung at Ashta. She easily blocked it, stepping inside and slicing his belly open with her other sword.

The man dropped to the ground. The other four watched him in silence. Then looked at her with wary eyes.

This time all four men charged at once. Ashta parried and sliced as best she could at the men.

Carien screamed when one man swung at Darkling's head.

Ashta flinched and didn't move out of the way fast enough. She felt the familiar bite of cold steel in her arm.

Ignoring it, she quickly threw her one half sword into his throat.

He fell backwards, the sword pinning him into the sand.

Before one of the remaining men could use the opening, Ashta pulled a dagger out of her hair and threw it into the next man's throat.

She reached back again for a dagger this time. She kept parrying the two remaining men, sweat mixing with salt water down her back.

The men split, one on either side of her. They took a break, eyeing her as she watched them.

She feinted towards one before dropping to the ground and kicking the other man's legs out from under him.

Before he scrambled up, Ashta rolled onto his back, sliced his throat, and rolled the rest of the way. The other man's broad sword swung down, past where her shoulder had been, and lodged into the dead man's head.

Swearing, the berserker tried to pull the sword out. But Ashta had already got to her knees and shoved her half sword up into his chest and twisted.

The man gasped before falling to his knees.

Ashta pulled the sword back out. For a moment she surveyed the carnage around her. The image would be forever burned into the back of her eyelids.

She felt the telltale acid at the back of her throat.

Fighting past the need to puke, Ashta shut herself off from the bodies littering the sand and back to Carien and the boat.

"Let's go." Ashta's voice was as cold as her soul.

Carien dumbly nodded, not able to look away from all the blood. She had known her guard was deadly, but the proof surrounding her cemented it into her mind. Darkling was dangerous.

Ashta stepped passed her and to the boat. She threw her bloodied sword into the hull and braced herself on the edges. She pushed against the soft sand, the early morning light warming her back. Finally, the boat edged into the water.

Her heart broke at the tell-tale swish that followed.

She stopped and glanced into the bottom of the boat. Holes. Tens of hundreds of them littered the walls and the bottom. Thin slices that she wouldn't have seen.

Before she could think about the how and the why, another shout from down the beach rose into the early morning air.

She felt a prickle of hot tears in her eyes. Frustrated and beaten, Ashta took a short breath. It felt as if the gods had now abandoned her. Why?

"Darkling?" Carien whispered, her eyes never wavering from the oncoming party of berserkers, much larger than the last. She pulled the warm bundle closer to her chest. This group carried torches, their swords glinting in the flickering flame.

They had been so close, Ashta despaired. So close.

She wouldn't let the princess go back to the berserkers without a fight. Her shoulders tightened as Ashta reached down and pulled the bloody half sword out of the hull.

She turned back to the oncoming party, blood dripping down her arm.

Her arm stung.

Her legs shook.

She carelessly wiped the half-sword off on her leather leggings. The party coming towards them was much bigger than the last.

Swallowing, Ashta stared at the bedraggled princess who stood beside her. Carien's hair hung limply around her shoulders. Dark circles ringed her eyes. But there was still a sliver of hope in those caramel depths.

Ashta had sworn to protect the princess with her life. And now, she would do exactly that.

CHAPTER THIRTY-NINE

⌘

Black Teeth

THE MEN, OVER a dozen, fanned out around Ashta and Carien, not sparing more than glance at the bodies that littered the sand.

Ashta groaned internally. Five had been just barely manageable, but fifteen? It would take a miracle to beat them without major injuries to herself. And even if she did, there was no guarantee that she and Carien would find a way off this island without being caught.

The tallest of the group, a man with a white streaked beard, stepped forward.

"Princess Carien," he called out, his voice carrying across the sand. Ashta winced, hoping it didn't carry all the way back to the tents.

"Give up now and we won't kill you."

Ashta laughed, was that supposed to convince Carien to go with these men? Ashta didn't even have to glance back to know Carien's response.

"Never." Her voice was firm, threaded with the confidence of being a princess of an ancient and powerful kingdom.

The man shifted his gaze to Ashta, "The King said not to kill you, princess Svetlana, but he said nothing about you needing all of your limbs."

Ashta hissed at the name and spat on the sand. "My name is Ashta the Lion Tamer. Remember it, berserker."

"We have over a dozen men and more coming from the docks. You cannot think you will actually beat us?"

Ashta grinned wide for him, baring her teeth. "I don't have to kill you to get away from you."

A blur from farther down the beach had Ashta glancing over the berserker's shoulder. There, in the distance, looked to be another dozen or so berserkers running towards them.

The smile slid off Ashta's face. The odds of escaping with the princess and Mina were getting worse with each moment.

She focused back on the men in front of her.

"Well, which of you men thinks they can beat a lioness?" She taunted.

A few of the men glanced at each other before four from the group stepped forward to take her on.

The only good thing with so many men was that they couldn't all attack her at once. Using her advantage, Ashta took a half step forward. But still from close to the princess

The men didn't have a chance to get in more than a few blows before she had cut open their legs.

One man tried to attack her from the ground. Ashta easily lopped his head off before turning back to the tall berserker. He only grimaced before nodding to four more men to jump forward.

The longer Ashta fought, the more her arms and legs burned with exhaustion. She wouldn't be able to keep this up much longer.

To her dismay, the second party of a dozen men had arrived and fanned out. Behind them, an even larger gathering of men was slowly walking towards them. She had had the slimmest hope of beating the first group, but the entire island?

Ashta wiped the sweat off her brow and continued to strike and parry, always keeping Carien a half step behind her. The men tried to edge closer to her back. Each time they did, Ashta threw one of her hair daggers.

But she was running low. Soon the only blades on her would be her half swords. Even the daggers from her boots had been thrown at the crowd.

For each body that fell, another stepped forward and replaced him. The sand was heavy with blood and bile, a sticky mess that sucked everyones' feet down.

Ashta stood atop a pile of bodies, using the height and uneven ground to strike the oncoming berserkers down. But she was slowing.

Soon, it would end, she worried.

Then she slipped and fell to her knees.

She looked up into black eyes filled with blood lust.

She watched as the blade swung down and time slowed.

She was ready to die.

Her only regret was not being able to get the princess out of her father's clutches.

Before the blade came down, an unearthly scream tore across the hushed island. Ashta shivered involuntarily, the hairs on her neck standing on end. There was only one thing that could make that noise.

Ashta threw herself to the side, watching the sword glide by her and bury into the body she had tripped over. Before she could raise her arm to defend herself, an unearthly shadow jumped over her and tore into the man.

Another horrible scream filled the air, as the torash ripped into the man's shoulder. It shook him before throwing him over the rest of the gathered men.

The berserkers scrambled back as more than one dropped his sword in shock and fear.

Torash weren't well known in Bbrski, but all men knew the night tales of men going missing with only a lock of hair left on the beach.

Ashta watched in shock as the torash, its lithe black body, ran threw the party. It ripped bodies apart as easily as a sickle fell through a grain field. Swathes of bodies now littered the once white sandy beach.

Finally, when every man was dead, the animal calmed and stepped towards Carien. Its red eyes blazed as blood dripped down its long onyx fangs. The blood lust hazed the creature's vision, as all it saw was another living human. Food.

Ashta pushed her mind onto the creature.

No. Friend.

The male torash stopped short, it's mane still glistening with sea salt and blood.

An idea began to form in Ashta's mind. Before she could second guess herself, she heard a shout from the much larger party. The one coming from the tent city.

The berserkers at the front had begun running down the beach.

With a grim smile, Ashta stood up and grabbed onto the torash's face. She pressed her forehead against his and pushed the image of the cliff entrance into the palace into the torash's mind. He snorted in understanding.

She held that image for another second then turned to Carien.

The princess was clutching Mina, her knuckles white and her eyes rounded as she stared at the torash. She had not forgotten her last fateful ride on the back of such a creature.

"It's okay," Ashta said in a calm voice to the princess.

Carien was already shaking her head.

"We have to," Ashta begged, "It's the only way."

Carien glared at Darkling before glancing back at the huge incisors. Her mind flashed back to memories of that afternoon. Of how close she had come to dying.

She had prayed never to see one of these creatures again. And now one stood before her.

Despite her fear, she watched the blood lust clear from its gaze as the creature watched her curiously.

"We don't have time," Ashta warned, taking another step towards the princess. She glanced nervously at the group of men who were fast approaching. Another couple of moments and they would be almost in throwing distance. "Please, Carien," she begged.

At the sound of her given name the princess took a step forward.

Indesion still warred across her face. Ashta didn't let her think about it for another moment. She stepped forward, picked the princess up, and threw her over the torash's back.

Carien spread her legs automatically and gripped the torash's mane with her free hand. Before she could freak out, a familiar whizz in the air had her gripping the torash for dear life.

Ashta fell to the ground, an arrow staking her to the blood-soaked sand. She watched in horror as the torash reared, three arrows sticking out of its flank. The princess just barely held on.

Without looking back, Ashta pushed her mind one last time on the torash.

Go.

The creature didn't wait. It reared once more, then galloped straight across the water. It's hooves just scratching the surface of the ocean.

As she watched the princess ride to safety, Ashta knew the same would not be true for her. But she had done her job. She had protected the princess with everything she had.

The clank of swords behind her warned her that the party was almost upon the carnage. She couldn't help but smile.

Let them take me, she thought. Because they could never break me. They could never turn me back into a princess.

She was now a white lioness, down to the white of her bones.

CHAPTER FORTY

⌘

The Boat Rocked

ASHTA WATCHED AS Carien and Mina disappeared into the horizon on the torash's back. Safe.

She kept watching even as the men pushed her head in the blood-soaked sand, binding her wrists together behind her back. The berserker had barely pulled her to her feet when she cried out from the arrow still in her leg.

"You deserve worse, slut," he mumbled as he leaned down and broke the head off the arrow. He pulled the rest back out, not caring that the wound began to bleed in earnest.

Ashta held her tongue against the pain. These men were used to pain, even preferred it. She couldn't show any if she wanted to be treated with some respect.

"Time to return you to King Alerik. He won't be happy," the berserker warned as he shoved Ashta forward. She stumbled but managed to stay upright.

Her father.

She hadn't planned on seeing him again. Anger and fear began to roll and boil deep in her belly. No, he would not be happy to see her.

The red sand pulled at her boots. Her arm, stretched back, burned from its earlier sword wound.

Everything in Ashta ached.

But she had won, in her heart she knew this. Because of it, she kept her head high and glared at the men as she passed them.

As the large party came into the edge of the tents, more berserkers stood outside their tents, making a makeshift hall for her to pass through. At first, they were quiet.

Slowly the crowd began to yell and jeer at her.

One berserker ran in front of her, naked and shaking his cock at Ashta.

Ashta kept a blank face but couldn't stop the slight smirk when the berserker behind her punched the other man in the face. The second man fell back, his eyes rolled up in his head.

The flasher wasn't the last on the long walk up the steep incline.

The higher up they got, the angrier the crowd became. Some men began to throw old food and slop.

With only twenty paces more to walk, a man stepped forward and threw shit, still warm at Ashta. It splattered across her chest, its smell making Ashta gag involuntarily. She growled at the man as she passed him. The rest of the walk was the most disgusting minutes in her life. Her hair, face, and even her open wound were splattered with feces.

Finally, they got to the tent.

One of the berserkers from the beach party, pulled the flap aside while the one behind her gave her one last shove. Ashta stumbled and fell to her knees just inside the tent. The flap fell closed behind her.

At first the only sound in the tent was her labored breaths, and the slow drip of shit and slop onto the carpet floor.

Ashta forced her eyes up. Her father, King Alerik, stood across from her. His face was of stone except for the sneer that was plastered across it.

He stepped forward and slapped her hard enough that her head snapped back to the ground and shit from her face sprayed across the tent.

Grinding her teeth, she pushed herself back to her knees.

"Iskra!" her father bellowed.

Another berserker from behind King Alerik stepped forward.

"Wash her down," he ordered dispassionately.

The man nodded before disappearing further inside the tent.

"I should have killed you last time," he continued in an even tone. "When I had the chance. Once more, you have ruined my plans."

Ashta said nothing, staring with unseeing eyes down at the carpet.

Her father continued in his cold voice. "The princess would have made everything go faster."

Iskra returned to the room with two overfull buckets.

Her father stepped back with a nod.

Before Ashta could say anything, the man had dumped a bucket of warm water down her back. The second bucket he threw at her front.

Ashta gasped at its chill. She was grateful for some semblance of clean. Not that she would say it aloud.

Iskra returned to his station behind the King.

Her father crouched down beside her and whispered into her ear. "But I don't need her. Now I will just drag out the siege and starve the city out. Because of you."

Ashta shivered. Before she could say anything, he stepped back again and straightened to his full height.

"I made a mistake, daughter of mine, the last time we met. I had underestimated you and your time in Tripsia. But this time, I won't." He snapped his fingers at Iskra, "Strip her. Of everything."

Another berserker joined Iskra, holding Ashta as she struggled against the men.

Iskra pulled out a wicked blade and cut straight through the breast bands. He continued down, cutting through the skirt, watching with a flare of something in his eyes. Ashta shivered and fought harder as the first of her ruined clothes fell to the ground.

Knives clattered onto the carpet.

Iskra continued downward, cutting the leggings and boots as well. Her father's one eyebrow rose as he watched more daggers and short blades clatter out of her pants.

Ashta had used up quite a few of her knives in the battle. But not all of them.

"Check her hair," Her father warned.

Ashta glared at him as Iskra smiled grimly, reaching his thick fingers into her hair. Ashta winced as he pulled and tugged. The throwing knives she had used all up.

"Clear, your majesty."

"Bind her."

Ashta's blood ran cold, as the men easily bound her arms, her legs, and her whole body. In the end she lay naked, bound and gagged in front of her father. It was humiliating beyond anything done to her in Tripsia, in the Nursery.

The King shrugged out of his fur coat and placed it over her naked body. As he was still crouched over her, his face softened and he whispered, "This time I will forgive you."

He stepped back and stared at the two berserkers. "Have her tied to the ship mast. If anything happens to her, it will be you two who pay the price."

The men winced. Iskra gently lifted Ashta into his arms, keeping the fur around her. Suddenly, Ashta was to tired to fight anymore. She lay limp in his arms, her eyes never leaving her father. He leaned forward, pushing a lock of her black hair behind her ear.

"Next time, daughter, I will not be so kind," he warned. Then he turned away.

Ashta tried to keep her eyes open as the men carried her through the tents and down to the dock. The crowd had dissipated, the king's warning keeping the men in line. For now.

Her father's warning still tickled down her back as Iskra tied her around the mast. He arranged the fur over her before disappearing inside the ship.

Her mind finally forced her into dazed sleep as the shouts of sailors and the creak of the ship surrounded her.

Some time later she woke to the sight of stars. Looking up at the night sky and the first sliver of the new moon, Ashta thanked her grandfather for looking over her. For protecting Carien. For only her grandfather knew about the torash on the beach.

Ashta then prayed to her mother's soul, to look out over her only daughter, as Ashta had no idea what awaited her in Bbrski.

Her home.

The End, For Now…

Ashta's story continues in **Darkling the Broken Slave**

Acknowledgements

First off, I would like to thank you the reader. Without you, this whole process would not have been possible. Writing is a lonely job, but knowing that one day it will shape and create worlds for you, the reader, to escape into makes it all worth it. I myself am a reader first and a writer second, and I appreciate the efforts of all the authors whose works of love I have read.

I want to thank the writing community at large. I can't count on my hand how many times I went in search of formatting issues or character development and found a writer who had the answer. We are a small community, but we are mighty! For those of you not published yet, I wish you all the luck on this crazy journey. And know that hard work and dedication pays off. Don't be scared of it.

To Google, thank you for indexing all the answers a crazy author could ever need. I can't count on my hand how many times while I was editing, I would open up a Google search on some crazy random topic or a word I couldn't remember.

To Fiverr and your endless resource of great editors, formatters, and illustrators. Thank you! The editing experience was wonderful. Also, the cover art is gorgeous.

Thank you to my family who puts up with my crazy mood swings and doesn't let me get distracted from writing. I know it's not easy dealing with someone with as wide of a creative streak as me. I can't even count how many times you guys took my phone away so I could focus. Jokes aside, knowing you all loved and supported me no matter what I do is a blessing. I appreciate it more than you all can ever know.

About The Author

Morena Stamm grew up in central Alberta as the third of four kids. She has her Bachelor of Communications degree at MacEwan University, in Edmonton, Alberta, in 2017. After graduating, she moved back to her home in rural where she completed her Masters in Intercultural and International Communication at Royal Roads University, in Victoria, B.C. online.

She grew up reading every book she could get her hands on, for hours on end. This started her love for authors like Tamora Pierce, Rick Riordan, Scott Westerfield, Gail Carson Levine, and many countless more. These sparked her passion for the fantasy genre and sucked her into the endless world of fantasy and science fiction books, which she has yet to emerge from.

Want to read more from the Named Again Series? Keep up to date on Morena's new releases on her website <u>morenastamm.wordpress.com</u> or Facebook page @morenastamm.

Made in the USA
Middletown, DE
31 December 2020